B.R.E.A.C.H.

B.R.E.A.C.H.

EDWARD GRAY

CANADIAN AUTHOR

Contact Info:

 www.EdwardGray.ca

Editor: Lauren Lewis

Author Photo & Book Cover: Emil Mateja

First Edition

10 9 8 7 6 5 4 3 2 1

ISBN: 978-1-0696802-0-4 (eBook)

ISBN: 978-1-069802-1-1 (Paperback)

ISBN: 978-1-0696802-2-8 (Hardcover)

For my wonderful wife and amazing daughter.

You make every part of this life worth living.

PROLOGUE

The Central Intelligence Agency.

Also known as the C.I.A.

Sometimes called "The Company" or simply "The Agency."

Created on September 18, 1947, by President Harry S. Truman, its mission has always been the same: protect America from its enemies.

The C.I.A. gathers, processes and analyzes intelligence critical to national security. Its work stretches far beyond public view, into operations that rarely reach headlines.

Among its many divisions is the **Special Operations Group**—the Agency's covert paramilitary arm. When precision, silence and deniability required, units from this group are deployed.

From within that arm, a new team was formed. Four operators, chosen for missions where others could not go. Officially, they don't exist. Unofficially, they are called: **B.R.E.A.C.H.**

Black Ops
Reconnaissance
Espionage
Assassinations
Coercion
Hostage Rescue

FIRST

INTO THE BREACH

1

January 18 | 2:08 a.m. MST
Big Sky, Montana

The syringe expelled a sharp jet of clear liquid, just enough to purge the last trace of air. He slid the safety cap back on with practiced precision and slipped it into the breast pocket of his arctic camo jacket, his movements steady, deliberate, unhurried.

A howling wind swept down the valley, dragging sheets of snow with it and rattling the pine branches overhead. It whistled through the rocks and into the treeline, where the faint glow of a fire reflected against the glass of a mounted spotter's scope.

It was a dark and frigid Montana winter night. Through that scope, a sprawling log mansion stood out against the storm, its wide windows glowing with the pulse of a fireplace. The structure leaned against a wall of pine forest and jagged outcroppings, perched at the end of a long, winding gravel road. Remote. Isolated. Untouchable. To most, it might have looked like a fantasy getaway. To its owner, Congressional Representative Robert Barkley, it was simply another refuge from Washington's constant noise, another stronghold where he could vanish from the public eye.

The watcher didn't blink. Snow crusted over his hood, clinging to his balaclava, while he lay half-buried beside his partner. They had been there for nearly five hours, still as statues. The cold gnawed at their bodies, but neither man stirred. Through the glass, they watched Barkley move in the lamplight, a bourbon in one hand as the other shuffled papers across his desk. For over an hour, he had remained rooted in that chair.

A vibration broke the silence. Barkley's phone buzzed once on the table, the screen flashing. A message unanswered. He didn't reach for it. He didn't want to think about the reporter tonight, or about the dangerous task he had sent her chasing in another part of the world. That weight could hold off until morning.

In the treeline, one of the men shifted slightly. It was time.

They rose together, slow and deliberate, shapes peeling from the snow. Arctic camo blurred them into the storm, their white balaclavas and suppressed pistols painted to match the terrain. Ghosts breaking free of the drift. Snow slid from their uniforms as they checked chambers, brushed down weapons, and readied themselves for the approach.

Snowshoes crunched softly against the frozen ground as they pushed out from cover. The scent of pine faded behind them, replaced by the raw bite of wind pouring off the mountain slopes. Each gust battered their advance, but it also masked their noise. With the house unlit outside and no neighbors within miles, their confidence sharpened. They were invisible.

At the porch steps, they bent low, slipping out of their snowshoes and drawing pistols. The taller man glanced at his partner, his breath clouding in the night air.

"*Vamos. Silencioso.*"

Together they ascended, movements controlled and exact. Every step pressed into the storm-muted wood. At the wide living room window, the shorter figure scanned the interior, raised a hand, and signaled all clear.

At a smaller side window, the other knelt and pulled a black device from his jacket. The wind shrieked as he pressed it flush to the glass. A flick of the switch, and the pane fractured inward with the faintest whisper, the storm smothering the sound.

He slid inside, smooth as a phantom, dark eyes sweeping the room. His target lay within arm's reach. A girl.

She was sleeping deeply, her face soft against the pillow, lips parted in steady rhythm. Her chest rose and fell in small breaths. A stuffed fox, fur worn, one ear missing, rested beneath her arm. Her hand, small and pale, clutched it even in unconsciousness.

The man moved to her side, lowering to one knee. His gloved hand pressed over her mouth as the cold steel of the syringe touched her skin. The sharp tang of antiseptic filled the room. With a steady push, he depressed the plunger. Her body slackened instantly, her breath catching before settling into shallow rhythm. The custom benzodiazepine compound would hold her quiet, sedated, pliable for the long journey.

At the window, his partner hefted a silver thermal bag inside. Its metallic skin caught the faint lamplight. Opening it wide, he held it steady as they lifted the girl together, wrapping her into the insulated lining. The material cocooned her, preserving her warmth and concealing her form while making transport effortless.

They retraced their steps across the open field. Snow lashed their faces, but the wind that punished them also cloaked their retreat. The girl's limp weight swayed between them as they pressed toward the forest. At the treeline, their forms melted into shadow, swallowed whole by the storm and the endless dark of the pines.

Behind them, the broken window gaped open. The wind hissed through the jagged frame, curling around the curtains and spilling cold air inside.

On the carpet, the stuffed fox had fallen. It lay abandoned on its side, stitched eyes fixed on the empty bed. Snowflakes drifted inward, dusting its fur. They melted one by one in the room's heat, leaving dark patches on the threadbare toy.

January 18 | 12:25 p.m. AST
Tarim, Yemen

It was 78°F on the patio of a café in Tarim, the desert sun warming James Hopper's face. Heat shimmered in the air, warping the edges of the market beyond. The faint scent of spices mixed with the ever-present desert dust—a taste, a smell, and a grit that seemed woven into every corner of life here. No matter where you went, it followed.

Hopper brushed the tabletop clean with his hand before lifting his coffee. The Arabic blend was rich, smooth, carrying the faint bite of sand, as though the desert itself had slipped into the cup. He swallowed, eyes scanning casually, every sense alert.

Behind him, an old, beaten radio hissed through static.

From its weak speaker came fragments of a report—a missing Western journalist in South America. Hopper barely caught the words, but they settled in the back of his mind. He strained to hear more, parsing through the static and the marketplace chatter. His Arabic carried him only so far before the overlapping shouts of vendors drowned the rest. Someone else's problem, he told himself. Still, the voice lingered, a ghost in the noise.

He set his cup down. His hand trembled. A sharp pain lanced across his temple, and in an instant he was elsewhere—heat, fire, the deafening crash of an explosion, the screams of his team, and then the suffocating weight of silence.

His breath hitched. He pressed a hand against the scar on his temple, eyes squeezing shut as he forced the ghosts away. Focus. Not now. Not here. He drew in a long breath, exhaled, and steadied his hand on the cup.

The mission.

His gaze swept the courtyard beyond the patio, counting vendors and civilians, mapping lines of sight. His left ear hummed with the low voices of his teammates, quiet comms delivering status reports and probability calls.

The courtyard formed a rough U of stalls, painted bright with rugs, pottery, jewelry, and spices. Foot traffic surged shoulder to shoulder, a dozen escape routes crisscrossing through the chaos. Exactly the kind of cover Hopper wanted.

From the second floor of a crumbling apartment at the north end, Ezekiel Jones waited five feet back from a balcony rail, inside the building, scope trained on the crowd. Zeke was the eye in the sky, murmuring movement patterns and threat markers with the calm rhythm of a man who had done this a hundred times.

To the east, parked discreetly at an intersection, the team's van idled. Inside, two more operators watched the approach routes. Ready. Waiting for Hopper's word.

Hopper himself—mid-thirties, salt-and-pepper hair, beard grown long enough to help him blend into Arab streets—sat still, the picture of a traveler enjoying the market. Sixteen years of service, most of them as a Navy SEAL, had etched steel into his posture. Master Chief Petty Officer. Now field commander of a unit that officially did not exist. **Call sign: One**.

The team was new. Covert. Born from the CIA's Special Operations Group. Known internally as BREACH.

"One, this is Two. Eyes on Qasim, entering the courtyard from the east. You got him?"

"Got him, Two. East side," Hopper whispered into his mic, his voice a rasp carried low against the hum of the crowd.

Colin "Finn" Finnigan, 31, replied from his position near the van. Blond hair cropped close, lean frame, quick hands. A former Navy Corpsman turned SEAL, Finn was the team's medic and Hopper's second-in-command. **Call sign: Two**. History bound them—years of firefights, late-night patrols, and too many close calls. Finn had patched Hopper's wounds more times than either cared to count. Irish, New York bred, a family of cops from Queens, men who believed in the job above all. For Finn, everything was black or white: you do it, or you fail.

"I've got the bodyguard," a voice cut in. "Ten paces back. Black shemagh, sunglasses, AK slung."

"Copy, Three. I see him," Hopper murmured. His eyes scanned, settling on the man shadowing the target.

The courtyard swelled with bodies, vendors hawking wares, children darting through the crush. Hopper had chosen the timing carefully. The peak hours gave him the cover he needed—noise, chaos, and too many moving parts for anyone to track.

Qasim was here. The bomb maker. A man who sold death to the highest bidder. Suicide vests in Kandahar. Car bombs in Baghdad. American soldiers had paid the price. Hopper's SEAL team had paid the price. The CIA had tracked him to Tarim, and BREACH was here to end his work.

"Snatch and Grab" was the plan. Quiet if possible. Permanent if not. Hopper didn't lose sleep either way.

From the balcony, Zeke's calm voice filtered through. An African American, former Army Ranger, from a family of proud service members. Marksman, comms, tech wizard. **Call sign: Four**. He carried youth, but never weakness. Anything inside a thousand meters, he owned. His words cut through the comms, clean and precise, anchoring the team in the storm of the crowd.

Each operator had a specialty. Each had a purpose. And Hopper, scarred but unbroken, was about to lead them straight into the fire.

From his sniper perch, Zeke Jones knew if he fired, no one would trace it back to him. The suppressed MK12 beneath his cheek, the storm of market noise below, the chaos of voices and haggling—it would swallow the sound. In the crowd, even the echo of death could vanish.

Through his scope, he tracked the target. The sway of bodies forced him to adjust in tiny increments, crosshairs drifting, settling, waiting. At twenty-four, he had pulled a trigger more times than he could count, but always, it was the seconds before the shot that mattered most. His finger hovered. His heartbeat slowed to the rhythm of the reticle. He reminded himself of the same truth he carried into every mission: don't miss, because if you miss, someone else pays.

The thought burned his nerves. He bit down, let the candy bar soften and melt across his tongue, and forced his eyes to stay on the glass.

The speaker crackled in Hopper's ear.

"Say the word, boss, and I'll drop him like a bad habit."

Hopper gave the faintest smile. He wouldn't mind seeing Qasim's skull snap back from a round.

Another voice cut in, roughened by a Texas drawl. At twenty-seven, Jackson Williams was the second youngest on the team, trailing only Zeke. His palms were hard from ranch chores, later hardened more by explosives training.

"Four, you can't even drop the candy bar I hear you chewin' on."

Zeke peeled his cheek from the stock, glared at the half-eaten bar in his hand, and set it down on the floor.

"Easy, cowboy. You didn't spend the last twenty-four hours flat on your belly, pissing in bottles, to hold this perch. I'm hungry, alright?"

"Sounds like you need more patience, son. Old Wolf drilled that into me back on the ranch—wait for the right shot, don't rush it."

Zeke swiveled his rifle off target for a moment, aligning the crosshairs on the van parked at the curb. "Yeah, keep talking, cowboy. I've got eyes on you too."

Through his scope, he saw a single finger rise inside the van, pressed against the glass.

"Real cute, Jacks."

Jacks chuckled. But the sound had an edge, hollow at the back. Joking was easier than remembering the last charge he set, the last buddy he didn't bring home. Humor kept the silence away. When silence hit, it got too loud.

Jackson Williams—Green Beret. Texan. Weapons and explosives specialist. **Call sign: Three.**

In the van, Finn sat beside him, eyes on the crowd. He kept the banter short.

"Alright, swap dick jokes later. Focus up."

His tone was businesslike, almost flat. Almost.

Discretion mattered more than bravado. Qasim couldn't disappear in a way that screamed "American snatch team." If it did, every cell in this city would come hunting, and Hopper's men wouldn't make it ten blocks.

Hopper had chosen these men himself. Trusted their scars, trusted their skills. Six months of training had bound them into something sharp, but Hopper still kept a sliver of distance. He had learned the price of letting men get too close. Sometimes it was hearing a voice in your ear one night and never again the next. Sometimes it was scrubbing blood off gear that wasn't your own. Bonds cut deep, and when they tore, they left holes.

On the street below, Qasim moved slowly from stand to stand. He fingered scarves at one stall, set them back. The crowd pressed, shifting between him and his bodyguard. For the first time, a gap opened.

The van rolled forward, settling into a new slot just ahead of Hopper's position. From here, Finn had a line of sight to both Hopper and the target.

Hopper's voice carried across the comms. "Two, move the van. Get closer."

"Wilco," Finn answered.

The courtyard swelled with bodies. The air smelled of hot bread, grilled meat, incense curling from a brass burner. Hopper rose, dropped bills on the café table, set his mug on top, and drifted into the crowd. He moved slow, casual, a traveler blending into the crush. His eyes never left Qasim.

The bodyguard struggled to keep a clear line. The swell of the market was closing gaps, choking sight lines. Still too close, still too tight. Hopper wanted space. A distraction would make it.

He dipped his head, lips barely moving. "Four, give me a distraction. Make him look the other way."

Zeke's eye left the target, pivoted to the bodyguard. The man stood beside a pottery stand, stacks of vases big and small arranged in neat rows. Hand-painted clay, days of work in each piece. A shame.

Zeke racked the action, slid a round into chamber, and thumbed the selector to fire. He gave Hopper a soft click in reply. Ready.

He keyed the long-range comms.

"Reaper One, Bravo Zero Four."

"Bravo Zero Four, this is Reaper One. Send traffic."

"Status on hostile elements in the vicinity if we go loud?"

"Negative, Bravo Zero Four. Area's cold."

"Copy that. Appreciate it."

He settled back onto the rifle, breath steady. "One distraction coming right up, Boss. Call it."

Hopper angled through the crowd, closing the distance. Qasim moved toward him, guard lagging. Timing was everything.

"Three, ready on the door?" Hopper asked.

"Ready."

"Open it."

"Four—distraction. Now."

Zeke's finger curled. He exhaled, squeezed.

The rifle cracked. A vase exploded in a plume of clay dust and shards.

The bodyguard flinched hard, pivoted toward the blast.

That was the moment.

Hopper lunged. His shoulder crashed into Qasim, folding him with a grunt. They tumbled together into the van's side door as Jacks yanked it open. The metal slammed shut behind them.

Finn dropped the shifter. Tires screamed as the van clawed forward, spitting gravel, smoke, and sand.

Finn's voice cut sharp across the net. "Three, EXFIL, EXFIL, EXFIL."

"Copy. Rally point in twenty."

The van roared out of the market, swallowed by the dust and noise behind it.

January 18 | 4:00 a.m. MST
Big Sky, Montana

Congressman Robert Barkley woke to a sharp chill pressing against the back of his neck. His body shuddered with an involuntary shiver. The fire had burned out hours ago, leaving behind only the acrid scent of charred wood. The hearth was cold, nothing but blackened stone and ash—no flicker, no ember, no warmth.

The air bit harder than it should have. A draft, maybe? His eyes flicked toward the windows—old frames, half-rotten, some that never shut right—but all of them looked closed. His frown deepened.

The house was silent. Too silent.

A faint creak broke the stillness.

He froze, pulse tightening in his throat. Floorboards settling in the cold? Or something else? The sound didn't return.

Barkley rose from the chair, joints stiff from a night of fitful sleep. He stretched, cracked his neck from side to side, his back groaning at the strain. The chair had long ago lost any pretense of comfort, but he had fallen asleep there anyway.

As he passed the mantel, his gaze caught on the photo at its center. He stopped.

The family portrait had been taken two years ago, just before cancer took Terri. Sarah stood between them, auburn hair unbrushed, half-tucked behind one her ear. Freckles scattered her pale face like flecks of paint. She wore no makeup, only that crooked, stubborn smile, her small hand gripping Terri's so tightly it blurred the photo's edge.

Barkley barely recognized the man beside them. His jaw had been firmer, his posture straighter. His suit had fit. His smile had looked real.

He hadn't let himself stare at that picture for weeks. It carried happiness, yes—but also the weight of what had been torn away.

The air in the room thickened. His nerves sharpened. A thin unease dug into him, though he tried to dismiss it. Early hour. Lack of sleep. Tricks of the mind.

He turned toward the hallway. The living room light reached only partway down. The far end was shadow, dark and still. His daughter's door was shut. His stomach clenched.

Sarah never slept with her door closed.

A thousand thoughts came at once.

Sarah.

His daughter. Resilient, quiet, tougher than she had any right to be after losing her mother—but grief still flickered in her eyes sometimes, and he'd been too busy, too consumed by work, to notice when it did. God, when was the last time he had really looked at her? Had he just seen her in passing, crossing between meetings and phone calls, mistaking proximity for presence? Was he failing her—not just as a father, but as the only parent she had left?

Could she have run away? In this weather? Alone? The thought of her out in the snow made him shiver again. Fear, this time, not cold.

He crossed the living room, feet dragging across the

hardwood until he stood at her door. His pulse hammered. He could feel it in his temples, beating heavy and uneven. His breath thinned, shallow, like his body already knew what he would find.

You're overreacting.

She's fine.

She's curled up asleep.

He pushed the door. It creaked open. He didn't step inside at first. Something in him resisted. The dread was thick, suffocating.

Did I miss something?

Did I push her too far?

Was all she wanted just… time?

Then his eyes landed on the bed.

Empty.

He scanned the room fast. The window. Shattered. Jagged glass glittered across the floor like shards of ice, cold and merciless.

His gut sank. This wasn't a runaway. This wasn't rebellion.

He rushed forward. Snow gusted through the opening, carried by the night wind. On the floor, amidst the wreckage, lay Sarah's stuffed fox. One ear torn, glass dust clinging to its fur. The toy looked abandoned, left behind like a witness.

Barkley bent, snatched it up, and clutched it to his chest.

She was gone. Taken.

His panic flared. He spun toward the living room, hands fumbling as he grabbed his phone. The screen blurred through shaking hands, his thumb stabbing the numbers. 9-1-1.

The device almost slipped from his grip as he pressed it to his ear.

The operator answered. Calm. Routine. "9-1-1, what's your emergency?"

His throat tightened. For a moment, no words came. His lips trembled.

"My daughter's gone," he rasped. "Someone took her."

Silence.

Then the operator's voice, clipped but steady: "Stay on the line, sir. Help is on the way."

The words were meant to calm, to reassure, to hold him together. But even as he heard them, Barkley's chest sank. He knew the truth already.

It was far too late for help.

2

One week prior...
January 12 | 8:23 p.m. BOT
San Lorenzo, Bolivia

The jungle swallowed her whole. Foliage clawed at her clothes, each branch lashing her arms and face, vines wrapping her legs like snares. Every step was a fight against roots and mud. The humidity pressed in, thick and suffocating, draping her body in sweat. When the rain came, it came hard—sheets hammering down, plastering her hair across her face, flooding her eyes, turning breath itself into labor.

Kaitlyn Thompson pushed forward. Fifty miles behind her. Hills, cliffs, swollen rivers, mountain ridges—she had left them all in her wake. Her body burned, her lungs rasped, but she kept moving.

Lean and wiry, a runner's build. War correspondent.

Marathoner. Danger had been her companion for years, but this—this was survival. Her accent might have marked her as foreign, but her gear told a different story: worn leather straps, frayed canvas pouches, boots cut and patched. She looked more explorer than reporter, something torn straight from an old adventure reel.

Sixty miles more. Brazil was the finish line. Safety, maybe. If she could reach it before Rocha's soldiers reached her. She hadn't heard them in hours, but she felt them anyway. A second heartbeat, pounding just behind her own.

Her luck cracked.

A foot jammed between two slick rocks. The rubber sole slipped. Her ankle twisted. Her bag tore loose. Gravity ripped her from her path.

She tumbled, body flailing, rocks scraping skin raw. Her elbow struck stone—pain bright and blinding. Branches whipped past, slammed her shoulders, ripped her clothes. Her head clipped a branch, her vision splintering. She rolled until momentum hurled her toward a ravine's edge.

She stopped hard, breath gone, chest heaving shallow. The world tilted around her. Her eyes opened just enough to catch the sight of her shoulder bag spinning free, bursting open as it crashed against a rock. A laptop tumbled out.

Her cry tore silent in her throat.

The machine flipped into the air, cartwheeled, and vanished into the torrent below.

Gone.

Not just hardware. Not just notes. It had been her tether—backup, archive, shield. She felt the loss like a blow to her ribs.

Pain came in waves. Ankle twisted, maybe fractured. Elbow swelling. Blood stung her eye. Her muscles screamed for stillness. She pressed her face into the dirt, let the rain mix with tears she hadn't wanted to show.

London flickered in her mind—tea steeping on the stove, her father's old record player scratching out jazz on Sunday mornings. Comforts she had left behind, lies she had told to protect him. He had never known how deep she was in.

She snapped herself back. No time.

The bag still lay nearby. Precious. Inside—stolen documents, passport, photos, names, graves. Rocha himself, caught in frame, smiling above the dirt he had filled with bodies. The laptop had been backup. The bag was everything.

Every rustle sent her pulse racing. Every snapped branch made her throat tighten. Were they already here? Had they seen her fall?

She grit her teeth, forced her body to move. Her ankle screamed, nerves firing white-hot. She bit her cheek until she tasted iron, forcing herself not to cry out.

People were counting on her. Families with no names, lives buried in ditches. She had promised to tell their story, to drag it into the light. That promise had carried her across deserts, through firefights, out of trafficking dens. It would carry her here.

Night drew close. The jungle would cloak itself in black, leaves sealing out sky. That darkness might be mercy. Maybe the soldiers would camp. Maybe she had one more night to live.

She dragged herself against the gnarled bark of a tree, trying to steady her breath. Shelter, she told herself. Find shelter. Dry off. Bind the ankle, cradle the arm. One hour of strength could mean survival. Blind running would mean death.

Her eyes pulled east. Brazil. That was her finish line.

Thoughts drifted home. Her father, alone. She had lied to him—hadn't told him what this assignment truly was, or where it had taken her. He would've tried to stop her. He always did.

Too late now.

This wasn't just reporting. It was reckoning. A dictator laid bare. Every grave, every body, every lie catalogued. She could save lives, but only if she survived Bolivia with the truth intact.

She had faced worse before. Wars. Drug lords. Cartels. She had walked into trafficking rings with only a fake ID and a recorder sewn into her bra. She was good. Damned good.

But a single slip had cost her.

One unsecured call. Just one. Enough to turn her from predator to prey.

And the man responsible for her being hunted through this jungle?

Congressman Robert Barkley.

January 18 | 7:25 a.m. MST
Big Sky, Montana

Congressman Robert Barkley paced the living room, voice low and strained as he repeated the same sparse details to the local deputy for the third time. Each retelling scraped nerves raw, pulling on guilt he didn't know how to quiet. He kept glancing toward the door, waiting for the FBI. Almost relieved, in a way. At least when they arrived, something might finally happen. But the thought of starting from the beginning again made his chest tighten.

The deputy stayed composed, her notebook balanced in one steady hand, pen scratching quietly. Her calm wasn't detached—it was practiced. She had seen fathers like him before, standing in the ruins of a night that had stolen too much. She offered no false comfort, only order, and in some small way that helped.

The house itself no longer felt like his. Sterile movement filled every hallway. Forensics techs in pale-blue Tyvek suits moved like ghosts, brushing gloved fingers across surfaces, murmuring into radios. Cameras flashed. Evidence bags sealed. Every drawer opened, every corner illuminated. Privacy did not exist here anymore.

The front door creaked. A pair entered, coats wet with Montana sleet, gold badges clipped to lapels, catching the light. They carried the quiet gravity of people who had done this before.

The deputy nodded toward them. "The Feds are here. If you need anything, here's my card."

"Thank you, Deputy. You've been thorough." His voice cracked slightly at the edge of the word.

The agents closed the distance. One, mid-forties, dark hair just starting to gray, extended his hand. "Congressman Barkley. I'm Special Agent Matthews. This is Special Agent Johnson. I won't waste words. If we seem cold, it's because time matters. The faster we work, the better chance we have."

"I get it. Let's get on with it."

Matthews flipped open his notepad, eyes moving over the deputy's report, confirming details as Barkley answered again. Johnson drifted down the hallway, scanning rooms the bedrooms.

The congressman exhaled hard. So little to give them. The abduction had been swift, surgical. No noise. No warning. That silence haunted him more than anything—how close he had been. If he hadn't fallen asleep in the chair, if he'd walked down the hall just once more…

Johnson returned minutes later. "Probably too broad, sir, but—anyone come to mind? Political rivals? Personal grudges?

Anyone who'd push this far?"

Barkley shook his head. "Plenty don't like the votes I've cast. That's part of the job. But kidnapping my daughter? No. Nothing like that."

Before the silence could settle, one of the forensic techs entered from the hallway. Young, focused, latex gloves tight on his hands. He carried a clear evidence bag.

"Sir, two things. Partial print on the window frame. And this." He held up a translucent red cap, no bigger than a pen tip. "Safety cap from a syringe. Found it under the girl's bed."

Matthews didn't pause. "Get it to the lab."

"Already in motion. Mobile unit's live at the curb. If the print hits, we'll have results in twenty."

The tech vanished, swallowed by the storm of voices and movement. Outside, the hum of generators carried through the open door where the white trailer sat parked, lights glowing against the snow.

Matthews turned back. "Congressman, one more angle. Threats your security filtered out. Anything that didn't make it up the chain to you?"

"My detail vets everything. If there'd been a credible threat, I'd have been briefed. Lately… it's been quiet. Too quiet, maybe."

Matthews jotted. "We'll need their names. Direct, not filtered."

"You'll have the list." His tone clipped, tired of circling the same questions.

The lab tech reappeared, moving fast, tablet in hand, face set.

"We've got a problem with that fingerprint."

Matthews straightened. "Problem being?"

The tech held out the tablet. "It matched almost instantly. But the match triggered a classified firewall. CIA-level. Access denied. The only contact showing is Deputy Director Tom Conley. Past that, locked."

Barkley's body went rigid.

The CIA.

The word rattled inside him like a stone in a jar. His chest felt tight, the air in the room thinner. He knew what this meant. If they dug—and they would dig—they'd find out. About the reporter. About the assignment. About what he had set in motion. And if they connected those threads, her life was in danger.

Matthews raised an eyebrow, then turned to Barkley. "Looks like we're taking this to Langley. Congressman, you're coming with us."

Barkley hesitated. "Shouldn't I stay here? In case—"

"Sir," Johnson cut him off, voice calm but firm, "with respect, this stopped being a local crime scene the second that print hit the CIA. You're not just a witness anymore."

January 19 | 2:35 a.m. EST
Langley, Virginia

Late-night Virginia felt abandoned. After the corporate lights went dark, the streets gave up their noise. No cars. No chatter. Just the Pentagon, the Potomac, and silence stretching between Ronald Reagan International and the George Bush Center.

Inside the blacked-out van, the silence had soured into irritation. After a clean op in Yemen and a long flight home, the team had wanted a pit stop. Jacks insisted— "real food" was non-negotiable. Nobody bothered to tell him that drive-thru chicken barely counted.

Now he sat in the back, barbecue sauce on his knuckles,

grinning through grease.

"So let me get this straight. Flawless op, no casualties, Qasim bagged and tagged. Instead of rack time, we're back here at ass-o'clock in the morning?"

Finn didn't look up from his wrapper. "Orders were waiting when we landed. That's all we know."

The van slowed to a crawl, headlights off, before pulling behind a plain structure at the edge of the CIA campus. Unmarked, unremarkable—exactly the point. BREACH liked it that way. A space apart from the "Big Building" across the lot, with its swarms of analysts and bureaucrats. This was their place.

They grabbed their packs and filed inside.

The briefing room greeted them with shadows and chill. Monitors blank. Chairs lined up like an interrogation. No staff, no noise. BREACH was new, barely stood up, and support hadn't caught up yet.

"This better not be a joke," Jacks muttered.

Hopper flicked the switch. Fluorescent bulbs buzzed overhead. "Relax. We're early. Sit down. Keep licking your damn fingers."

The room's design was barebones, functional—just the way Hopper and Finn had planned it. Comms equipment, intel terminals, nothing extra. No clutter. Efficiency first.

They waited. Ate. Watched the monitors flicker to life in a slow crawl. The rhythm was familiar.

Hurry up and wait.

Thirty minutes later, the door opened.

A woman strode in, sharp-angled posture, tablet balanced on one hand. Blond hair cropped short, glasses framing eyes that scanned the team before she spoke.

"Morning, gentlemen. Melinda Taylor. Sorry for the early call."

Zeke looked up from his notes. "Mindy. Knew it was you. You have a way with satellites."

A smirk, thin and quick. "And you've got a way with comms. Zeke, I assume?"

Before anyone answered, the second door opened.

Deputy Director Tom Conley stepped inside. Clean-cut, mid-fifties, steel in his stare. Hopper felt the shift immediately. Conley didn't waste his time on standard SOG briefings. But BREACH wasn't standard. It was his baby—conceived, protected, and watched over.

"Solid work in Yemen," Conley said, voice flat but carrying weight. "Pentagon's pleased. Qasim's talking. Good intel. You made me look good."

No pause, no chance for thanks. The tempo was his, not theirs.

Mindy moved back to the door, ushering in three more figures.

Hopper stiffened. Outsiders shouldn't be in this room. Not without good reason. The first two were easy to read—FBI, crisp suits, bureau haircuts. The third man pulled the air from the room. Congressman Robert Barkley.

The team straightened as one. No chatter now.

Mindy gestured. "Special Agents Matthews and Johnson, FBI. Congressman Barkley. Ground rules: you don't get names. These operators don't officially exist. You'll call them One through Four. That's all."

The team sat opposite, Conley at the head of the table, command embodied.

Conley opened the briefing, but Barkley barely heard him. The sterile room, the clipped words, the scent of stale coffee—all of it blurred. What he saw was Sarah's empty bed. What he felt was the weight of failure. He had built a career on protecting families, but Washington was powerless against the silence that filled his house last night.

Matthews leaned forward, voice cutting through. "Straight to it. Sixteen hours ago, Congressman Barkley's daughter was abducted from his Montana home. No alarms. No tracks. Clean. Professional."

The word "professional" hung like smoke.

Zeke leaned forward, brow tight. "A stateside kidnapping? That's not a snatch-and-grab. That's black op territory."

The room went still.

Matthews nodded. "That was our read too. Forensics pulled a partial print off the window frame. It hit a classified wall. That's why we brought it to Director Conley."

Conley's gaze swept the table. "Which is why you're here. The fingerprint belongs to a foreign operative. Mindy will brief you on the details."

She tapped a folder against the tabletop, then slid it down the line. "Rodrigo Aguilar. Second-in-command of Bolivia's elite Special Forces. Direct subordinate to Teo Mendoza— who answers only to President Alejandro Rocha."

The team straightened, silent focus sharpening the air.

Mindy went on. "Mendoza's men aren't conventional. They're deniable assets—kill squads. They make journalists vanish. Protesters. Dissidents. Anyone Rocha wants erased."

Barkley leaned forward, voice tight. "Bolivia? That can't be a coincidence."

Hopper tilted his head. "Why call it a coincidence, Congressman?"

Barkley exhaled, shoulders heavy. "A month ago, I hired an investigative journalist. There were whispers coming out of Bolivia—rumors of things that made my staff sick to their stomachs. I wanted them traced back. I wanted proof Rocha was the one pulling the strings."

Finn frowned. "We monitor hot zones across the globe.

Bolivia hasn't been on the radar."

Barkley's jaw tightened. "It should've been."

Mindy interjected. "Let me give context."

Barkley gestured. "Go ahead."

"When COVID hit the West, governments fractured under the strain. Rocha capitalized on the anger. His campaign promised freedom from lockdowns, miracle cures, wealth for all. He sold hope, then weaponized it. He won in a landslide."

"And then slammed the door shut," Barkley added.

Mindy nodded. "Media blackout. No foreign press. No oversight. What's leaked is ugly. Forced labor in mines. Children in chains. Public executions as deterrent. Enough food and water to keep the population working—but nothing more."

Jacks whistled low. "So, he smiles his way into office, then builds a gulag behind closed doors?"

"That's the word," Mindy said. "But word isn't proof."

Barkley shifted in his seat. His voice dropped. "That's why I sent Kaitlyn Thompson. She goes places others won't. Ten days ago, she reached out. Said she had evidence—photos, files, names. Enough to bury Rocha. She was preparing to transmit." His throat tightened. "I haven't heard from her since."

The table stilled.

Hopper leaned forward. "Yesterday, I caught a radio broadcast. Western journalist missing in South America. That her?"

Mindy's fingers flew across the keyboard. "Checking."

Barkley's complexion drained. "I assumed she was laying low. Being careful. That's how it works, right? But if she's listed as missing—who even knew she was there?"

"Her guide," Mindy said, scanning her screen. "Miguel

Garcia. He filed a quiet report at the U.S. Embassy in La Paz. Redacted entry."

Conley's voice sliced through the room. "You didn't think the silence was suspicious?"

Barkley stammered. "I—I thought—"

"You don't think Rocha monitors calls to the U.S.? Especially in English?"

The silence after was brutal.

Barkley's voice cracked. "Did I get Kaitlyn killed?"

No one answered. The question hung heavy, unanswered by choice.

Finally, Hopper spoke, his tone steady. "Unlikely. If Rocha had her, there'd be no reason to take your daughter. They grabbed Sarah because they don't have Kaitlyn. Which means Rocha's nervous. Nervous enough to use leverage."

Barkley latched onto the words. "So, there's still a chance? For Sarah—for Kaitlyn?"

Conley gave a single nod. "Sarah's off-limits for us—we can't operate Stateside. But Kaitlyn? That's different. She's our way in."

Mindy tapped a final command. The central monitor blinked alive.

A grainy, time-stamped still filled the screen. A teenage girl being hustled up the steps of a private jet on a Big Sky airstrip. Two men flanked her. One in tactical gear. The other turned away, unidentifiable.

Barkley surged to his feet, frozen mid-breath.

Mindy didn't look away. "Director… I think we're staring at how they got her out."

3

January 19 | 4:35 a.m. EST
Langley, Virginia

"The signal analysis team just pushed this over," Mindy said.

The temperature in the room seemed to drop. Congressman Barkley stared at the monitor, his features rigid but unable to hide the fracture lines. His eyes told the truth—guilt hollowing him out, fear dragging him under. Guilt for sending Kaitlyn into Bolivia. Raw anguish for Sarah being pulled into it too.

Onscreen, the CCTV still was grainy and distant, but it didn't need to be high-res. A private jet waited on a strip of asphalt. Two men hauled a zip-tied girl up the stairs, one hand locked on each of her arms. Barkley didn't blink. He didn't need to. He knew.

It was Sarah.

Mindy narrated without emotion. "Timestamp's an hour

after the 9-1-1 call. Private airfield outside Big Sky, Montana."

Finn leaned forward, squinting. "No masks. Do we have a positive on the visible face?"

Mindy tapped her tablet. "Already confirmed. Teo Mendoza on the left. Based on the fingerprint lifted from the Barkley residence, the one on the right is Rodrigo Aguilar. He's the one forcing her onto the aircraft. Angle's not ideal, but match is strong."

Barkley's voice cut through, low but absolute. "It's her."

Hopper frowned, memory stirring. "Mendoza… why do I know that name?"

"Agency's tracked him for years," Mindy said. "Long before Rocha consolidated power. Sadist. Torturer. Analysts call him the Bolivian Butcher. Every attempt to snare him abroad failed—he moves too quickly."

Hopper looked to Conley. "If they don't have the reporter, then Sarah is leverage. Insurance policy. If Kaitlyn surfaces with the documents, Rocha needs Barkley muzzled. Sarah guarantees that silence. That's his play."

Conley didn't flinch. His eyes flicked toward Barkley, catching the spark of fury rising through grief. Then he turned back to the team.

"Prep for South America. You're going to Bolivia. Retrieve Sarah. Analysts will track the reporter separately. Operation codename, we'll keep it simple, Bravo Sierra. You're dismissed."

Four chairs scraped against tile in unison. The sound was sharp, metallic, final. No questions. No hesitation. They moved as one.

The sterile white hum of the hallway fading behind them, down two corridors and one flight of stairs, until the air thickened with oil and cordite.

The cage room.

Concrete walls. Steel racks. Rows of caged lockers. This wasn't an improvised cache on foreign soil—this was home turf. Every weapon cleaned, tagged, catalogued. Every inch of the room smelled of gun oil and sweat.

The lockers creaked open. Four cages, four men.

Finn thumbed cartridges into a magazine with steady, precise motions. The rhythm was almost meditative—click, press, slide, repeat. He carried sixteen years of ghosts. Operators he'd patched back together. Operators he hadn't. His role wasn't just to fight; it was to hold the fragile line between breathing and not. Hopper trusted him with that burden. Finn wasn't always sure he trusted himself.

Zeke cracked his knuckles, pulled a bundle of jungle netting from his cage, and ran a hand across its rough weave. He tucked it under his arm, then moved along the rack until he found his rifle. The stock rested in his palm like an old friend. His eyes flicked across the sights, the barrel, the weight—ritual, reassurance.

Jacks was already knee-deep in gear, desert pouches stripped, jungle kit checked and swapped. He ran his fingers across the stitching of each strap like checking scar tissue, then tossed them into his pack. His movements were quick but methodical—chaos with a purpose.

Hopper lingered a moment, watching. Six months of training. One mission in the books. Already, they were tighter than most teams he'd commanded in combat. They were learning each other's rhythms, instincts, silences. They weren't just operators. They were becoming brothers. And that scared him more than he'd admit. Closeness had cost him before.

The room hummed with a pressure they all felt. Mission clock had started. Every muscle knew it.

Hopper stepped to the central table, palms flat against the

cold steel.

"Bolivia. Rainy season. That means hot, wet, miserable. No airfields—we'd light up their radar and paint a bullseye on our backs. One option. We H.A.L.O. in."

His knuckle tapped the table once. A sharp, deliberate clack.

Zeke groaned, slinging a rig across his shoulder. "So much for the easy ride."

"High and slow's off the table," Hopper said. "We thread the needle. Fast, silent, blackout sky."

Jacks raised his hand half-joking, half-serious. "We bringing boom with us, or cooking our own once we land?"

"Ground-made only," Hopper replied. "Recon loadouts. Rations, optics, mags, ammo. Explosives if and when we set a base. Could be five days before we're dug in anywhere safe."

No hesitation. No complaints. Just nods. The rhythm of operators who had rehearsed this a hundred times in training and past careers.

Zeke checked his O_2 mask, then tore open a vacuum-sealed pack of jungle fatigues. "Guess we're back in the mud. And the bugs."

"You love the mud," Jacks said.

"I tolerate mud. I hate bugs."

"Pack DEET, princess," Finn said, voice dry as dust. Another magazine clicked into place.

Hopper allowed a rare smile—small, fleeting, but real.

Piece by piece, desert kit came off. Jungle kit went on. Deep greens, mottled blacks, streaks of brown. Zippers hissed. Velcro snapped. Boots stomped down on concrete. By the time the last strap cinched, they were a different team—camouflaged for a new war.

The drop crate sat at the center. Tracker armed, parachute rigged, gear strapped tight. Red diode blinking steady.

Jacks gave it a hard kick. Solid. "She'll follow us in. Land close. Same as training."

The overhead light flickered once, then steadied.

Hopper nodded. "Lima's moving our kit to the bird. Final checks. Van in twenty. Move."

They didn't answer. They didn't need to. The silence was its own reply.

One by one, they filed out, slipping through the back door, shadows melting into the Virginia night.

Gone like smoke. Like ghosts.

January 19 | 3:15 p.m. BOT
San Lorenzo, Bolivia

Teo Mendoza and Rodrigo Aguilar slowed to a stop at the checkpoint just beyond the rusted iron gates. The afternoon sun bore down, relentless, casting sharp shadows across the cracked concrete drive. Heat shimmered in waves above the hoods of parked vehicles, sun glinting off the steel barrels of mounted weapons. The morning rain was long gone, but the ground still steamed, turning the compound into a cauldron of humidity. Dust spiraled up beneath the truck's tires, disturbed for the first time in hours.

The compound didn't exist on any official maps. Hidden deep in the Bolivian interior, shielded by jungle that stretched in every direction, it was fortified by concrete walls, razor wire, and men whose loyalty belonged not to a flag but to Mendoza. His private army—brutal, unquestioning, and entirely off the books. One of many black sites scattered across the country. In some, soldiers lived and trained. In others, miners were housed like livestock, worked to exhaustion before being dumped back into villages as reminders of who ruled them.

Aguilar's eyes flicked toward the flatbed. The girl was still motionless, her limbs slack, face turned slightly away from the glaring sun. For a second he thought she was gone—but then her chest rose faintly, shallow breaths dragging through parted lips. Still alive. Still usable. Their leverage against the American remained intact.

Mendoza pressed the accelerator. The truck crept through the yard, past walls crowned with barbed wire and guard towers that loomed like watchful predators. At the far end stood a weathered building that looked a century out of place. A jailhouse stripped to its bones. Rust streaked down its walls in jagged lines. Iron bars clung stubbornly to the windows, their edges eaten through by time. Concrete crumbled in chunks, leaving pale scars across the ground. The structure had survived war, storms, and decades of decay—but barely.

"Take her inside," Mendoza ordered.

Aguilar gave a curt nod and moved to the back of the truck.

Mendoza didn't wait. He strode toward a cluster of men gathered near a burn barrel at the yard's center. A flame licked lazily inside, useless against the sun's glare. Smoke drifted upward in oily ribbons, carrying the acrid scent of scorched wood and garbage. The soldiers stiffened as he approached. No one wanted to be the one caught slouching.

"Status of the journalist?" Mendoza asked.

The men exchanged glances—silent, nervous. Finally, a junior officer stepped forward, his boots dragging in the dust. He couldn't have been older than twenty-five. Sweat smeared his face, streaking with grime, and his eyes betrayed a fear he couldn't mask.

"Sir," the young man said, voice catching. "The team has been tracking her through the jungle—almost fifty miles.

Terrain is difficult. Rain hasn't stopped. She—she's still ahead of us."

Mendoza stopped. His boots scuffed the dirt, sharp in the silence.

She had avoided capture.

He inhaled once through his nose, then let the breath out slow. Controlled. A reporter. And she was making fools of his men.

The officer pressed on, desperate. "Sir, the men are exhausted. Three days without rest. Food is gone. We're doing our best, but—"

Mendoza raised his hand.

The yard froze. Even the insects seemed to pause. The crackle of the burn barrel died beneath the sudden weight of silence.

A pistol barked once. The sound tore through the heat, then vanished into the jungle canopy surrounding the compound.

The young officer collapsed like a marionette with cut strings. One hole centered in his forehead. Blood sprayed across the rim of the barrel, sizzling as it struck the hot metal. His body hit the dirt with a dull thud. Limbs twitched, quivered, then went still.

No one moved. Not even to breathe too loudly.

Mendoza's expression remained unchanged. He hadn't fired to make an example. He had fired to correct an error, as casually as snapping a twig beneath his boot.

He looked at the others, his voice cold, steady. "No more excuses."

His gaze lingered on the corpse, then lifted, his tone dropping to a near-whisper. "Send reinforcements. Find her. Aguilar will go with you. And somebody clean this up."

The soldiers didn't hesitate. They scattered at once, boots

pounding against the dirt, tripping over one another in their haste. Better to vanish on the trail than risk being the next body in the dust.

Inside the jailhouse, the air changed. Aguilar carried Sarah's limp form through a narrow corridor into a room that smelled of mildew and iron. He laid her on a rusted infirmary bed, its frame spotted with corrosion, its thin mattress torn and water-stained. The walls were blotched with mold, green and black veins running through cracked plaster. Overhead, pipes hissed, dripping into shallow puddles on the floor. The air was wet, suffocating, laced with the reek of old blood that clung to every surface.

He tied her wrists with a heavy rope threaded through the bedframe. Tight enough to hold. Not cruel. A precaution.

Sarah stirred as the rope pulled at her skin. Her eyes fluttered open.

Confusion hit before the fear. The ceiling above was mottled and dark. Not her room. Not home. Her breath quickened. Panic followed.

She jerked against the rope. "What's happening? Where am I? Where's my dad?"

Her voice cracked, thin, trembling.

Aguilar's face softened briefly, but only slightly. His English was jagged, rough-edged with accent. "You quiet here. You good. We feed you. Nothing happen. You go home. *Comprender?*"

Sarah's eyes welled, red and glassy. Tears streaked down to her jaw, drying in salt lines. Her lips were cracked, pale. She didn't believe him. Not for a second. But she nodded, small and shaky. What else could she do?

Aguilar turned. The iron lock clanked as the door shut. His footsteps faded down the corridor, leaving her in the stink and the silence.

She was alone.

No idea where she was. No one she could understand. Everyone spoke Spanish—the guards outside, the shouted orders, even the angry voices that rose and fell through the walls. None of it belonged to her.

The mattress beneath her was damp, rank with mildew. The rope bit her wrists every time she shifted. A pipe above spat, drops falling in irregular taps that made her flinch.

Her chest ached. Her heart thudded so hard it seemed to shake the bed. This wasn't a nightmare she could wake from. This was real.

Sarah curled onto her side, eyes fixed on the stained ceiling. She trembled—not from cold, but from the vast, terrifying unknown. She was a prisoner in a place that didn't even know her name.

She closed her eyes, searching for something— anything—to hold onto.

Her dad's voice. His hand on her shoulder. The memory of one night when she'd cried for her mother and he sat beside her bed, telling her, *"I've got you. Always."*

The memory steadied her breathing. Just enough.

One thought burned through the fog of fear.

Dad will come.

He has to.

January 20 | 2:43 a.m. ACT
Brazilian Airspace

The team huddled around the soft glow of a laptop screen, strapped into webbed seats along the cargo bay of a modified C-17 built for covert operations. The cavernous hold vibrated with the heavy drone of engines, a constant thunder rolling through steel ribs. The air carried the familiar mix of jet fuel, warm oil, and metallic tang—an odor these men knew as well as the smell of their own sweat.

On the screen, Mindy's face appeared grainy, washed in the dim light of her laptop back at Langley's command center. The reflection off her glasses caught the glow, her sharp eyes locked on the team. Every word she spoke mattered. Her Intelligence briefs had already steered the team through fire once. Now, she was their compass again.

"Through the satellite network and ground intercepts, I've narrowed Sarah's location to two possibilities," she said, her tone clipped. "First, a compound outside San Lorenzo. High probability she's being held there. It's isolated, shielded by jungle, close to the mines. No civilian foot traffic—only Mendoza's men and the mine workers. Some workers live inside, so P.I.D. your targets. The second is northeast, in the Santa Maria mountains. More like a temporary camp than a fortified site. Less likely, but it's in striking distance of the first."

Hopper leaned over his chest rig, eyes scanning the terminal mounted there. His jaw clenched once. "Drop zone?"

"Coordinates are already with your pilots. You'll be jumping near Chobareca—dense canopy, plenty of cover. GPS waypoints for both the DZ and the compounds are uploaded to your devices. Shouldn't be a tough hike for you boys. You can scope the Santa Maria camp en route. Your call, Hopp."

Hopper gave a short nod. "Copy. Looks like a stroll through the bush."

From behind the sealed equipment crate, Jacks' head popped up, hair mussed and palms dusty. He slapped the side of the box like it was a horse. "Crate's rigged and chute's armed. She's riding with us. All green, boss."

"Good work, Jacks."

Attention swung back to the laptop. The team waited as Mindy glanced aside at something on her secondary monitor.

"Anything else we need to know?" Hopper asked, voice flat, no wasted breath.

She shook her head. "That's it for now. I'll be live until you hit blackout. If anything changes, you'll hear it first from me."

Hopper turned back toward the three faces around him. His tone shifted, firm and anchoring. "Alright, boys. Final checks. Talk to me."

Finn leaned forward, elbows on his knees. His voice stayed low, but steady. "If the reporter's still breathing, she'll be pushing east. Brazil's her lifeline. The chatter said she was staying in Roboré before she bolted. If she's smart, she'll already be moving toward our DZ. Hell, she might've crossed it by now."

"Good catch," Hopper said. His eyes flicked across the bay, cataloguing his men. "We stay alert for signs. Tracks, campsites, anything. We keep her vector in mind as we move. What else?"

The silence that followed was broken not by a teammate, but by the aircraft itself.

A burst of static hissed through the P.A., sharp enough to rattle the team's nerves. Then came a voice—tight, edged with strain. One of the pilots. And if a pilot sounded tense, Hopper knew to brace.

"Commander Hopper, are we expecting company on the Brazilian side of the border?"

The words dropped like a weight. Hopper looked to his

team—blank stares, tense jaws. Finn's brow furrowed, Jacks mouthed a silent curse, and even Zeke's usual smirk had drained away. On the laptop screen, Mindy leaned forward, her face a shade paler. She hadn't sent them into friendly skies expecting this.

"This can't be good," Hopper muttered.

Without waiting for an answer, he unclipped his harness and moved. Boots pounded the grated deck as he climbed the steep ladder, swung the cockpit hatch open, and stepped into the glow of instruments and the wide, cold view ahead.

Through the reinforced glass, the horizon stretched endless and dark. And then he saw them.

Two silhouettes slid into focus, hard to see, tank gray against black sky. Sleek. Predatory.

Fighters. One off each wing.

"Two tallies," the pilot said, voice clipped, hands tight on the yoke. "Yak-130s. Light attack birds. And we haven't even crossed into Bolivia yet."

Hopper's gut sank. That meant one thing. Someone knew they were coming—before they were supposed to.

"They're not Brazilian." Hopper's voice was calm, but iron edged it. "We had clearance. Nobody should know we're here. This isn't friendly. Prep for evasive maneuvers—now."

The pilot didn't argue. He flicked switches, alarms whining as lights blinked across the cockpit panels.

Down in the cargo bay, Mindy's voice came through the laptop speaker, her tone sharp with concern. "What's going on, guys?"

Hopper dropped back into the bay, breath tight. "Two fighters shadowing us—twenty miles out from the Bolivian border. Pilots were about to climb for the jump."

Mindy blinked, the screen reflecting raw data feeds across

her glasses. "Bolivia doesn't have jets."

"Exactly," Hopper said. "And Brazil wouldn't tail us after greenlighting the flight."

Her voice cracked, rising with urgency. "Then who the hell—"

The P.A. system roared, cutting her off. The pilot shouted, his voice jagged through static.

"Commander! They've got lock. Countermeasures hot. Brace!"

The C-17 heaved into a violent bank. Its bulk groaned, wings shuddering under the strain. The cargo bay erupted into chaos. Loose gear tore across the deck. The laptop spun out of sight, Mindy's voice fracturing into static before vanishing.

The team slammed against walls and crates, grabbing for straps and rails. Zeke caught a rolling duffel, hugging it like ballast to keep himself grounded.

"Gear up!" Hopper bellowed over the roar.

Training kicked in. Jacks lunged to the chute crate, snapping the latches open. Finn was already in his rig, buckles snapping tight with practiced speed. Zeke cinched his harness, knuckles white on the straps. Hopper moved between them, checking locks, anchoring hands against the swaying deck.

From the cockpit came the pulsing scream of alarms. The pilots fought the controls, but the C-17 wasn't built to dodge hunters. It was a target—slow and heavy.

Finn shoved to a porthole, eyes wide. Against the black sky, a sharp white streak tore toward them. His gut flipped cold.

"SMOKE IN THE AIR! SMOKE IN THE AIR!" he roared.

The jet dove again, hard right this time. Gravity slammed every man sideways. Shoulders cracked into steel. A spray of countermeasure flares burst from the belly, dozens of burning stars spinning into the night. They turned the dark sky into false daylight, heat signatures meant to trick the missile's eye.

For a second, hope.

Then the sound hit.

BOOM.

The concussion rattled the airframe, shaking every rib and rivet. The C-17 bucked like a wounded beast, alarms overlapping into a screaming chorus. One wing dipped, threatening to roll the whole craft, before the pilots muscled it back level.

Zeke hit the deck hard, ears ringing. Jacks sprawled flat, one arm locked on his chute. Finn cursed, spitting blood where his teeth had cut his tongue. Hopper braced against the wall, steady through it all.

"Report!" Hopper shouted.

"Proximity detonation!" the pilot barked back. "Wing's peppered, controls sluggish but holding! We won't outlast a second strike."

Another streak lit the sky. Faster. Closer.

The pilot's voice cut through the P.A., urgent, final. "We can't shake this one. Prepare to bail!"

Hopper didn't waste a second. He shoved upright, one hand gripping a harness strap. His voice was steel.

"BREACH! Masks on, rigs tight, move to the ramp! We're jumping early!"

The explosion didn't bring fire at first—only a crushing thud that reverberated through steel and bone, followed by a guttural growl under their boots. The aircraft lurched like a dying whale. The entire frame rattled, groaning in protest as rivets screamed in their sockets.

Warning lights strobed across the cargo bay, slicing the

haze into jagged flashes. Shadows jumped and twitched across crates and steel walls. A siren wailed from the cockpit, shrill and unrelenting, cutting through the roar of engines fighting for life.

Then came the smoke. Thick, acrid, suffocating. It rolled in fast, turning the bay into a dull, choking fog. Burnt plastic stung the nose. Scorched metal coated the tongue. The bitter tang of jet fuel filled their throats, searing as they breathed. Hopper coughed hard, eyes burning. He dragged an arm across his face, but the haze only thickened.

"We're hit! We're hit!" the pilot's voice cracked over the intercom, raw with panic.

Zeke stumbled toward a porthole, gripping the frame with white-knuckled hands. He barked through clenched teeth, "No shit!"

Through the glass, the right wing burned like a torch. Fire ripped outward from the engine housing, flames tearing back along the wing's length, shredded by the slipstream. Smoke poured into the night sky, a thick black flag flapping behind them.

Then the engine let go.

It shrieked like metal ripping in half as bolts tore loose. With a final, violent wrench, the engine dropped free of the wing, spinning into the dark.

The C-17 bucked, hard. The sudden imbalance pitched them sideways. The deck tilted steep, sending gear and bodies sliding. A crate slammed against the bulkhead, metal screeching on metal. Finn hit the deck, rolling until he snagged a tie-down strap, coughing through the smoke. Jacks cursed, one hand locked on the chute crate, the other clinging to a rail.

The cargo bay rattled like a can of bolts. Harness buckles

clanged against steel. The airframe vibrated so violently Hopper felt it in his teeth. He braced against the wall, planting both boots wide. His voice ripped above the chaos.

"STAY STRAPPED! WE'RE LOSING HER!"

The siren's pitch rose, merging with the low mechanical groan of a giant dying.

They weren't flying anymore.

They were falling.

4

January 20 | 2:12 a.m. EST
Langley, Virginia

The video feed cut to black.

Shock hit Mindy like a brick. Her hands moved anyway, fingers hammering the keyboard with controlled violence. Every keystroke landed sharp, deliberate. No hesitation. She had the entire CIA network at her disposal—but her spine was rigid, shoulders locked, a coil of tension winding tighter behind her eyes and down her neck.

The aircraft's final words echoed in her skull: Finn's voice, jagged through static— *"Smoke in the air."*

Then nothing.

A silence so complete it felt like pressure on her chest. For Mindy, silence wasn't calm. Silence was failure.

Behind her, Deputy Director Tom Conley paced the

length of the floor, phone pressed to his ear, voice low and clipped. He wasn't asking questions anymore. He was issuing orders, demanding names, pushing teams into motion. His shoes struck the floor in a steady rhythm that matched the tempo of her typing. He'd been in crisis rooms before. He knew this was bad.

Very bad.

Her screens glowed like a warzone. Rows of tabs overlapped, feeds streamed, data crawled across black monitors. A dozen CPU fans hummed below her desk, their whir swallowed by the fluorescent buzz overhead. She cycled through channels—command nets, satellite relays, encrypted comms. Each window stacked over another, forming a digital wall that still gave her nothing.

Her desk was chaos—open mission briefs, folders bleeding paper, a half-drunk coffee long gone cold, Post-its scrawled with reminders she'd stopped reading hours ago. She even pulled up movements of U.S. support ships off the Pacific and quick-response teams in Central America. But it was all useless. Nobody could move into Bolivia without permission. Not with a man like Rocha in charge. One wrong step, and this became international.

Still nothing. No ping. No voice. No trace.

She cracked open new comms lines—Satellite Recon Unit, SIGINT, the South American Desk. Typed command strings, double-checked every field. Returns came back empty.

"Come on," she muttered, jaw tight, eyes darting from feed to feed. "Talk to me."

The room was full of sound—Conley's clipped orders, the hum of machines, static chatter from open lines—but not the one voice she needed.

Then, a flare.

One infrared screen bloomed bright against the dark. A sudden heat signature, raw and violent. Then another. And another—like wounds ripped open across the night sky. A smoke trail unfurled on her display, thick and jagged, bleeding southwest across Bolivian airspace.

Her pulse spiked. "I've got something!"

She sat up straight, adrenaline flooding her chest, fingers flying across keys. "Director—satellite capture, five minutes old. Black smoke trail, edge of Bolivian airspace. Tracking southwest. Trail runs across the country and Chile, ends in the Pacific."

Conley stopped pacing. His voice dropped half an octave, steady as a stone. "That's a start, Taylor. Good work. Trust your skills. We'll need more."

She didn't look at him. Didn't acknowledge it. Just swiped the smoke capture into a new window, overlaid grid coordinates, cross-checked time stamps. Her breathing had gone shallow, fast.

Conley moved closer. His tone softened. "Step away for five. Regroup. Clear your head."

"I'm fine." Her voice was steady, controlled. No tremor, no crack. But she hadn't blinked in thirty seconds. She rubbed her wrist across her eyes, then went back to typing.

The truth sat sharp in her gut. She wasn't fine. She couldn't even imagine walking away from the screens now. Four operators had gone dark. If they died, it would be on her watch. Her first real mission. And she hadn't even learned all their names yet.

"I'm sweeping for transponder signals," she said, forcing the words level. "If any of their emergency beacons ping, I'll catch it. I can't step away now. There's no time."

Conley studied her. His voice was flat, unreadable. "You sure?"

"I'm sure, sir."

Conley paused, studying her. He respected how much of herself she poured into the mission—at the same time, it unsettled him. Dedication that deep burned bright, but it could also burn fast.

"I'll head back to the main building," he said finally. His voice was firm, stripped of hesitation. "I'll get you more support—intel analysts, techs, whoever you need. You give the orders, I'll clear the path."

He turned toward the door, stride quick and deliberate, as if motion itself kept the weight from crushing him.

Mindy glanced up, just a flick of her eyes. No nod. No smile. But the silence carried its own thanks. He understood.

When the door shut, the hum of machines filled the void again. Banks of servers whispered and whirred, a low chorus under the sterile light. Her shoulders hunched tighter toward the screen, eyes locked on shifting lines of code and data streams rolling like stormfronts across the glass.

A sudden alert. Her breath caught.

She leaned closer. A burst of data scrolled across her terminal—then fizzled out. False positive. A civilian satellite ping, nothing to do with her team.

She exhaled through her nose, long and steady. Reset the scan. Fingers kept moving.

In the corner of her eye, she realized Conley hadn't left yet. He lingered in the doorway, watching her. Measuring the tension in her jaw, the rigid set of her shoulders.

Still no beacon. Still no signal. Just silence.

But she wasn't stepping away. Not for five. Not for one. If she had to sit there until her eyes burned out of her skull, she would. Because silence wasn't absence—it was threat.

She barely knew the operators beyond briefing notes and the mission profile. She'd been given this role months ago, tasked with running point on missions where failure wasn't allowed. She had told herself she could shoulder it, that her skill justified the responsibility. But the truth pressed on her chest every time a feed went dark: four lives tethered to her decisions. Four lives she could lose.

It gave her pride. It gave her fear. And it gave her no margin for error.

Her fingers reset the beacon scanner. Another sweep. A pause.

Then—

Ping.

Her pulse jumped. A dot blinked to life on the western edge of her display. Faint, almost lost in the noise, but there. Her analyst's eye caught it instantly.

She snapped open a new window, calling up satellite confirmation. Coded. Authenticated. Not a false positive. Not a drill. A live GPS signal.

Her heart kicked once, hard. She leaned in, pupils narrowing on the readout.

Drop Crate #A19 – Beacon Active.

Altitude: zero.

Status: grounded.

Motion: none.

Her throat tightened. She pulled a grid overlay across the map, magnifying the quadrant until she could see every ridge and line. Close to the original drop zone.

"They made it," she said, words spilling fast, almost breathless. "The crate's down. No fragmentation on impact. Beacon's stable. That means the gear's intact—they had to have made it out of the plane."

Conley finally stepped inside. Raised one eyebrow, the same skeptical look he had leveled at field officers for decades.

"Or," he said, voice flat, "the crate just fell out on its own."

Mindy froze. His tone wasn't cruel, but it cut through her surge of hope.

He let the silence hang for a moment, then added: "I hope I'm wrong. But we need more than a box on the ground before we make a call."

She sat back an inch, staring at the pulsing dot. Her fingers hovered uselessly above the keys.

"Yeah," she said quietly, almost to herself. "I know."

The dot held steady. Solid. Unmoving. A piece of steel, a bundle of supplies. Crate A19.

But a crate wasn't a man. And no dot on the screen could tell her if anyone else had survived.

January 20 | 2:45 a.m. BOT
San Tomás, Bolivia

Kaitlyn Thompson sat huddled near a flickering fire, her body curved inward against the damp chill of stone. The flames painted restless shadows along the limestone walls of the shallow cave, shapes that bent and swayed as if alive. Smoke curled upward in thin streams, hugging the jagged ceiling before leaking through cracks toward the mouth of the cave. The air was dry, metallic, and bitter, leaving the taste of ash and dust thick on her tongue.

It wasn't much, but it was shelter. The cave curved just enough to hide the glow from prying eyes in the jungle. At least, she prayed it did. Every sound outside carried weight—the constant insect drone, the chitter of unseen creatures—but no boots crunching on leaves, no guttural Spanish commands, no sharp stutter of gunfire. That silence was fragile. She clung to it.

Her ankle pulsed with pain, sharp and unrelenting. Against her better judgment, she had pulled her shoe free and propped the swollen joint on a folded strip of canvas. The skin was flushed red and puffy, stretched tight over bone that no longer sat quite right. The sight alone threatened to buckle her stomach. Each throb reminded her how far she still had to move, and how impossible that seemed. Brazil's border lay dozens of miles away. Days of crawling jungle, rivers, mountains. If she forced herself onward tonight, she risked collapse. If she stopped, she gave her hunters more time to close the gap.

She shifted her focus to the skewer in her hand. A crude stick, sharpened and blackened at the tip, held three palm-sized insects. Their shells popped and sizzled as they cooked, the tiny legs curling in toward the fire. The smell was acrid, almost chemical, but her stomach growled despite herself. A week ago she had been in Sucre, sipping bitter coffee and eating warm empanadas at a café table, her notebook open beside her. Now she was roasting beetles on a stick. Survival stripped away dignity first, then preference. Hunger didn't negotiate.

Outside, the jungle was absolute in its darkness. No glow of distant villages, no electrical hum, no headlights bouncing off dirt roads. Just blackness pressed tight against the cave, vast and suffocating. She strained her ears—every night sound layered over the next, a living wall of noise. For one fragile moment, she allowed herself to believe the silence meant safety.

Then she heard it.

A hiss. Low, stretched across the night air. At first faint, like a distant waterfall. Then louder, a growing vibration under the surface of jungle sound. Her grip tightened on the skewer.

She froze, every muscle tensed.

The hiss deepened into a rumble. A heavy pop followed—a muffled concussion that reverberated through the trees. It was wrong. Thunder carried a hollow roll. This carried weight. Intent.

Her pulse spiked. She lurched toward the cave's mouth, dragging her bad ankle behind her, ignoring the protest of pain. Smoke stung her eyes as she tilted her head skyward, searching through the canopy.

And there it was.

A fireball ripped across the sky, cutting east to west. Massive, incandescent, far too slow and jagged to be a meteor. It blazed like a falling star that refused to die, tearing the night in half. Flame and debris trailed behind, tumbling end over end in a broken chain of fire. For an instant, the jungle lit up in stark orange relief—tree trunks glowing like skeletons, shadows stretching long.

The roar followed, a tortured scream of engines in their death spiral. She caught a glimpse of twisted metal breaking away, glowing as it fell, vanishing behind the black wall of trees. The jungle swallowed the sound, but the echo stayed inside her chest.

Kaitlyn's breath locked in her throat.

For a second, instinct pulled her back into reporter mode. The reflex she had trained her life for. Questions rattled fast: Who had fired? Was it Rocha, finally tightening the noose? Had the military fractured into open conflict? Or was this foreign intervention, the beginning of something worse? A spark meant for Bolivia that could ignite far beyond its borders?

The fireball arced lower, disappearing behind the canopy with a dying glow. The silence afterward was louder than the noise had been.

She stood in the cave mouth, chest heaving, hand trembling around the skewer of charred insects. Ash crumbled from their shells into the dirt. She didn't move to eat. Hunger felt smaller now.

If her eyes hadn't betrayed her, then the world outside her cave had just shifted. South America wasn't simply unstable anymore. It was breaking apart.

Something had fallen out of the sky. Something that wasn't supposed to fall.

And Kaitlyn Thompson—alone, injured, exhausted— was standing at ground zero of whatever came next.

January 20 | 3:20 a.m. BOT
Bolivian Jungle

A crackle of static in his earpiece dragged Hopper back from the void.

He blinked once. Twice. Vision blurred, edges tilting, nausea rolling through his gut like a tide he couldn't fight. His skull throbbed—a heavy, pounding ache that grew sharper with every heartbeat. He tried to swallow, but his throat was sandpaper.

Where the fuck am I?

His breath came ragged, echoing in his own ears. Something clamped over his nose and mouth, squeezing each inhale until it sounded hollow and mechanical. His hand came up automatically, glove brushing plastic. The oxygen mask. He yanked it free, letting it dangle against his rig.

The night air rushed in—wet, pungent, full of rot and green. Damp bark. Decaying leaves. The musty odor of rain-soaked soil. He coughed against it, lungs burning, then realized why it felt so close.

Branches caged him. Jagged limbs, broad leaves, tangled parachute lines webbed around his body. His harness bit deep into his ribs, cutting circulation with each sway. The parachute had caught high in the canopy, suspending him like some gutted marionette forty, maybe fifty feet above the jungle floor.

He swayed gently with the wind. Beneath him, the ground was a black abyss broken only by shards of moonlight.

"Fuckin' trees," he muttered, voice hoarse.

He reached for the knife on his vest—then froze as his earpiece crackled again.

"Hopper, it's Finn. Sitrep?"

Relief hit like a shot of morphine.

"Finn, Hopper," he croaked. "I'm up... emphasis on *up*. Stuck in the damn canopy. Must've blacked out. More trees here than I saw on the way in. You read me?"

"Clear, Boss. We're spread out a little more than planned. Jacks dropped the crate before he bailed. Off-mark, but close enough."

"Copy that. Status on Jacks and Zeke?"

Zeke's voice cut in, strained but steady. "Banged up, but alive. Landed a couple klicks out. Moving your way."

"Glad to hear it," Hopper said. "Rally on me. I'm not going anywhere."

Before the jump, Zeke had rigged ATAK devices onto their chest plates—lightweight, encrypted, linked to the drop crate's beacon. Even buried under a jungle canopy, the system gave them a chance to find each other. Tech had its limits, but tonight it was doing its job.

Hopper adjusted his grip on the knife and worked it under the first riser strap. The blade sawed slow through webbing slick with humidity. His shoulder screamed with the awkward angle, but he kept cutting.

Snap.

The strap gave way, and his body jerked sideways. The harness twisted, ribs compressing so hard it stole his breath. He swung in a brutal arc, smashing against bark. His knife slipped in his sweaty grip. He froze, lungs burning, lines creaking above him.

One more cut would send him crashing straight down. Too far. Too high. Not survivable.

He hung there, chest heaving, blade shaking in his fist.

Leaves rustled below. Two shapes emerged from the brush—moving low, silent, pistols ready. Then a beam of silver moonlight cut through the canopy and caught the outlines of helmets.

Jacks and Zeke.

Both carried their chutes slung across their shoulders. No way they'd leave them behind for Mendoza's men to find. Jacks limped, face tight, but still moving with purpose. Zeke's face was streaked with mud and sweat, chest rising and falling fast, but his stride never faltered.

Hopper let out a shaky exhale.

Jacks looked up, hand raised. "Hopp, hold it!"

No questions. No wasted breath. Just action. Jacks dropped to one knee, already stripping cord from his chute lines, cutting and tying with fast precision. Zeke worked beside him, anchoring into a thick root that jutted from the ground.

"Rope loop and counterbalance," Jacks muttered, fingers flying. "Anchor here, run it over a branch. You tie in, we lower you slow. That's the plan."

Zeke tugged the line hard, bracing with his weight. Then Jacks cupped his hands and shouted up. "Ready to catch, boss?"

Hopper steadied himself. "Send it."

The rope arced upward, cutting through the leaves. He snatched it mid-air, looped it twice through his D-ring, and yanked hard. Solid.

Below, Zeke called, "We're set!"

Hopper looked down again. The jungle shimmered silver and black, a chaos of shapes and shadows. In the gaps of moonlight, he could just make out movement—Finn pushing through the brush, weapon angled low, eyes scanning.

"All three of you better be ready." Hopper tightened his grip on the knife. "And this shit better hold."

His chest rose once, deep and deliberate. He braced, turned the blade, and pressed it against the final strap.

The harness creaked. The jungle floor waited. His team below stood taut, every muscle wired for the catch.

Hopper slashed the strap.

And let gravity take over.

January 20 | 3:55 a.m. BOT
Bolivian Jungle

Kaitlyn sat quietly beside the dying fire, her silhouette caught in the faint orange glow of the last embers. The flames had collapsed into blackened wood and weak, pulsing light. Smoke drifted upward in thin ribbons, clinging to the cave's limestone walls before escaping through the jagged mouth above.

She rubbed her swollen ankle, jaw tight as pulses of pain stabbed up her leg. Every throb reminded her of the mistake that had set all of this in motion.

The phone call.

She knew better. She had trained better. Secure lines existed for a reason. She should have waited, should have swallowed the panic and stuck to protocol. But she hadn't. The excitement—the urgency—had overridden her judgment. She'd reached for the phone like a rookie and dialed Barkley on an open connection.

The second she hung up, she knew it was a mistake. A desperate, reckless act. And desperation was death in this part of the world.

How could I have been so careless?

The call hadn't just exposed her. She might have painted a target on Barkley too. He had a family. A career. A name big enough to echo in the wrong ears. He hadn't signed up for this. And now, because of her, Mendoza's men would know. They wouldn't stop with her.

She shifted against the cave wall, forcing the guilt back down. Regret wouldn't save her. Regret wouldn't carry her through the jungle.

The safe house in Roboré had been perfect—Miguel's find. Hidden among other homes, forgotten and crumbling. It should have been invisible, buried in plain sight. Until she made the call. One slip, one open line, and the whole disguise burned away. By the time Mendoza's unit swept in, she was already gone. But the loss gnawed at her. The safe house had been more than walls; it had been her one point of control. Now she had nothing but the jungle and her own failing body.

Her hand dropped from her ankle to the pack beside her. The weight inside was more than gear. Documents. Photos. Names. Evidence of what Rocha's regime was doing to its own people. Faces of the dead. Proof of the prison camps, the mines, the children forced to work until they collapsed. Proof that would burn him if she got it into the right hands.

Rocha's power depended on silence. She carried the noise that could tear it apart. And for that, they would kill her.

She drew in a shaky breath, her chest tight against the

thought. It was too late to turn back now. Too late for second thoughts. The only path left was forward.

She glanced back down at her ankle. The swelling had worsened, stretching the leather of her boot until the laces bowed outward. The joint was hot to the touch, each movement sending sparks of agony up her calf. But it wasn't broken. Not yet. She could still walk. And walking meant living.

Her mind turned to the choice that had stalked her all evening: stay and rest, or move. Stay, and the swelling might ease. But staying meant giving Mendoza's trackers the time they needed to close the distance. Move, and the pain would only get worse. But every mile forward was another mile between her and their guns.

She clenched her teeth, decision hardening.

She'd move.

Pain would be her companion, but so would progress. Each step would stab, but each step would matter. Survival wasn't comfort. Survival was motion.

She pulled her bag close, stuffing the last of her gear inside. There wasn't much—maps, canteen, the battered camera she refused to abandon. She smothered the fire with the heel of her boot until nothing remained but faint wisps of smoke curling from the ash. Then she cinched the strap of her bag tight across her shoulder, fingers brushing the compass strapped to her wrist.

The needle quivered, she faced east. Toward Brazil. Toward freedom.

She stepped out of the cave and into the dark.

The jungle swallowed her whole.

No path. No light. Just instinct, direction, and the thin line of determination keeping her upright. Branches clawed at her sleeves, ripping fabric. Vines slid cold across her skin like living things. Mud sucked at her boots, heavy and slick. Insects whined in her ears, crawling beneath her collar. The jungle pressed against her from all sides, unrelenting.

Each step shot fire up her ankle, but she forced her body forward. She couldn't let the thought of pain root her in place. Somewhere out there, armed men were cutting their own trail, searching for her heat, her scent, her shadow. And if the jungle claimed her instead, Mendoza wouldn't care. He'd call it finished either way.

She gritted her teeth and pushed harder. Her breath came shallow, chest heaving with each drag of humid air. Sweat rolled down her face, salty and burning. Her heart hammered in her chest, not just from the exertion but from the weight of what she carried.

She glanced back once, through the narrow slits of moonlight between the canopy. Nothing but leaves and blackness stared back. But that didn't mean she was alone.

The jungle never let you forget that it was alive. That it was watching.

She pressed forward anyway.

Every step hurt. Every step was another reminder of how far she had to go. But every step was also defiance—against Mendoza, against Rocha, against the silence they tried to enforce with bullets.

Pain was constant. But so was purpose.

And tonight, purpose had to win.

January 20 | 5:00 a.m. BOT
Bolivian Jungle

The team pushed through the jungle in a loose wedge, moving southwest toward the crate. Without it, the mission was already dead. Radios only covered short range. Sidearms and a couple spare mags each weren't enough to push against Mendoza's men. They needed their weapons, optics, rations—the spine of their operation.

The jump had scattered them farther than expected, slamming bodies into trees, rocks, and mud. Injuries were obvious—limps, burns, bruises—but they kept moving. There was no alternative.

Zeke cut the way forward, machete slicing low arcs through curtains of liana and thick palms. Each swing released a spray of damp leaves and the sharp scent of sap. Cicadas buzzed like static. Howler monkeys roared faintly in the distance. The jungle wasn't quiet—it never was—but every snapped branch under their boots felt loud. The trail they left behind was obvious. But stealth didn't matter. The second their bird lit up the sky, any chance of subtlety was gone. They'd conceal their track later. Right now, the only thing that mattered was the crate.

The beacon placed it about a mile ahead, on the far side of a narrow ravine. Nothing on the map—no villages, no farm plots, no roads. That was good. No civilians. No witnesses. Just jungle.

Hopper's GPS blinked steady from the chest rig strapped over his aching ribs. Each throb under the harness reminded him how hard he'd hit during the jump. His skull pounded too, a deep ache behind his eyes, but he forced his pace steady. Finn limped behind, face blotched red from flash burns. His sleeve was scorched from the engine fire. Zeke's own limp hadn't improved, one knee swelling under the strain. Jacks looked like he'd fought a tree and lost—scratches across his cheek, swelling closing one eye. But they were moving. Still together. Still a unit.

The canopy overhead was a wall of green and shadow.

Ceiba trees towered more than a hundred feet high, buttress roots jutting out like natural fortifications. Creepers as thick as wrists wrapped every trunk. Waist-high ferns brushed against their ready pistols. The ground alternated between slick red mud and shallow pools that stank of rot. Mosquitoes swarmed their arms and necks, feeding at will.

The ravine appeared ahead, more trench than canyon—filled with runoff from days of rain. Brackish water sat unmoving, a film of green scum dancing on the surface. Clouds of mosquitoes hovered above it. They prayed the crate hadn't landed there.

Zeke raised a fist at the edge of a wide clearing. They froze.

The canopy parted just enough to let weak morning light spill through. Long grass swayed in the wind. Humidity pressed down heavier than before. The crate's signal placed it dead ahead, maybe a hundred meters into the clearing.

Hopper clicked his mic. "Signal's strong. Eleven o'clock. Keep it low and tight. Move."

They spread out, a staggered line with ten meters between each man. Pistols up, eyes scanning. The clearing felt wrong—too open, too exposed—but the signal didn't lie.

The crate sat just beyond the grass line, parachute draped and tangled around a clump of brush. Miraculously intact. No sign of tampering.

"Thank Christ," Jacks muttered.

"Alright," Hopper said, stepping forward. "We grab fast, then disappear. Patch up once we're under cover."

Zeke hauled a ruck free. Hopper followed, eyes on the buckles. His rifle was still lashed to the side, sealed in its waterproof wrap. He cut it loose, checked the action with a pull, then slung it across his shoulder. The weight settled into place, familiar. Balanced.

Finn snapped open a Pelican case, pulling free a med pouch and clipping it to his belt. His face twisted with pain, but his hands moved smooth, automatic. Jacks dug out his own gear, fingers brushing each pouch for moisture. Zeke tugged his pack on, shoulders sagging with relief.

No words. Just a shift in the air.

This wasn't just gear. This was their edge back. Control. Capability. A lifeline in steel and Kevlar.

Hopper adjusted his sling, breathing easier for the first time since they hit the trees. Control was thin, but it was there. The mission lived.

Zeke checked the ATAK map strapped to his vest. "We're way off DZ. Couple klicks at least."

Hopper pointed southwest, toward the faint outline of mountains behind the canopy. "Ridge system's our goal. Caves or cliffside shelter near the line—we dig in, rest, treat injuries. Then San Lorenzo. Intel says that's the best shot. We don't have the time or manpower to split and check both sites."

Jacks shouldered his machine gun, already moving toward the far treeline. Finn gave him a nod.

"Moving," Jacks said.

The others followed, Zeke taking rear. His voice carried just loud enough. "At least it's not raining."

The sky cracked open.

Rain slammed down in sheets—hard, fast, relentless. Within seconds, uniforms were soaked, boots sloshing, rifles dripping.

Hopper turned slowly, water running from his beard, glare fixed on Zeke.

"You asshole."

Zeke grinned, blinking through the downpour.

The jungle was going to drag them mile by mile, soaked

and bruised. But this was what they did. They kept moving.

And tonight, no matter the mud, the pain, or the storm, they would move until the mission pulled them under or carried them through.

4:35 p.m.

Each step was a battle. Kaitlyn dragged herself through the mountains, hour after punishing hour, burning with every incline. The morning had already cost her: descending the slope from her cave had eaten her strength, and the two ridge-lines that followed drained what little was left. Uphill climbs were brutal. Every shift in elevation lit her ankle on fire, even with the strips of fabric she'd tied tight around it. The makeshift wrap offered structure but not relief. Her pace was pitiful—just under two miles for the day. At that rate, Brazil might as well have been another continent.

By late afternoon, the jungle went still. No birdsong. No insect drone. Even the monkeys had gone silent. A blanket of quiet pressed down on the ridgeline. She stopped on a narrow outcrop of rock, sweat cooling along her spine, and listened hard. Silence in the jungle was never a gift. It meant something bigger was coming.

Her chest tightened.

Then—

A low thrum. Distant, faint. Mechanical. Not thunder, not an animal. It grew with every second, swelling in the air. A tremor built in the stone beneath her boots.

Her breath caught. Helicopter blades.

She spun, scanning the horizon, her heart pounding against bruised ribs. Then she bolted forward—half-limping, half-stumbling—driving herself downhill, ignoring the screaming in her ankle. Panic surged through her blood like fire. The sound was building, rolling through the mountains. They were sweeping. They were hunting.

They were hunting her.

Ahead, at the base of a cliff wall, she spotted it: a dense lattice of brush and vines. A knot of cover thick enough to swallow her whole if she could get there. It was her only chance. She locked onto it, shut everything else out, and pushed. Boots slipped in loose red earth, mud streaking as she staggered.

The noise grew louder. No longer faint. The air itself seemed to vibrate inside her chest.

Her ankle buckled under her weight. A white-hot spike of pain shot through her leg. She fell hard, ribs slamming the ground, palms scraping raw against wet earth. A mouthful of mud choked her. She spat, groaned, and forced herself up, crawling forward on hands and knees. Her body screamed for her to stop. She didn't. Couldn't.

The first helicopter crested the ridge behind her. Its silhouette rose above the canopy, dark and menacing, blades chewing the air like a predator closing in.

Kaitlyn risked a glance back. Not one. Three. Three helicopters, flying tight, low, and fast. Blades thundered in sync, carrying them over the ridgeline she had just crossed. A straight line. Their path aimed directly at her position.

Her stomach sank. She couldn't outrun them. That wasn't even a possibility. All she had left was the hope of vanishing into the jungle.

Ten feet.

She dragged herself the last stretch, elbows driving into the earth, shoving her pack ahead of her as she crawled. Thorns raked her sleeves. Branches snapped against her shoulders. She pushed until the wall of green closed over her and the canopy shielded her from the sky.

Her breath came ragged. Her chest heaved.

She forced herself deeper, crawling until she was swallowed by leaves and vines, until the foliage pressed against her face and back, until there was no open air above her. Mud clung to her arms. Sweat burned her eyes. Her ankle throbbed with every twitch.

The jungle swallowed her.

And then the sound hit.

The helicopters swept overhead, rotors hammering the air so hard the ground trembled. Branches rattled against each other. Leaves shook loose and spiraled down on her head and shoulders. The roar pressed into her skull, vibrating in her teeth.

Kaitlyn curled tighter, wrapping her arms around herself, trying to vanish into the brush. She clamped her mouth shut, held her breath, forced her body still.

They're looking for me. They know I'm here.

The thunder of blades rolled back and forth as the helicopters crisscrossed above the treeline. For a moment, the entire mountain felt alive with their roar.

She closed her eyes, praying to anyone who might listen. Not like this. Not now. She'd come too far, seen too much, carried too much evidence to die here in the dirt. Rocha's men wanted silence, but she carried truth. And truth had to live.

She prayed the brush was enough. That she had moved fast enough. That in the sea of green stretching mile after mile, she was invisible. Just another speck swallowed by the jungle.

Her pulse hammered in her ears, louder than the rotors.

Don't breathe. Don't move. Don't get found.

And she lay there, locked in the foliage, waiting for fate to choose—life or capture.

Praying this wasn't the end.

5

January 20 | 4:40 p.m. BOT
Bolivian Jungle

Kaitlyn lay motionless beneath the crush of tangled foliage, pressed hard between a wall of dripping vines and the slick stone of the cliff. Rainwater pooled beneath her ribs, soaking straight through her shirt, but she didn't shift. Every breath came shallow, rationed into quick bursts she tried to bury in the patter of rainfall. She couldn't risk moving. Not with death still circling the sky.

The rotor wash had passed minutes ago, but it clung to her nerves. Blades thundering overhead, branches thrashing like a storm, twigs snapping against her cheeks as the downdraft kicked debris in her face. Now the helicopters had rolled east toward the next ridge. The noise was fainter, distant, swallowed by trees. But a minute earlier it had been deafening, like the entire jungle was being torn apart above her head.

Her chest tightened.

Did they see me?

Is this over?

Her thoughts came sharp, jagged, as if her mind itself were clenching into a fist. She hadn't blinked for over a minute. Her eyes burned, refusing to close, as if a single split second of darkness would invite discovery. Even now, with the patrol fading, she didn't trust the quiet. She pressed her chin lower into the mat of leaves and mud, trying to erase herself.

The sound of blades echoed on the far ridgeline. Not circling back. Not yet. But she didn't move. Didn't breathe beyond what her lungs forced.

Stillness was safety. Stillness was life.

Her ankle throbbed, pulsing heat that spread up her calf in vicious flashes. The strips of cloth she'd torn from her undershirt had soaked through, rain and muck turning the wrap into a useless weight. Mud crept inside her boot and rubbed her skin raw. She felt it squish when she flexed her toes. The fall on the last incline had left damage worse than she admitted. A deep ache more. The pain told her she could still move, but every step would be a gamble.

Insects moved freely through the underbrush around her. Something skittered across her forearm, then vanished into the mulch. She didn't flinch. Couldn't afford to. The ground was spongy with moss and rot, damp with decades of decay, the smell of bark and wet earth thick enough to choke her. Rain traced rivulets down her neck and into her collar, chilling her chest. Her face was streaked with runoff and grit, camouflage she hadn't planned but earned.

She adjusted just enough to slip her mouth against a gap in the brush, drawing cleaner air through the screen of leaves. Beyond it—only shadows. Dense green, occasional shafts of dim evening light. No movement. No voices. No dogs.

Not yet.

She glanced back toward the cliff wall. She couldn't climb it. The stone was near vertical, slick with moss. Turning back would mean retracing ground she had nearly died to cross. Running wasn't possible with helicopters still prowling. This hollow, this narrow slit between rock and jungle floor, was all she had. Not safe. Never safe. But safer than open ground.

Her ankle screamed as she shifted slightly, easing her weight deeper into the brush. Hunger clawed at her gut. She hadn't eaten since dawn, and even then it had been little. She ignored it, let the pain settle into her like background noise. This would be her refuge for the night.

Kaitlyn had slept in war zones before. On rooftops in Aleppo, in burned-out apartments in Mogadishu, under shell-fire in Donetsk. But not like this. Not with silence pressed in like a coffin lid, and not with the certainty that no one was coming. In those other places she'd had colleagues. Fixers. Men with guns to watch her back. Here, she had nothing.

This wasn't reporting from the edge. This was the edge.

No fixer. No armored convoy. No evac plan. Just her, a wrecked ankle, and whatever luck remained. She thought of the drive that had been lost in the river, evidence gone in seconds. Everything left was in her bag, pressed against her ribs. That, and the thin thread of faith she held in the man in D.C. who had set her on this path.

Kaitlyn, you're not done yet.

The jungle around her never truly quieted. Rain softened everything, dulled sound, muffled movement, but it didn't erase it. Birds called cautiously, muted. A deep croak rolled from the canopy above. Then a rustle off to the east—sharp, wrong. She froze, heartbeat climbing, ears straining. Too soon for the forest to return to normal. Too easy for movement to be masked behind the rain.

She stayed still. Muscles locked. Breathing slow and measured. Cold water ran over her lips, pooled in her shirt, dripped from her elbows. The urge to run clawed at her nerves, hot and insistent, every fiber screaming to move. But she ignored it. She couldn't run. Not now.

Stillness was the only answer.

She blinked, finally, the first time in minutes. Rain traced down her lashes. The jungle pressed in tighter. And she let it.

As the night would come and conceal her further.

4:42 p.m.

Hopper's jaw was tight, his eyes fixed on the helicopters as they thundered east and dissolved into the horizon's green blur. He should've killed the beacon sooner. But without the crate, that had been impossible. Now they were dealing with an unknown variable—a set of three gunships cutting search patterns overhead.

It was one problem too many. If those birds backtracked along their trail, the mission wouldn't just be compromised. It would be over.

He turned to his men, his voice calm but carrying steel.

"Sun's dropping. We take the ridge before dark. From the top, we get eyes on the ground and somewhere to put our heads down. Let's move."

The rotors faded, but the threat hadn't. Every distant beat of their blades lingered like a countdown, a reminder of how fragile their window of safety was.

The team began the climb. The ridge wasn't high, but it was unforgiving. The slope rose steep and slick, a lattice of roots and vines tangled across it like snares. Each foothold had to be tested, every reach calculated. Rain dripped through the canopy in steady threads, soaking leaves until they sagged and slapped across faces. Mud sucked greedily at their boots. Loose stone shifted under their weight. Every step forward was paid for in effort.

A sudden scrape echoed ahead—rubber sliding against wet rock. Hopper froze mid-step, hand raised. The line stopped dead. Rain pattered in uneven rhythms. For a heartbeat the jungle seemed to hold its breath.

Then Finn steadied himself against a trunk, crouched low, breathing hard but controlled. His eyes met Hopper's. He gave a nod. No injury, no noise beyond what had already slipped.

They moved again.

Breathing grew heavier, shoulders pulling with strain. It wasn't fear—they'd left panic behind long ago. This was exhaustion, creeping in at the edges, whispering through their muscles and slowing their pace. The soaked cases strapped to their backs felt twice as heavy, dragging like anchors.

Zeke brought up the rear, machete low. Every few steps he brushed their trail clean, dragging vines back into place, masking footprints where the mud was softest. His movements were quick, practiced, almost invisible. A branch out of place was a signal. A footprint could be a flare.

"Keep the spread," Hopper muttered.

No one answered. They didn't need to. Formation shifted naturally, each man sliding into the rhythm of silence, pistols loose in their grip. They moved like shades—slipping forward, unseen but always listening.

The canopy thickened the higher they climbed. Ceiba roots rose from the ground like the walls of a fortress, forcing them to weave through narrow channels. Sweat ran freely, mingling with rain. The jungle pressed against them from all sides—heavy air, dripping vines, the stink of wet rot. It was like walking through a curtain of damp cloth that never ended.

But the real weight wasn't the heat. It was the sound of the helicopters, now faint but close enough to haunt. The team listened for the next burst of thunder, the signal that their time had run out.

At last, they reached the crest. They paused, bent slightly under their gear, catching hard breaths. Every muscle burned. Their uniforms clung heavy with rain. The jump, the scramble, the climb—it was all written into their faces now.

Shelter wasn't optional anymore.

Hopper scanned the ridgeline. Rain smeared the distance into a green blur, the jungle shimmering as if made of glass. No movement. No glints of metal visible. Just trees, and water, and shadows that promised nothing.

"Eyes up," he said. "We find cover, reset, and patch what we can. Then we figure out the next move."

The men adjusted their gear and followed him down the far side, their shapes vanishing into the gloom. The ridge gave way to deeper jungle. Shelter waited somewhere ahead. And they needed it before the sky swallowed the last of the light.

5:00 p.m.

Three helicopters hammered into a swampy ravine, their rotors tearing at the rain-heavy air. The downdraft churned mud and water into spiraling waves, bending grass flat and hurling arcs of spray through the clearing. The ground shook under the weight of the machines as they settled. Engines wound down in a stuttering hum, blades slowing but still chopping until they bled into silence. The quiet afterward was heavier than the noise.

Rodrigo Aguilar stepped into the field with twenty men

at his back. His voice cut through the hiss of rain.

"Spread out. We're losing daylight. Find the source!"

The soldiers moved instantly—no hesitation, no wasted words. Veterans all, they waded into the muck, rifles at the ready. Boots sank ankle-deep with every step, sucking sounds lost beneath the patter of water on helmets and gear. Their AK-74s gleamed wetly in the dim light, rain streaking down barrels and stocks. Aguilar had fought hard to get these rifles—illicit Russian stock, smuggled and paid for in blood and favors. Reliable. Deadly. Extensions of their own bodies.

Fuel fumes from the helicopters clung to the air, mixing with the sharp musk of drenched earth. Frogs croaked from the ravine, insects buzzed like static, but the storm pressed everything down beneath its weight. Water poured in shimmering sheets, pooling in low ground until every step was a slog.

For ten minutes the search dragged on, each man combing the swamp with disciplined urgency. The only sounds were rain and the subtle clicks of safeties and radios. They knew what was at stake. A signal this close could not be ignored.

Then a shout broke the stillness.

"Over here, sir!"

Aguilar turned, boots sagging through mud as he moved fast. A soldier stood over a large crate, half-hidden by grass and bent reeds.

Aguilar knelt. Rain streaked across the dented lid in rivulets. A discarded GPS unit lay beside it, screen dead, water speckling the glass. Someone had powered it down. He pressed a hand to the crate, inspected the seams. Inside: shredded parachutes. No gear. No identifiers. Nothing but a message.

His lips curled into a hard line.

"Americans."

The intel team had briefed him earlier—an aircraft hit near Bolivian airspace, written off as a spy plane. But this? A supply drop, cut chutes, powered-down beacon? This wasn't reconnaissance. These were soldiers. Special forces.

Before the thought could settle, another soldier jogged up, mud splattering at his boots. His hand thrust out, pointing beyond the crate.

"Tracks, southwest. Toward the mountains."

Aguilar's eyes narrowed, following the gesture. The jungle ridges loomed, cloaked in mist and storm. The Americans had survived. They were on foot. And they were close.

His fingers tightened around his rifle as he rose. He could already picture Mendoza's face when he brought back proof—dead or alive. This was no longer a search. It was a hunt.

He strode back to the helicopters, shielding his eyes against the rain. Pilots leaned from their cockpits, waiting. Aguilar didn't waste words.

"Return to base. The Americans are here. Update Mendoza. We'll track on foot."

He turned to his soldiers, grouped tight in the clearing.

"We know this land. We cut them off. Surround them. End them."

The men nodded, faces hard. Purpose burned in their eyes.

Engines roared again, rotors lashing the swamp as the helicopters lifted and peeled away. Rain swallowed their thunder until only jungle remained. A jagged flash lit the mountains white, followed by a roll of thunder that shook the ground beneath their boots.

Aguilar raised his hand, signaling forward. Rifles clicked, gear shifted, and the men pushed southwest—toward the mist, the ridges, and their prey.

The hunt was on.

6:30 p.m.

The last veins of daylight drained into the western sky, smothered by low clouds. Evening cooled the jungle fast. Mist drifted from the valley floor in pale streams, curling upward like the earth exhaling. Visibility shrank by the minute—just enough ambient glow left to sketch the outline of the next valley ahead.

The far ridge bristled with jagged rock, teeth against the horizon. Dark patches marked the cliffs—shadows, maybe caves. Hard to tell. Either way, it was the first chance at real shelter since the drop.

The four men sank to a knee beneath the dripping canopy. Water slid from their helmets and shoulders in silver drops. The rain had passed, but the jungle still bled. Their breaths came as thin plumes of vapor, swallowed fast by the damp air.

"Game plan?" Finn asked, his voice low.

Hopper didn't answer right away. He studied the slope like a problem to be solved—angles, shadow lines, possible firing positions. Smoke from the C-17 still burned in his eyes, and fatigue pressed down hard, but clarity was duty. Mission first. Always.

"We push west. Those cliffs are cover. If there's a cave, we hole up, patch wounds, rest. We move at first light. If the helos found the crate, they've got boots in the hills. They'll be pushing uphill toward us."

No one argued. Their bodies already hurt—ankles swollen, ribs bruised, gear pulling heavy—but exposure was worse than pain.

"You heard him," Finn said, tapping his helmet. "NODs down. Jacks, you're on point."

Jacks slipped ahead, low and fluid, descending the slope like he'd been born to it. The others followed in staggered spread, rifles up, eyes cutting across every shift of foliage. Every shadow was treated as a threat.

The jungle pressed in tight. Vines snagged at gear, mud pulled at boots with every step. The air reeked of earth and wet moss. Each inhale tasted green and rotting.

Ten minutes into the descent, Jacks' voice cracked through the radio, muffled and low.

"Hold one. Hold one."

The line froze. Hopper dropped to a knee, rifle tight. "Talk to me."

Static. Then Jacks again: "Movement. Cliff wall. Behind brush. Unconfirmed."

"Zeke," Hopper said, eyes forward. "With him."

Zeke nodded once and vanished into foliage. He flowed downslope, quiet as mist, curving wide along the ridge until he found Jacks crouched in cover. He tapped his shoulder—silent contact.

Jacks flicked a hand signal: **flank left, flush it out**. No words needed.

Zeke dropped to a knee, flipped down his NVG optic. The world shifted green. The brush ahead sharpened. Movement—small, low to the ground. Not military posture. Not armed.

He whispered into comms, barely audible. "Visual. One figure. Civilian."

***

Kaitlyn crouched behind the brush, every nerve ablaze. Her ankle pulsed like a second heartbeat. Mud coated her arms and soaked her torn pants. Her breathing was shallow, ragged. She pressed her fists into the earth to stop the trembling.

Voices drifted near. Male. Low. Not Spanish, not clear enough to parse. Her panic spiked. Her body overruled her brain—fight or flight on instinct alone. She shifted weight to her good leg, bracing. Even five stumbling steps would be better than surrender.

SNAP.

A branch cracked close—too close. Her body bolted before thought could stop it. She lunged from the brush, a gasp ripping from her throat. Her ankle failed instantly. She crashed into the slope, mud grinding into her face. She clawed, scrambling, trying to get up, limbs flailing for traction.

Then—

"Kaitlyn Thompson?"

The voice cut through the chaos. Not Spanish. No foreign cadence. English. Steady.

She froze mid-crawl. Turned, blinking through mud.

Two silhouettes emerged from the undergrowth, rifles angled low. Flashlights clicked on, beams tight against the ground. One stepped forward, calm, measured.

"We're American," Zeke said, lifting his light and giving a quick up-down wave.

Kaitlyn collapsed back into the mud. Her body broke with sobs she couldn't stop. Hands rose instinctively, trembling, palms open to the light. Tears carved streaks through the grime on her face. Relief hit so fast it hurt.

Not Bolivians. Not hunters.

Saviors.

For the first time in ten days, hope cracked through the

fear. For the first time since the call, she believed survival was possible. That there might be an end to the nightmare.

6

January 20 | 11:30 p.m. EST
Langley, Virginia

Congressman Barkley's SUV rolled to a stop in front of the BREACH operations building at CIA headquarters. He dragged himself out, every step heavy from stress and too little sleep. His body moved on habit, but his mind was frayed. The moment Conley's assistant had called him back for an in-person update, he'd known it wouldn't be good news.

Mindy waited just inside the entrance, posture rigid, hands clasped in front of her. She didn't waste words.

"Good evening, Congressman. If you'll follow me."

Barkley waved off his security detail with a tired flick of the wrist as they stepped to follow. No need for bodyguards here. This was the safest building in the country—outside the White House itself.

Mindy led him down a hushed corridor, the sound of

their footsteps swallowed by thick carpet and humming ventilation. At the end of the hall, she pushed into a briefing room where Deputy Director Conley sat alone at the long table. A single file lay open in front of him. His eyes didn't move until Barkley entered.

"Have a seat," Conley said, gesturing to one of the empty chairs.

Barkley lowered himself slowly, shoulders slumped, bracing for the worst. Mindy slid into the chair beside him and placed a folder in front of him, identical to the one Conley had been reading. She didn't speak, and she didn't need to. Their faces told him enough.

"Where do we stand?" Barkley asked, the rasp in his voice betraying both fatigue and dread.

Conley didn't soften it. "We lost comms. Aircraft confirmed down—last known position near Brazilian airspace. No word from the team since impact."

Barkley's chest hollowed. "My God…" His voice dropped to a near whisper. "Do we know who hit them? Any survivors?"

Mindy leaned forward, hands laced tightly together. Her tone was steady, but her eyes betrayed strain. "No confirmation. No emergency beacons. Just the equipment crate so far. We're scraping every channel—satellites, intercepts, partner networks. Whoever took that plane out did it clean and fast. We don't even have positive ID on the jets. It was over before we had a chance to react."

Barkley's throat constricted. He forced the words out anyway. "And my daughter? Sarah… she's still out there?"

Conley's mouth opened to respond—but the desk phone rang. The sharp, jarring sound froze the room. All three turned toward it.

Mindy's eyes widened. "It's their SAT phone." She

lunged for the button.

The line clicked, and a voice broke through—rough with static, but alive.

"This is One. All four accounted for. Banged up, but alive. Located gear. Off the original DZ, but we've got shelter in the mountains."

Conley gripped the table's edge. Relief mixed with suspicion. "Good to hear your voice, One. What the hell happened up there?"

"Fighter jets took us down," Hopper's voice replied. "No idea who or why. But by some miracle, we picked up a stray after recovering the gear."

There was a pause long enough that everyone in the room leaned closer.

"Kaitlyn Thompson. She's injured, but alive."

Conley's gaze cut straight to Barkley. The congressman froze, his pulse hammering. For a beat, he thought he'd misheard. The silence of ten days crashed back all at once—he'd assumed she was dead. Could it be true? His mind clawed for answers. Why had she gone dark? What had she endured?

"She's with you?" Conley asked.

"Yes, sir," Hopper said. "Twisted ankle, dehydrated. But she ran fifty miles alone through jungle with Mendoza's people chasing her. Tough as hell. We're bedding down for the night. Charlie Mike at first light."

"Copy," Conley said. "Continue the mission."

Mindy leaned in. "Transmit your grid. I'll reposition satellites for overwatch. I'll also check naval assets for drone coverage."

Hopper rattled off coordinates. "Appreciate it. One out."

The line cut to silence.

For a long second, no one spoke. Then Conley slapped the table with his palm and let out a sharp grin.

"Well—it's about damn time we caught a break."

Barkley leaned back, breath finally releasing from his chest in a long, shuddered exhale. Kaitlyn was alive. The team was alive. Against all odds, the mission wasn't broken—it was moving forward.

Mindy's fingers were already flying across her keyboard. "Redirecting satellites now. I'll notify SouthCom. We'll get eyes overhead."

"And task a grid over the Pacific," Conley added. "I want our pilots found and brought home."

"Understood, Director."

Barkley pushed to his feet. The relief on his face was unmistakable, but the exhaustion was still there, thick as concrete. "If anything changes—anything—call me immediately. Day or night. And if my office can provide support, you let me know."

"You have our word," Conley said. "Go get some rest."

Barkley nodded once and turned toward the door. Rest might not come, but tonight at least, he carried something he hadn't in days—hope.

January 20 | 11:35 p.m. BOT
La Paz, Bolivia

Colonel Teo Mendoza climbed out of the SUV and paused at the base of the Presidential Palace steps. Palacio Quemado. The towering stone pillars loomed like sentinels, watching, judging. He adjusted his collar, steadied his breath, and began the long walk toward a meeting he knew would end in humiliation.

Yes, his team had taken the American girl. That victory would please Rocha. But the failure to capture the reporter—

two weeks without progress—would outweigh everything else.

Each step across the grand entrance cut deeper. Gilded archways stretched overhead, chandeliers gleamed, and the polished herringbone floors amplified the sound of his boots like a drumbeat of failure. Every echo reminded him how precarious his position had become.

The palace was beautiful—vaulted ceilings, sweeping staircases, stained glass spilling fractured light across marble. Mendoza had walked these halls many times, but tonight the grandeur felt cold. It no longer welcomed him. It judged him. Beauty meant nothing when your worth was being measured in failure.

A young staffer intercepted him near the entrance. Rocha's assistant. Elegant, expressionless, clipboard in hand.

"This way, Colonel," she said, turning briskly.

He followed, jaw tight. They ascended the marble stairs, each step heavier than the last. Passing beneath the stained-glass skylight, Mendoza allowed himself a fleeting glance upward. Brilliant colors washed across the sky. A reminder of glory, of permanence. He felt neither.

At the top, the staffer rapped lightly and pushed open the massive wooden doors.

"Mr. President, Colonel Mendoza, as requested."

She stepped aside. Mendoza hesitated for a single breath, then crossed the threshold. The doors closed behind him with a heavy thud that felt more like a cell locking shut.

President Rocha stood by a wall-sized map of Bolivia, hands clasped behind his back. His gaze lingered on the preserved parchment, but when he turned, Mendoza saw it— contempt. Controlled for now, but deep.

"Colonel Mendoza," Rocha began, voice low, deliberate. "I gave you command. Men. Weapons. A budget larger than your last three posts combined. And after all of that, two weeks later, I still have no reporter."

He stepped out from behind his massive oak desk, lamplight glinting off polished wood.

"What am I paying you for?"

Mendoza swallowed hard. Heat crawled under his skin—humiliation mixed with fury. Rocha had gutted the military after his rise to power. Half his officers defected, the rest purged. Mendoza was left with green recruits and conscripts more afraid of him than loyal to him. Yet Rocha dared blame him for their failures.

"Mr. President," Mendoza said carefully, choosing each word. "Since the transition, veteran officers have been... removed. The men left to me are young. They follow orders, but they lack experience. I am shaping raw stone, sir."

Rocha's hand moved fast. The slap cracked across Mendoza's cheek, echoing through the office. Pain burned, humiliation sharper still. Mendoza kept his hands at his side, jaw clamped tight. He pressed one palm briefly to his face, then spoke again—steel edging his words.

"No disrespect intended. Only context. This isn't any reporter. She's resourceful. But we now have a lead. My best man, Aguilar, found an American supply crate in the jungle. Whoever was on board the downed aircraft—Special Forces, CIA, DEA—we're not certain. But they're here. On our soil. We're tracking them now."

That cut through Rocha's anger. His eyes narrowed, fury replaced by something colder, sharper.

"Americans," he repeated, tasting the word.

Mendoza nodded once. "Aguilar's team is already on foot. They'll find them."

Rocha turned back toward the desk. His hand curled into a fist against the polished wood. For a long moment, silence filled the room—just the sound of rain against the palace windows.

Finally, he spoke, voice hard as stone.

"This is unacceptable. Find the reporter. Find the Americans. Kill them all. Do not fail me again."

He waved Mendoza away like dismissing an insect.

Mendoza snapped a sharp nod and turned. His cheek still throbbed, but the fire inside him burned hotter. Each step down the marble staircase fueled it further. Rage. Resolve.

He would fix this. Not for Rocha. Not for the so-called Republic. For himself. To prove he was still indispensable. To keep himself from being discarded—sent not to retirement, but to rot in the mines like the men he once commanded.

This wasn't about loyalty anymore. It was survival.

January 21 | 1:25 a.m. BOT
Bolivian Jungle

The cave was damp, narrow, and cold—but to these outcasts, it might as well have been a five-star hotel. They huddled around a small, flickering fire while water dripped steadily from somewhere deeper inside. The flames threw long shadows across the stone, washing their battered faces in a wavering orange glow. It gave off little heat, but anything larger risked drawing attention.

While they patched themselves up, introductions came in short, clipped exchanges. No formalities. Real names and CIA protocols didn't matter here. Kaitlyn learned only nick-names—each close enough to the real one, but different enough to keep safe. She sat among them now as if she'd always belonged. Her face was gaunt but alert, her breathing shallow, her ankle wrapped. The presence of others seemed to dull her pain.

Hopper studied them in the firelight. They looked wrecked. Burned, stitched, limping, hollow-eyed. But alive. Still breathing. Still here.

Finn leaned back against the wall, the left side of his face slick with antiseptic gel that glistened across burns running from jaw to collar. His pale hair was plastered to his forehead, and a rough stubble shadowed his jaw. He looked beat to hell, but Hopper had seen him worse—and seen him keep moving anyway. Finn didn't break. He endured. The firelight exaggerated the rawness of the burns, but the man behind them was steady.

Zeke crouched nearest the flames, rubbing at his knee when he shifted. The limp looked like it would fade by morning, but Hopper logged a mental note to check again. Zeke's lean frame was taut with energy, his dark skin catching the flicker of light, close-cropped beard defining the sharpness of his jaw. Always scanning, always calculating. He said little, but every move had intent. Hopper trusted that.

Jacks sat quiet, face stitched and tugged by Steri-strips that pulled his skin into a permanent scowl. Zeke had cleaned the wounds, sealing them in place. Even bruised and cut up, Jacks had the bulk of a breacher—broad chest, heavy forearms, a man built for force. His broken nose and Texas drawl only added to it. He absorbed pain like it was part of the job.

Finn had rigged a splint for Kaitlyn using gauze, elastic, and sticks scavenged outside. It wasn't pretty, but it let her test weight on the ankle. She hadn't stopped thanking him.

The mood in the cave was subdued—not just fatigue but a deeper frustration. They all felt it. The mission already carried more weight than any of them expected. Their ride in shot down. Endless hours in the rain. No guarantee they weren't being tracked. Still no confirmation of Sarah Barkley's location. The silence pressed on them harder than the cold stone.

Hopper's gaze lingered on Kaitlyn. Knees drawn close, face pale under streaks of mud, hair matted flat. She looked less like a journalist and more like someone dragged through captivity. But despite everything, she was still in the fight.

He leaned toward her, voice low enough for only her.

"You did good making it this far. Most wouldn't have."

Her head turned, startled by the softness in his tone.

"I didn't have much choice."

"Still, you didn't quit. That matters."

She gave a short nod, eyes back on the fire. He let the silence settle and didn't push further.

Rising, Hopper moved to the cave's mouth. A thin mist clung to the valley floor below, curling upward like breath from the jungle. Through his NVGs, the world washed into grainy shades of green—treetops dripping, the slope they'd descended faintly visible. For now, it was still. Too still. Quiet in the jungle never lasted.

"Once we're safe in Roboré," he said over his shoulder, "I'll want to see that evidence. We'll get you and Sarah out, but if we're walking into a shitstorm, I need to know what kind."

"I'll show you everything I have. Just get us there."

"That's enough for now."

He turned back to the fire. His team looked like shadows curled against stone, gear piled around them. Soaked, burned, stitched up, dead on their feet.

"We need rest," he said flatly. "Two-hour shifts. I'll take first. Finn, you're next. Everyone else—get some sleep."

No one argued. They slid down to the cold floor, using packs as pillows. Sleep claimed them before the cave even fell silent.

At the entrance, Hopper settled with his rifle across his lap, back braced against rock. Night vision flipped down, painting the valley in green. Nothing moved. Only the faint hiss of rain beyond the mouth of the cave. Behind him, slow, steady breathing filled the space.

He pulled a strip of gauze from his vest and wrapped the cut along his forearm. It stung, but compared to what the others carried, it felt like nothing. His pain could wait. Their survival couldn't.

For tonight, the cave held. The fire burned. And for the first time in days, the team had a moment to breathe.

January 21 | 3:50 a.m. BOT
San Lorenzo, Bolivia

Silence. Stillness. Absolute dark.

Sarah lay curled on the narrow bed, her spine pressed to the cold concrete wall, her body contorted in a way no one should have to sleep. Her wrists burned, the skin rubbed raw where ropes had chewed deep. Every shift sent fire shooting up her arms. Sleep had not been rest—it had been collapse. A brutal surrender. She'd fought it, clung to consciousness, but exhaustion dragged her under anyway, into fever-dreams that blurred with memory.

When her eyes snapped open, she didn't know where the nightmare ended.

Then came the sound.

A scream.

High-pitched, ragged. Wrong.

It cut through the walls like a blade. Her heart slammed into her ribs. She jerked upright, eyes wide, searching the dark for its source. The room gave her nothing—just pitch blackness heavy with mildew, sweat, and fear. Her pulse hammered in her ears. She had no sense of time anymore. Time didn't exist here.

Another scream. Closer.

She blinked hard, forcing air into her lungs. Reality returned in pieces: concrete walls, rusted bars, the reek of damp rot.

She wasn't alone. She wasn't free.

Her hands trembled as she crawled toward the tiny, barred window, dragging her bound wrists against the cot's edge. She knelt awkwardly, one knee slipping into something wet—water or piss, she didn't care. Her cheek pressed to the bars, the rust cool and sharp against her skin.

Outside, a single security lamp flickered, its amber glow sputtering across cracked pavement and dirt. The bulb stuttered, casting long, warped shadows that shifted with every pulse. Guards moved through the dark, their rifles catching glints of light as they ran.

Spanish voices barked orders, fast and overlapping. She couldn't understand the words, and that made it worse.

Her chest tightened.

Then—

A small shape in the lamp's reach. A boy. Curled in the dirt, one arm twisted beneath him, legs at unnatural angles. Still.

Her breath caught. Dead? Dying? No shots—at least none she heard. But here, there were other ways to kill. She couldn't tell. She didn't want to.

The guards didn't stop. Didn't check. They swept past, rifles ready, eyes on something else. The child might as well have been invisible.

Her eyes adjusted further to the dark. She caught more

movement at the edge of the yard, near the perimeter fence. Two figures, low to the ground. A man and a woman, clutching hands. They crept along the wall, steps slow and desperate.

Hope stirred inside her chest for the first time since waking in this place. Maybe they knew a way out. A gap in the fence. A hole in the wall. Maybe escape was possible.

But it lasted seconds.

A voice barked from the tower.

A spotlight blazed to life, searing her vision. It locked onto the couple, freezing them in its glare like animals on a road.

Shouts erupted. Boots thundered across mud.

The couple ran. They sprinted for the far gate, bodies straining against age, slush splattering underfoot.

Sarah gripped the bars until her knuckles went white. Her lips moved in silent prayer. Please.

Above them, a guard stepped forward with unsettling calm. He leveled his rifle on the railing, tracking. Waiting.

Then he fired.

The first burst cut the woman down. She pitched forward, body flipping sideways, skidding in a spray of mud and blood.

The man kept running for half a heartbeat. Then a second burst ripped his back apart. He collapsed mid-stride, scream torn away as he hit the dirt.

Sarah staggered back from the window, her own cry strangled in her throat. She fell onto the cot, hands clamped over her mouth to smother the sobs. Gunfire echoed off the concrete—loud, merciless. Tears streamed unchecked down her cheeks.

It wasn't just the killing. It was the precision. The cold patience.

And the boy—still motionless in the dirt. Not even a glance. Forgotten. That detail hollowed her out more than the gunfire.

This wasn't an execution.

It was a message.

Sarah curled into herself on the cot, ropes biting deep, body wracked with tremors. She would never be the same. The filth, the fear, the helplessness—they had seeped into her skin. Even if she escaped, her life would never be untouched again.

She pressed her face to her sleeve, sobbing quietly. Long. Hard.

Not only for the strangers she had just watched die.

But because she knew—

They could do the same to her.

Maybe already planned to.

Sleep was gone. Not tonight. Maybe not ever.

January 21 | 5:45 a.m. BOT
Bolivian Jungle

The first light bled through the scattered clouds, stretching across the valley floor. It wasn't much, but to Jacks—perched on a flat rock just outside the cave—it was enough to make the morning feel less suffocating. Every minute it brightened, soft gold pushing back the jungle's weight.

The calm unsettled him.

The sky was clear for the first time since their boots hit dirt. No rain. No mist. Just a thin glaze of dew on the undergrowth, every leaf glistening. The jungle didn't feel like it was trying to kill them. Not today. That was progress—but progress usually meant something worse waited around the bend.

His autorifle lay across his lap. He cycled the chamber, thumbed away dried mud, checked bolts. Not because it needed it—because idle hands got sloppy, and sloppy got you killed.

His face still throbbed. Steri-strips tugged each time he exhaled, bruises swelling beneath like something alive. But he didn't flinch. His turn on watch meant no excuses.

Birds chirped low in the brush. Uneasy, but still present. The jungle wasn't silent, which was good. Silence meant predators. But too much sound could be a warning too. He listened, weighing every note like a poker player watching tells.

Jacks raised his optic and scanned the far slope. He panned slow, steady, trained. Nothing but trees and a tide of sunlight rolling through the canopy. No shimmer of metal. No movement.

Then the SAT phone buzzed against his chest rig.

It wasn't loud, but in the stillness it hit like a gunshot. He jolted, cursed under his breath, and fumbled it free. For one terrifying second, it almost slipped from his grip—an inch more and their only lifeline would've vanished into the trees below. He caught it, steadied his breathing, checked the screen.

Mindy.

He thumbed it on. "Go for Three." His voice was hushed, clipped.

"Jacks, where's Hopp?"

"Everyone's racked out. My shift on watch. Talk to me."

"You need to wake them. Now." Her tone was sharp, urgent. "The search team that found the crate—they're here. East hillside. I lost satellite coverage for ten minutes. When the feed came back, they were practically on top of you. I'm sorry."

His gut tightened, cold and fast. "Copy. I'm on it."

So much for calm.

He killed the call and bolted into the cave.

Inside, the dim light painted everything in shades of ash and ember. The fire had burned down to coals, shadows flickering along the stone. The air was thick with smoke, sweat, and damp clothes—stale, clinging, lived-in. The others slept in clusters, gear within arm's reach, boots half-laced. No one ever truly relaxed. Not out here.

Jacks crouched beside Hopper and pressed a sharp nudge to his shoulder.

"Boss—hey—"

Hopper exploded upright with a strangled gasp. His pistol cleared leather before his eyes were even open, arm extended, muzzle shifting and locked inches from Jacks' chest. His hands trembled.

Jacks froze, palms up. "Whoa—easy. It's me."

Hopper blinked, wild-eyed, chest heaving. Sweat tracked down his temple. His gaze cut around the cave like he didn't recognize it. Then, with a slow exhale, he lowered the weapon. His hand dragged down his face—not to wipe sweat, but to cage the nightmare, to force it back down where it belonged.

"Bad dream, Boss?" Jacks asked, voice low, not mocking.

"Something like that."

The tension broke, but only for a breath.

Jacks leaned in, tone clipped. "We've got company. East hillside. Mindy lost them in a SAT gap. She thinks it's the unit from the choppers. They're right on us."

The fire popped, wood splitting in the silence.

Hopper holstered the pistol in one smooth, controlled motion. Whatever ghosts had been on him were gone. His voice was steady again, all command.

"Get them up. Now."

7

Jacks moved fast through the cave, nudging each man awake with the urgency of a fire drill. His voice stayed low but hard, the kind that burned away sleep in seconds. Mindy's warning erased any hope of a quiet morning.

The cave sweated with damp. Cool drafts slid along the stone, carrying the faint smell of wet moss. Drips echoed deeper inside. Whatever sense of refuge the cave had given them was gone now.

At the entrance, Hopper crouched tight behind a slick boulder worn smooth by centuries of runoff. Rifle braced, jaw locked, lips pressed to a line. His eyes cut through the tree line without blinking, cataloguing every twitch that wasn't from the wind.

Groggy and sore, the others slid into position, gear

whispering, breaths still heavy from half-sleep. It wasn't much rest, but it would have to carry.

Finn guided Kaitlyn deeper inside, a steady hand on her shoulder. His voice barely more than breath. "Stay here. Around that bend. If it goes bad, you don't move. Don't make a sound. Clear?"

She nodded once, eyes wide, lips drained of color.

The cave didn't stretch far, but the bend was enough. From there, she'd be hidden from the line of fire. If they were overrun, maybe she could stay concealed long enough to survive. Finn didn't promise her more than that.

The rest of the team locked into firing positions at the mouth. Eroded ridges. A stone lip like a rampart. Cracks deep enough to tuck into. They settled in, rifles out, breathing steady. They didn't have luck on their side, but they had high ground—and skill. That was enough to start.

Zeke dropped prone behind a basalt slab, bipod out, scope dialed for range. His cheek found the stock. Exhale. Hold. The glass steadied. Through the trees, movement cut the green—military uniforms flashing for split-seconds.

"What've we got, Boss?" Finn murmured, rubbing grit from his eyes, muzzle already sweeping gaps.

Hopper eased back from his scope. "Seventeen. Maybe more. Far ridge. Staggered movement."

Zeke shifted, focus tightening. "Aguilar's with them. Forty meters back, giving orders."

A dry note in Hopper's voice. "Guess they sent their best."

Finn's reply was thin, almost hopeful. "Maybe they'll pass us by."

Hopper's look was flat. He reseated his mag with a hard slap. "Doubt it. Our tracks point here. If they're worth a damn, they've already read the trail. They'll follow it straight to us."

He pointed into the valley. "Pick your lanes. Cover good sectors. We hold until we can't. Zeke, you start it. Aguilar first if you get the shot."

"Copy."

The cave hushed. Only insects droned. Water dripped slow in the rock. From outside came faint metallic clicks, rifles shifting, and the muted bark of Spanish orders passed through the trees.

The enemy moved like soldiers, not conscripts. Clean wedges. Good spacing. Weapons low but ready. Eyes working. Trained. Disciplined. Mendoza hadn't sent regular troops—this was his elite.

Through Zeke's scope: boots dark with dew, trouser cuffs muddied, vines swept aside with practiced cuts. Aguilar halted to confer with a man, half-hidden by brush. Zeke had his torso and left arm. Not clean, but enough.

"Taking the shot."

He breathed out, steady. The rifle cracked, sound muffled by the suppressor. Brass spat across stone, skittering to stillness.

A burst of pink lifted off Aguilar's shoulder. He pitched sideways into cover.

"Hit," Zeke reported. "Kill not confirmed."

Hopper and Finn's rifles coughed in quick rhythm. Three figures folded in the green, bodies swallowed by ferns.

Then the jungle erupted.

Spanish commands cut sharp from two angles at once. Muzzle flashes tore through foliage. Rounds chewed into stone, spitting chips that stung bare skin. Dust and grit clouded the cave mouth, thick in their throats. The air turned hard with gunfire.

"Contact left, high!" Jacks barked from cover, snapping off a short, mean burst.

"Watch your flanks!" Hopper shouted back.

Rounds hammered the rocks. Leaves shredded into confetti across the cave mouth, green debris raining down and choking the air.

Jacks leaned out, fired, then ducked. A round screamed past his ear, ricocheted off a boulder, and a shard came back at him. It punched low, burning like fire.

"Ah—fuck me! He got me in the ass!"

"Suppressing!" Hopper leaned out, sent a hard burst downhill. Chips of stone sprayed across his cheek as a round shaved rock inches from his eye. His mag clicked dry. He dropped it, slapped a fresh one in from his vest, and was firing again before the brass from the last shot hit the ground.

Finn crawled to Jacks, dragging him behind a thicker slab of rock. Belt loose, hands working fast. "Round's still in. Clean entry. I'll pack it for now."

"Just don't touch anything that makes me wanna punch you," Jacks groaned, sweat dripping into the dirt.

"MG, two o'clock, mounted!" Finn called, peeking while he packed Jacks' wound.

Zeke swung, scope hunting. The gunner was hunched behind a fallen tree. Zeke's first shot went wide. The reply came fast—a brutal burst that hammered the stone lip, dust flooding his mouth.

Second shot—dead center mass. The gunner folded.

Third—straight through the skull. The body slumped over the log.

"Got him!" Zeke yelled. "Only I get to shoot Jacks, motherfucker!"

Fire raked the cave mouth again. A team pushed in from the right—fast, low rifles, bounding pairs, crisp like drill.

Hopper fired twice. Missed. A branch exploded ahead of him, shards splintering across his sleeve.

"They're moving like pros."

"We've dropped at least a dozen," Zeke said, sharp breaths cutting his words. "Still coming."

Hopper caught it—voices, too close. Too damn close.

"Zeke, hold the right. I'll check the slope."

He crawled to the edge, peered down. Four enemy soldiers were climbing fast, fifteen, maybe twenty meters below.

"Frags—now! Four below us!"

Three pins yanked. Spoons snapped free. They let gravity do the rest.

BOOM.

The first grenade ripped the slope, soil and roots erupting in a dark spray.

BOOM.

The second slammed the air, a shockwave punching the cave mouth, grit pelting their faces, ears ringing.

BOOM.

The third tore brush and vine apart. A helmet pinwheeled into the green. Smoke boiled upward, echoes stacking in the valley. For a moment, all sound was a high, thin whine.

Hopper edged out again. The slope below was shredded raw—branches stripped, roots torn, bodies tangled in the mess. Two moved, barely.

"Zeke, you see the far ridge?"

"Negative. No movement."

"They might've peeled," Finn said.

"Not taking chances." Hopper slung his rifle. "Cover me."

He slid down fast, boots slipping in blood and dew. The air was heavy, thick with iron and churned soil. Two survivors gasped among the wreckage. One clawed weakly at his vest, eyes already glass. The other curled half onto his side, lips moving without sound. Barely more than kids. Faces too young for the gear they carried.

Hopper's chest heaved. The wounds were mortal. Leaving them meant minutes of agony, maybe hours. Not a way anyone deserved to die.

He drew his sidearm, hand trembling under the weight of choice.

"*Lo siento*," he whispered.

Sorry didn't quite cut it, but it was better this way.

Two muffled cracks. The chests stilled.

The jungle settled. No gunfire. No shouting. Just the rustle of leaves, and the swelling drone of cicadas in the canopy.

A few minutes later, Hopper hauled himself back to the cave. Finn's eyes met his. No words passed. There weren't any.

The fight was over.

For now.

The mission wasn't.

8

January 21 | 12:30 p.m. BOT
Bolivian Jungle

The jungle had swallowed them whole hours ago. Sunlight filtered through the canopy in fractured beams, golden shards breaking across leaves slick with dew. Heat clung to the air, thick and buzzing with insect wings. Every breath carried weight. Every step dragged them deeper into green shadow.

The team moved with purpose, trekking for hours toward Roboré—a small town near the San Lorenzo compound where Kaitlyn's safe house once stood. Recon of the suspected compound could wait. Right now, they needed shelter. Somewhere to lay low, treat wounds, and reset. Again.

Kaitlyn walked near the center of the formation. Her ankle, bound with gauze and braced by a crude splint, was less of a hindrance than the day before. She limped, but she kept pace. She said little, saving her breath for the climb and letting her eyes track the shifting jungle. Every sound mattered out here.

Jacks scouted a few minutes ahead, Hopper led the rest in single file, staggered spacing, rifle ready. His men mirrored the pace—measured, deliberate, silent. They were burned, bruised, bleeding. But still lethal. Still professional.

He'd drilled them in ghost-walk: toes down first, avoid brittle branches, let your body ride the rhythm of the jungle. No unnecessary noise. No wasted movement. The forest would hide them if they respected it.

They weren't just moving toward Roboré. They had to arrive intact, combat-effective. Kaitlyn had warned him—there was still a tracker team out there. Eight men, maybe more. Enough to end this mission if even one caught their trail.

Hopper slowed, one hand braced on a tree trunk, the other twitching by his side. He clenched it into a fist, dragged it up to his temple, eyes clamped shut. A familiar ache bloomed behind them. Not fatigue. Not hunger. Memory. His fingers brushed the scar carved across his face, tracing it like proof he was still alive.

Kaitlyn noticed. She stepped closer, voice low.

"Hey. You all right?"

He didn't look at her. His hand trembled once, then stilled.

"Fine. Keep moving."

She studied him for another second, but let it go. She'd seen fatigue before, seen men and women fray under pressure. But this was something deeper, older. She filed it away.

Jacks' voice crackled over comms, steady and low.

"Movement ahead. Southwest. Tracker team."

Hopper raised a fist, halting the line. The jungle went still except for the buzz of insects. He guided Kaitlyn beneath a squat tree wrapped in vines and heavy fern growth. With one finger to his lips, he pulled greenery across her shoulders, hiding her completely.

"Stay low. No matter what."

She nodded, eyes wide.

Hopper pressed his throat mic. "Jacks, we're moving to you. Hold your glass until we're set." Then to the rest: "Finn, fifteen meters left. Zeke, right. I'll take center. Horseshoe."

They peeled off in silence, fanning wide. No chatter. No wasted sound. Bellies skimmed moss. Muzzles pushed through fern. Sweat ran cold down ribs as they crawled. Spanish murmurs drifted from the trees—boots scuffing roots, gear clinking soft, rifles shifting.

Zeke crawled under a deadfall and lined his optic through fern fronds. A flash of metal—enemy chest rig—slid behind a trunk. He steadied, slow breaths, patient.

Finn crouched behind a mound veined with roots, barrel rotating clean arcs across his field of fire.

Jacks was already prone, MK46 braced across his forearms, breathing steady. Hopper slid in beside him. Jacks gave the smallest nod, never breaking sight picture.

"Eight targets, boss. Tight group. Thirty meters. No eyes on us."

Hopper flicked open his ATAK. The grid lit with their positions—a clean arc above the patrol. Textbook. He keyed his mic.

"Sound off."

"Two, eyes on."

"Four, set."

Hopper tapped Jacks' shoulder twice. On you.

Jacks tracked their rhythm, watching the unit move. These weren't conscripts. This was a dedicated tracker squad. Rifles at the ready. Spacing tight. Eyes sharp. But they weren't expecting a team, an ambush. They were expecting a reporter, and for her to be alone. This was an advantage.

He raised his MK46, barrel sliding over a mossy root. Waited for spacing. Four men stepped into a narrow gap in the trees. Perfect.

The machine gun coughed. Sharp, clipped bursts.

The first man folded mid-stride, chest ruptured. The second pitched sideways, spine broken. The third collapsed in a storm of bark and blood. The fourth never got his rifle up.

The jungle exploded.

Zeke's rifle snapped, one shot. A throat ripped open. Another man dropped.

Finn's double-tap landed clean—sternum shattered, lungs gone.

Hopper fired four shots in quick succession. Two targets, two kills, bodies twisting into ferns with wet gasps.

It was over in less than ten seconds.

The jungle held its breath. Then only silence—broken by the steady drip of water from canopy to soil.

"Clear," Hopper said.

Finn retrieved Kaitlyn. She emerged slow, eyes darting between the sprawled bodies.

The team regrouped, moving among the dead with practiced efficiency. Safeties clicked. Pockets stripped. Radios, mags, scraps of intel bagged. Hopper scanned the clearing one last time. Eight men down. No satisfaction. But also, no regret. Just math.

The jungle would take care of the rest.

They gathered their packs, tightened straps, and slipped back into the trees. Ghosts moving toward Roboré.

Toward whatever waited next.

January 21 | 8:00 p.m. EST
Langley, Virginia

Congressman Barkley arrived at CIA headquarters again, heading straight for the BREACH building tucked at the back of Langley. At this point, he half-considered dragging a cot inside and living there. He was certain there had to be one stashed in a closet somewhere; staff probably used them on long nights.

The briefing room was dimmer than usual. Monitors dark. No files. No folders. Just the ceiling lights throwing a pool of white across the long table. At the far end, Deputy Director Conley sat as always. In front of him rested a bottle of Woodford Reserve and two glasses.

This wasn't a standard briefing.

Barkley slid into the nearest chair. Conley poured.

"Now that the dust's settled a bit—and we're not juggling a dozen disasters—I thought we could talk straight," Conley said. "Lay out next steps. Once we have the reporter's evidence. And whatever the team pulls in."

Barkley accepted the drink, the bourbon warm against his palm.

"I'm no stranger to late-night bourbon meetings, Director."

Conley gave a thin grin. "Tom."

Barkley nodded back. "Rich."

They drank.

"So," Conley said, leaning back in his leather chair, "this evidence from Kaitlyn Thompson—how do you expect to receive it?"

"She has an encrypted laptop. Government-grade. The plan was for her to upload everything to a secure server tied to my office."

Conley's brow rose.

Barkley caught it. "It's locked down. Either she left in a rush and couldn't bring it, or she can't get signal. Could be satellite coverage. I'm not a tech guy."

"I'll have Mindy check," Conley said. "And once the files are in your hands?"

Barkley let out a breath. "That part's less certain now. The idea was to bring it before a congressional panel. Revisit the aid package to Bolivia. If the contents showed something serious, maybe elevate it to the International Court of Justice. But that's a long shot—and slow. At minimum, we'd have grounds to freeze funding, then dig deeper through official channels. None of it should've led to this."

He turned his glass slowly, bourbon catching the light. "Cutting off foreign aid is one thing. Kidnapping a congressman's daughter?"

Conley shook his head. "Overkill. Which means there's more here than we're seeing. And if that's true, we'd better uncover it before the window closes."

Barkley stayed quiet. His jaw was tight. He was thinking the same thing. Whatever Rocha had set in motion wasn't finished yet.

They drank in silence at the edge of the light, shadows pressing around them.

"Stick with the plan," Conley said at last. "When the files come in, send them through your panel. I'll have Mindy keep watch on Bolivia."

Glasses touched down on the table. Phones came out. Messages sent. The unspoken urgency hung between them like fog—heavy, close, undeniable.

Whatever Rocha was building, they had to get ahead of it. Before it got worse.

January 22 | 10:30 a.m. BOT
San Lorenzo, Bolivia

The sharp, rhythmic crack of hammer on wood echoed through the courtyard, each strike cutting the heat like a metronome for death. Soldiers had been at it for hours.

Colonel Mendoza stood under the glare of the morning sun, sweat sliding down his neck as two soldiers raised the final beam. Rough timber. No finesse. Just a rope, crude and heavy. The gallows rose like a warning in the center of the compound, its noose swaying with the faint wind.

The mine workers had grown sluggish. Restless. Whispers of escape. Hidden caches of food. Last night, two men tried to run. One was beaten and dragged back. The other had vanished. This would remind the rest who held power.

Let them whisper. Let them panic. Fear had always been the best motivator.

A shout burst from the front gate. Mendoza turned sharply, eyes narrowing. Guards rushed toward the commotion.

Heat shimmered over the dirt road, warping figures into hazy silhouettes. Three men staggered toward the gate in a lopsided formation—two upright, one limp between them. Their pace was wrong. Uneven. Weighted.

As they drew closer, details broke through the blur: torn uniforms, mud caked thick, a dark stain spreading across the chest of the one in the middle.

Mendoza's boots crunched hard against the gravel as he quickened his pace. Then recognition hit like a blow.

Aguilar.

The others were jungle patrol. Faces he remembered from briefings. They'd been sent with him—the tracking teams. Choppers in, pursuit on foot. No radio calls. No warnings. And now here they were: bloodied, empty-eyed, dragging Aguilar back like cargo.

At the gates, Mendoza barked.

"Get them inside! Call the medics!"

Guards rushed to comply. Aguilar's head lolled between his escorts, face gray, lips moving without sound. Blood seeped steadily through the fabric at his collar, soaking dark down his chest. His boots dragged, legs gone useless.

"Take them to the infirmary. Now."

Two more soldiers lifted him and hurried off. The other patrolmen stumbled after them—gaunt, dehydrated, their eyes hollow.

Mendoza stayed rooted for a moment, jaw set. Questions piled fast and heavy.

Behind him, the gallows groaned as the noose swung. Beyond the walls, the faint ring of pickaxes carried up from the mines. The sound merged with the creak of fresh timber. Flies gathered in the heat.

Aguilar might live if the bleeding stopped. The patrolmen needed water and rest. He'd allow both. But only briefly. After that, he wanted answers.

He turned to his nearest lieutenant.

"Inform the intel team. I want every intercept in the last twelve hours—chatter, satellite pings, coded bursts. And sweep their route. I want to know what happened, and where I'm sending the response."

The soldier saluted and sprinted for the comms hut.

Mendoza's gaze drifted back to the gallows. The workers had seen it now. Soon they would grasp its meaning.

His jaw tightened. Rocha's last call had been as brief as it was humiliating. No reinforcements. No patience. The president's silence since then was worse—heavier than pressure, suffocating.

Mendoza needed results. Something to spin. Even a small

victory. Anything to prove he hadn't lost control of the men, the workers, or the region. Because if Rocha thought he had, Mendoza knew exactly how it would end. And it wouldn't be a clean execution. It would be slow. Public. Unforgettable.

The gallows weren't only for the miners.

Not anymore.

9

The team reached the outskirts of Roboré just as the sun baked the road into a mirage of dust and heat. They crouched in the last strip of jungle cover, where thick foliage gave way to a dirt track leading into town.

Beyond the treeline, squat one-story houses dotted the road, a few two-story ones here and there. Their walls faded to pale beige and sun-bleached yellow. A few leaned beneath rusted tin roofs that shimmered in the glare. Crooked satellite dishes perched like vultures on balconies. The faint smell of frying oil drifted on the breeze, mixing with diesel fumes from an unseen truck.

Zeke raised his optics and studied the bend where the first cluster of homes began. No uniforms. No rifles. Just townsfolk moving slowly in the heat, heads bowed, shoulders hunched, as if trying to go unnoticed in their own lives.

"Seems quiet," he muttered.

It was the kind of quiet Hopper didn't trust. No carts creaking, no trucks grinding their gears. Just heat waves dancing off the road and the stillness of a place that looked too ordinary.

The team all knew the problem. With their gear, camo, and rifles, they'd light up the second they stepped out of the green. Civilians could turn into informants with a single phone call. Every open street meant exposure. In the jungle they could vanish. Here, blending in was impossible.

Hopper crouched low, eyes on Kaitlyn.

"How much do you trust Miguel?"

Her answer came quick, no hesitation. "With my life. He set me up here, kept me clear of trouble. Warned me when to lay low. I wouldn't have made it without him."

"Any way to reach him?"

"I know where he lives. Fifteen minutes on foot. If I don't get stopped."

Hopper searched her expression, weighing more than her words. The last time he'd leaned on local help, it had nearly burned them. But Kaitlyn wasn't a variable he could second-guess right now. She knew the town, its rhythms, and—more than anything—the enemy's presence.

"If you can reach him without drawing eyes, do it. See if he's still on your side. Maybe he can get us wheels, something low-profile. Four armed Americans walking into town is a non-starter."

She nodded. "If my safe house is blown, he'll know. If not, we can set up there."

Hopper slid a compact radio from his pack and pressed it into her palm. "Channel's preset. You feel anything off, you cut and run. Straight back here. Don't second-guess."

"Got it."

She let out a long breath and rose, smoothing her hair with one hand, wiping her palms against her pants. The limp in her ankle was obvious if you knew where to look, but she tried to hide it as she stepped into the open. One stride, then another. Her figure shrank against the road as she walked into town alone.

Zeke tracked her through his scope. "She's got balls, I'll give her that. Walking into the same town she just escaped from? Damn."

The others gave low, tired chuckles—short, but real. The comment was true. What Kaitlyn was doing wasn't reckless; it was calculated. She moved like one of them now. Measured. Sharp.

The laughter faded fast. Hopper gave a silent hand signal: fall back, eyes on.

One by one, the men melted deeper into the brush. Jacks climbed to a higher ridge off the right flank, positioning himself for overwatch on the road bend with his MK46 locked in. Zeke slid behind a fallen tree, scope trained on the first line of houses. Hopper and Finn spread across the slope, rifles up, their sightlines overlapping into a tight kill zone net.

No talking. No wasted motion. Just breathing in rhythm with the jungle.

The foliage swallowed them whole. Insects hummed in their ears. A crow shrieked from the canopy above, the sound harsh, mocking, almost like a warning.

They would wait here, shadows in the green, until Kaitlyn came back—or until the town told them what kind of ground they were walking into.

2:18 p.m.

Kaitlyn walked through Roboré as if she belonged.

Her pace was steady, shoulders relaxed, hands loose at her sides. The sun pressed down, thick and heavy, and the air carried dust and the faint smell of frying oil from a food stall somewhere nearby. To anyone watching, she was just another local moving through her day. Nothing unusual. Nothing to track.

But under that façade, her nerves were tight wire. Her eyes worked every angle—windows, rooftops, parked cars, open doorways. She treated every corner like it might hide danger.

She couldn't afford another run-in.

The town itself hadn't changed. Same cracked sidewalks, same sunbaked stucco walls, same tin rooftops rusting in the glare. Motorcycles buzzed in the distance like angry wasps. But the weight was different now. Heavier. Every glance from a stranger lingered too long. Every silence seemed loaded.

Two men leaned against a shuttered storefront, cigarettes burning down to their fingers. One looked up as she passed and muttered to the other. She didn't break stride.

Keep walking.

A dusty Toyota pickup rolled past her. It slowed—too much. The passenger leaned out, dark glasses hiding his eyes, gaze cutting toward her. Adrenaline surged in her chest. Then, just as suddenly, the truck carried on down the road.

She released a shallow breath. False alarm. But enough to set every nerve on fire.

At the corner, she spotted Miguel's house at the far end of the block. Low brick wall. Faded metal gate. A curtain fluttering in the front window. No uniforms. No rifles. No obvious signs of a search.

Still, that meant nothing.

She didn't stop. She walked straight past, circled the block, then came in from the alley. The back lane was quiet. Chickens scratched the dirt behind a nearby home. A child laughed faintly somewhere, a sound out of step with the knot in her gut. A tinny radio played in the distance. Life carried on, even in shadows.

Doubling back, she approached the gate again. Her hand hesitated mid-air.

Not because she doubted Miguel. He had always been solid. But she knew how this worked—locals tortured, neighbors questioned, families pressured until they broke. If his home had been compromised, stepping through that gate might doom him, his family, everyone close to him.

She checked the street again. Clear. Then she knocked— three quick taps.

The door swung open almost at once.

"Kaitlyn!" Miguel pulled her in, voice breaking with relief. His arms locked around her like a brother clinging to a ghost. "You're alive."

The embrace caught her off guard. For a second, her arms hung loose, then she returned it, breathing against his shoulder.

"I thought maybe—"

"I know," she said quietly. "It wasn't easy. They hunted me for days. But I made it."

He stepped back, eyes raking her face, her torn clothes, the limp she tried to hide. "How? How did you escape them?"

"I didn't—on my own. I ran into a team. Americans. They're here for an extraction. Mendoza and Aguilar took a U.S. congressman's daughter. That's who they're after."

Miguel's expression darkened. Shame mixed with anger. "Those bastards... dragging a child into this. *Dios mío.*" He shook his head, then squared his shoulders. "Tell me what you need."

"A vehicle. Something big enough for four men and gear. Low profile. And I need to know if the safe house is still secure."

"No question. It's untouched." His voice was firm. "And I can get you a truck. Covered cargo bed, marked for the mine. My cousin drives for them. The paperwork is clean. Soldiers won't look twice."

Relief hit her hard enough to make her knees weak. A safe house and transport. Finally, a break.

***

Later, as the truck rattled along a back road, neither spoke much. The engine growled, tires grinding over gravel, the cargo frame bouncing on rusted shocks.

"Turn here," she said, pointing at a narrow dead-end track. Jungle pressed tight on both sides.

Miguel slowed, frowning at the overgrown cul-de-sac. "Where are they? I don't see anyone."

Kaitlyn allowed herself a thin smile. "You will."

She pulled the compact radio from her pocket and keyed it. "One, this is Kay. Transport secured. Approaching now."

The pause was long enough for Miguel to glance at her, uneasy. Then the brush ahead stirred.

Figures rose from the green, deliberate and silent, rifles angled low but ready. Faces streaked with mud. Eyes hard. Predators stepping out of cover.

Miguel's jaw went slack. "*Dios…*"

The truck halted. Kaitlyn pushed open the door, stepping down onto the gravel. She looked back at Miguel with the faintest grin.

"Told you they were good."

2:35 p.m.

As they approached the truck, the team exchanged glances—half impressed, half amused. No words, just nods and raised brows. Jacks let out a low whistle under his breath. Kaitlyn had moved fast, and the cargo-bed truck was exactly what they needed to slip into town.

Zeke gave her a slow, theatrical clap. "Hell of a find."

"This'll do just fine," Hopper said, circling the truck with a practiced eye. The mine's logo stenciled on the side panel, the canvas cover stretched across the bed—it was as close to invisible as four armed Americans in Bolivia were going to get.

They tossed the Pelican cases into the back, gear clattering against metal, then more carefully set down the rifles and remaining kit. With shoulders finally unburdened, they climbed inside. Jacks dropped the canvas flap, sealing them into shade and shadow. The relief was instant. No more hauling eighty pounds of gear through the jungle. No more endless uphill climbs. For the first time in days, their backs could rest against steel instead of roots and rock.

Kaitlyn leaned forward through the open cab window where glass used to be. "Guys, this is Miguel. He's solid. Wants the military gone and the mines shut down as much as we do."

Hopper leaned toward the opening, giving a small nod. "Glad to have you, Miguel. Call me Hopper. That's Finn, Jacks, and the baby face down there is Zeke. Appreciate the lift."

Miguel grinned. "Anytime, my friends. For the future of Bolivia."

He was shorter than they expected—barely five-foot-two—but broad through the shoulders, built like he'd spent his life hauling stone. A trimmed goatee framed his weathered face, and an off-white fedora shaded his eyes. The sweat-darkened band told its own story—years of sun, rain, and hard labor.

He shifted the truck into gear, the old engine coughing before settling into a steady growl, and they rolled onto the road toward town.

"It's not far," Miguel said, hands steady on the wheel. "And as far as I know, no one ever discovered Kaitlyn's safe house. I'll take you there. But we should stop before we reach it—watch until dark. Make sure it's still clear."

"I like your thinking," Hopper said.

Finn leaned forward from the bench, resting his arms on his knees. "Why haven't they forced you into the mines, Miguel?"

Miguel caught his eyes in the rearview. "Because I make sure they still have water to drink. I monitor the wells—levels, contamination, maintenance. Without me, the whole operation dries up. Even dictators understand you can't work men to death without giving them water first."

"Makes sense," Finn said, sitting back. His tone was flat, but his eyes lingered on Miguel with a touch of respect.

The truck slowed, tires crunching on gravel, and Miguel pointed ahead. "Seven houses down. The two-story with the balcony. That's the safe house. But for now, we wait."

Hopper studied the street, then nodded. "Daylight's no good. Too many eyes. We slip in at dark."

The truck rolled to a stop off the side road. The team

settled into the stifling heat beneath the canvas, the air thick with dust and sweat. Cicadas droned in the treeline, their shrill song filling the silence. Afternoon light crawled across the floorboards as the hours dragged.

They had four left until sundown. Waiting was the only move.

Time to get comfortable.

January 22 | 5:15 p.m. BOT
San Lorenzo, Bolivia

Mendoza stood in the barracks doorway, arms crossed, watching the medic peel back the bandages from Aguilar's shoulder. The air inside was stifling, heavy with the stench of blood and antiseptic. Bunk beds lined the walls beneath a single flickering bulb that sent twitching shadows across peeling paint.

Aguilar hunched on a stool, sweat pouring down his face, jaw tight as the medic probed the wound. Hours earlier, the round had been dug out of him, stitched closed. The bullet sat in a shallow metal bowl on the table, mute proof of failure.

"Your stitches are holding," the medic said. "It's going to hurt. Watch for infection."

Aguilar gave a slow nod, his face twisted with pain—and, Mendoza suspected, shame. More than a dozen men dead, only three survivors. Aguilar had failed, and he knew it.

Mendoza finally spoke. His voice cut through the room like a blade.

"Rodrigo… what happened out there?"

Aguilar shook his head, eyes low. "They got the drop on us. We were close. We knew it. Must've been hiding in one of the caves on the ridge. High ground. Better view. They waited for us to walk into it."

"How many?"

"I can't say for sure. We tracked four, maybe five sets of prints. Could've been doubling up to hide their numbers, though. I never saw them, not once. Just muzzle flashes."

Mendoza's expression hardened. "You took twenty men into that jungle, well trained men. Only three returned. That is unacceptable."

Aguilar didn't argue. His voice was flat. "They're good, sir."

The words stung worse than the wound. Mendoza let silence hang, then turned toward the door. Was it possible? Were these Americans truly that good—or had Aguilar simply been outplayed?

"Rest," Mendoza said. "We'll plan in the morning."

Aguilar shifted, wincing. "What about the girl?"

"What about her?"

"Maybe it's time for a ransom video. Something to scare the Americans off."

Mendoza paused, considering. "I'll think about it. But fear doesn't stop men like this."

He left, pulling the door closed behind him. Voices murmured down the hall, then flattened into silence. Mendoza leaned against the wall, rubbing at the tension in his brow. Twenty men gone. Still no reporter. And now Americans on the ground—moving like ghosts in his own backyard.

If Aguilar was right, these weren't ordinary troops. Mendoza had trained elite units himself. He knew what Special Forces looked like in the field. His half-trained conscripts wouldn't last seconds against them, and he just lost a whole unit. He had only so many professionals left.

His mind went to Rocha's last transmission, sent on the encrypted channel. The name whispered there, never spoken aloud over comms. A standby notification. If Rocha called them in, the game would change. Mendoza pushed off the wall and stepped out into the dying light.

The mine workers had been assembled in the courtyard. The gallows loomed at the center, crude beams and a swaying noose, the wood groaning like a living thing. A warning carved into the skyline. A woman pulled her child close in the back row. Someone coughed and fell silent.

At a guard's shove, a worker stumbled forward. An older man, hands scarred, eyes dull with exhaustion. He climbed the stairs as if each step drained the last of his strength. Soldiers bound his wrists, lowered the rope over his head. The crowd stiffened, but no one spoke.

Mendoza stepped into view, boots grinding the dust. His voice carried without need of a microphone.

"You are not working fast enough. You've become a problem. My problem. And I don't tolerate problems."

He let the silence weigh down on them before continuing, quieter now, but sharper.

"Unless I see progress—real progress—by tomorrow night, this man hangs. No more delays. No more escape attempts. You work, or you pay."

He turned and walked away, leaving the old man trembling beneath the noose. The crowd remained silent, fear hollowing their eyes. Some turned away, unable to watch. Others stared, broken.

Mendoza felt the weight of their fear. He needed it. It was one of the few tools he had left. But even fear had a limit. And he could feel those limits creeping closer.

January 22 | 8:00 p.m. BOT
Roboré, Bolivia

For six hours, they'd watched the safe house. No patrols. No shadows moving in windows. No soldiers. Only the still weight of the town pressed against the silence. Now, under cover of darkness, they were ready.

One by one, the men slipped from the flatbed, gear heavy on their shoulders. The street lay dead quiet, the night air broken only by insect hum and a far-off dog barking. A single streetlight buzzed at the corner, spilling its weak glow over cracked pavement. Most townsfolk were asleep by now— workers exhausted from days of forced labor. That exhaustion was the team's cover.

They carried the last of their packs up a narrow stairwell to the apartment that would serve as their base.

Inside, the space surprised them. Clean. Orderly. Kaitlyn's mark was everywhere—supplies stacked neatly, blankets folded, blinds tilted just enough to disrupt sightlines from the street. Practical. Careful. It was tight, but large enough for all of them.

Finn claimed the dining table without hesitation, clearing stray notepads and pens with one arm. "Jacks," he said, already digging through his med kit, smirk tugging at his mouth.

Jacks eyed him warily. "What?"

"Drop 'em. Face down, ass up. Table time, buddy."

Jacks groaned. "Well, shit."

He unbuckled, climbed up, and lay on his stomach like a man walking the plank. Finn leaned over the wound, gave a quick shake of his head.

"Slug's still in there. Tissue's sealing over. Gotta cut it out."

Jacks didn't flinch. He yanked the paracord bracelet off his wrist, shoved it between his teeth. "Do it."

Around them, the rest of the team spread out and set up. Hopper, Kaitlyn, and Miguel gathered by the window, heads bent over maps of Roboré and the Kaitlyn's hand drawn map of the nearby compound area. Zeke claimed the far corner, assembling a portable comms rig with the focus of a surgeon. Connectors clicked, cables wound, and the power pack gave off a steady hum. The SAT phone couldn't carry what they needed next—encrypted video feeds, recon imagery, bursts of data. Zeke's station would become their lifeline.

Finn worked fast. No anesthetic, no luxury of comfort. Just practiced precision—scalpel, tweezers, firm tug. Jacks bit down hard on the paracord, muffling a groan. A minute later, Finn stitched the small wound with neat, efficient loops.

"All done," Finn said.

"About damn time," Jacks muttered, spitting out the cord.

Across the room, Hopper listened as Kaitlyn and Miguel compared intel. Running into her in the jungle had been sheer luck. She knew the terrain, the locals, and the enemy. Miguel added what she couldn't—cover as a trusted townsman, invisible where they were obvious. Hopper knew luck like this rarely came twice. Tomorrow, they'd push on a fortified target. Without Kaitlyn and Miguel, their odds would have been cut in half.

Outside, Miguel had parked the mine truck two streets away in the shadow of a shuttered warehouse. Out of sight. Safe enough for now.

Zeke finally looked up. "Boss. Comms are live. Satellite uplink is stable."

Hopper moved to the table, opened the Toughbook, and patched into the agency network. The screen flickered, then steadied on a familiar face—Mindy, back in Langley. Thin, blond, black-rimmed glasses, her expression a mix of relief and focus.

"Hopp! Good to see you. How's the team?"

"Still standing. A little shot up, but nothing we can't manage. Just giving you an update."

"Go ahead."

"Team's at ninety percent. Medical handled. Safe house secured. Kaitlyn Thompson is with us. We've also got a local contact—Miguel. We're setting recon on Objective Sierra Lima for tomorrow. Skipped the mountain camp for now; needed time to recover. We'll hit it later if necessary."

"Copy. I'll brief the director. Good hunting. Base out."

The screen went black. Hopper sat back, exhaling.

They'd survived the day. But tomorrow, the real fight began. If they failed, none of them would walk out of Roboré alive.

8:55 p.m.

An old man sat on his porch, pipe clenched between worn teeth, the sweet bite of tobacco curling into the still night air. His rocking chair creaked with each shift of his weight, steady as a metronome. In the weeds along the roadside, insects sang their thin chorus. Beside him, a chipped ceramic cup sat empty, long since drained of tea. The day's heat had bled away, replaced by the cool breath of night.

He had labored in the mines earlier, same as every other day for weeks. Since being forced into San Lorenzo, these brief days of leave were rare—granted not as mercy but as calculated release. Now, in the quiet, he reclaimed his porch, his smoke, his watch of the town. But something unsettled the routine tonight.

A truck. Military-style. From the mines. It had parked down the road hours earlier, and his eyes had fixed on it ever since. Fear, not curiosity, made him notice. Trucks from the mines brought soldiers. Soldiers meant disappearances. Sometimes men came back hollow, silent shadows of themselves. Sometimes they never came back at all. He'd seen it too many times—neighbors, friends, fellow miners.

The truck stayed idle. Then, movement. A woman climbed out first, followed by four men. Foreigners. Not Bolivian. Not soldiers from Mendoza's command. Military, yes—but different. Their gear looked cleaner, their movements sharper. They crossed the street quickly and slipped into the shell of an old apartment. No shouting, no boots pounding on doors, no threats hurled into the night. Just a quiet entry, precise and deliberate.

The old man rocked once, slowly, pipe smoke trailing upward in a wavering line. Outsiders in Roboré were rare. Outsiders in uniform were rarer still. He didn't know if they meant ruin for the soldiers or ruin for the town—but either way, ruin was coming.

So he watched. His eyes never left the street, narrowed under the brim of his sweat-stained hat. In Roboré, information was the only currency worth more than food. A word whispered to the right ear could save a man. Or condemn him. He'd learned when to speak, and more importantly, when to wait.

He would wait tonight. Sit with his pipe, rocking chair creaking in rhythm with the cicadas, watching the apartment across the way. Because silence in Roboré was never safe. Silence was when the real trouble began.

9:30 p.m.

Most of the team was already asleep. After surviving a plane crash, two firefights, and a brutal trek through the jungle, they had earned it. Their breathing settled into a steady rhythm behind closed doors. From the comms rig in the corner came a faint, constant hum—Zeke's machine never entirely quiet—broken only by the occasional creak of settling wood. The rooms glowed faintly under dim red bulbs, an intelligent tweak Kaitlyn had made earlier: just enough light to navigate without tripping, but not enough to cast shadows across the windows.

Hopper couldn't sleep. He sat at the dining table with his sidearm disassembled in front of him, dragging a cleaning cloth through the barrel. Keeping his hands busy kept his mind from wandering—especially to places he didn't want it to go. The silence suited him. No distractions, only the soft clicks of metal and the measured movement of his hands.

He looked up when he sensed movement. Kaitlyn eased into the chair beside him, a mug cupped between her hands, though it looked untouched.

"Can't sleep?" he asked.

"I think I'm overtired. My body's finished, but my brain didn't get the memo."

"Fair enough."

Kaitlyn studied him for a beat, then tilted her head. "How did you even find me—in the jungle, I mean?"

Hopper gave a dry chuckle, eyes still on the pistol barrel. "Honestly? We didn't. We picked a jump point near where we thought Sarah was being held. Didn't know you were anywhere close, let alone on the run. Our plane took fire over Brazil, threw us off course. We landed where we did and started walking."

"So, it was just luck?"

"Mostly. The jungle's massive. Odds weren't in our favor."

"Well, I'm glad you did. I don't think I had much fight left."

Her shoulders tightened as she looked down into her cup. "Poor Sarah. I can't believe I dragged an innocent kid into this. All because of one stupid phone call. How could I be so careless?"

Hopper paused. For the first time, he set the barrel aside. He slid his chair closer and rested a steady hand on her shoulder.

"You couldn't have known. None of us ever do—not until it's too late. But you're here now, and we're going to get her back. That's what matters."

Kaitlyn swiped a hand across her cheek. "I know. I just... I can't stop thinking about what she must be going through."

He didn't offer false comfort. Just sat with her in silence, hand solid on her shoulder.

After a while, he picked up the cloth again. "So," he said, shifting the mood, "that accent of yours... London?"

She smiled faintly, grateful for the change of subject. "Born and raised. Right in the thick of it—crowded, loud, expensive. Probably why I got into journalism. I wanted to see the world. Get out of the noise."

"Seems like you did," he said, snapping a part back into the pistol.

"Everywhere from war zones to mud huts to presidential suites. Not the easiest life, but I love it. I can't imagine doing anything else."

Hopper nodded slowly. "Yeah. I get that."

Kaitlyn leaned forward, studying him. Until now, he had seemed stoic, unreadable. But here, stripped of the noise and company, she wanted to know more.

"What about you? How'd you end up in this world?"

Hopper didn't answer right away. He slid the magazine into the pistol, set it gently on the table, and exhaled.

"I come from a military family. Service runs in the blood. When 9/11 happened, I'd just graduated high school. I was angry, needed focus. The Navy felt like the only path that made sense. Fifteen years with the SEALs. Then the Agency came calling—gave me the chance to build a unit from scratch, to make my own calls. No more lives wasted because of people who've never seen combat. I handpicked this team. We're new, but we fit."

Kaitlyn rested her elbows on the table. "And before that? You don't talk about yourself. Not really. I've seen that look in your eyes—seen it plenty working with soldiers. Like something's still chasing you."

His jaw tightened. He hesitated, then nodded once.

"Afghanistan. Seven years ago. My SEAL team got sent into a building. Intel was thin. I said it felt wrong, raised concerns. Command pushed it through anyway—told us to secure it."

He went quiet. His fingers tapped once on the table.

"We breached. Took three steps. Then it blew."

Kaitlyn stayed silent, listening.

"The building collapsed. Buried the team. I was pinned under concrete—could barely breathe, couldn't move. I remember the sound of it: the explosion, the collapse, the screaming... then nothing."

His voice dropped. His hands fumbled with the rag.

"Finn found me. Dug me out. Cracked a few ribs doing it, but he got me free. Nobody else made it."

The room seemed smaller now. Hopper rubbed at the scar along his face. "That's how I got this. Since then, I keep people at a distance. Not because I don't trust them—I just can't watch it happen again. Losing people like that... it changes you."

Kaitlyn reached across, touching his hand briefly. "I'm sorry."

He shrugged faintly. "I've made peace with it. Doesn't mean it ever leaves you."

They sat a while longer. The silence between them was no longer uncomfortable.

Eventually Hopper stood. "We should at least try to get some sleep. Tomorrow's going to be a long one."

Kaitlyn rose with him. "Thanks for the company."

He gave a faint smile. "Anytime. Goodnight, Kaitlyn."

"Goodnight."

The quiet pressed in differently after she left—heavier. His instincts sharpened. Something flickered across the street: a faint orange glow. He stepped toward the window. Someone was smoking.

He lifted a night-vision scope from the gear table and scanned. An old man sat on a porch in a rocking chair, pipe in hand. Not moving. Just watching. Each draw lit his face in a brief, ruddy flare. His expression wasn't fear or curiosity, but a steady, unblinking appraisal.

The apartment inside was dark, only red light. No movement. Hopper shouldn't have been visible from the street. But the man's gaze locked on him—direct, precise.

Not a glance. Not a guess. Straight at him.

Coincidence? Maybe. Maybe not.

Hopper made a note on the intel pad: description, time, direction, pipe, posture, the unnerving accuracy of his stare.

Before heading to his room, Hopper checked again. The old man stood now, pipe extinguished. He opened the porch door, but turned once before stepping inside. His eyes met

Hopper's through the glass. Then he vanished into the house and shut the door.

Hopper stayed in the dark a moment longer, certain of one thing—he would remember that face.

January 23 | 5:30 a.m. BOT
San Lorenzo, Bolivia

Hopper and Zeke had set out before dawn, hiking six miles through dense jungle to reach their vantage point. Now they lay prone atop a wide earthen berm, half a mile from the San Lorenzo compound. From here, they had enough elevation to observe the camp while remaining unseen.

They were almost invisible. Thick tree cover shielded them from above, tall grass and underbrush cloaked them from the sides, and their ghillie suits blended seamlessly into the terrain. A patrol could pass within arm's reach and never notice. Recon was second nature to BREACH operatives, drilled into them across countless missions in their military careers.

The sun crept upward, painting the horizon deep orange. Hopper was already sketching the camp's layout, marking structures, fence lines, walls, and chokepoints. Zeke tracked guard movements and shift rotations, jotting in his clipped shorthand code. They needed everything—patterns, routines, weaknesses. Confirming Sarah's location was only part of it. Extraction meant getting her out alive and ensuring the team could escape, too.

Below them, the compound sprawled in a patchwork of weather-beaten structures and improvised barracks. Corrugated metal roofs sagged and rusted. Windows were boarded, barred, or missing altogether. Hopper squinted toward one building tucked near the eastern wall.

"You seeing that?" he asked.

Zeke adjusted his scope. "Which one?"

"Third row. Left of the motor pool."

He panned slowly. "Huh. That sign looks new."

"Not chipped. No rust. Still clean," Hopper noted.

Zeke zoomed in. "That's Cyrillic. Russian."

"Yeah. Doesn't fit."

They studied the building in silence. In a camp full of decay, one stood out—not because it was fortified, but because someone had labeled it clearly, recently. And in Russian.

Hopper penciled a note on the margin of his map. "Keep eyes on it. We're a long way from anyone speaking Russian. Might be nothing. Might be something bigger."

Zeke shifted his scope toward the courtyard. "Boss, they're bringing out prisoners. I count five with black hoods, coming from the white building on the north end."

Hopper raised his binoculars. "Eyes on. Maybe we'll catch a break."

Five prisoners shuffled single file into the courtyard, rifles jammed into their backs. Soldiers forced them into a row of chairs. Moments later, from the central barracks, Teo Mendoza emerged—grim-faced, marching toward the group. Rodrigo Aguilar followed close behind, his arm in a sling.

Hopper raised an eyebrow. "Well, look at that. Aguilar's still breathing. You slipping, Zeke?"

Zeke kept his eye glued to the glass. "Must've been the wind."

Hopper smirked at the quick comeback from his youngest operator.

A third figure climbed out of an expensive SUV and sauntered toward the gathering with arrogant ease. Short, dressed in a black suit, a multicolored sash draped across his chest. Medals gleamed along the fabric.

President Alejandro Rocha.

"Son of a bitch," Hopper muttered.

They activated the acoustic array, fine-tuning the gain until the courtyard voices came through. Rocha's morning address began like theater—a rallying cry about loyalty, unity, and the strength of Bolivia's soldiers. He promised rewards for capturing the Americans, and even offered civilians payment for information—money or time off from the mines. His tone, at first charismatic, hardened as he spoke.

He signaled to Mendoza. The colonel yanked the hood from the first prisoner: a young man, trembling, eyes wide. Sweat cut tracks through the dust on his face. His fingers locked around the chair's arms so tight his knuckles were bone white. Mendoza gripped his hair, yanking his head up to face the president.

"Do you think I've treated you unfairly?" Rocha asked.

Mendoza shoved his head back down. The prisoner shook violently, desperate, a whimper caught in his throat.

Without pause, Rocha raised his pistol and fired.

The crack split the morning silence, echoing through the compound. The man's head snapped sideways in a mist of blood. His body sagged, twitched once, and slid off the chair. A widening halo of red spread across the courtyard dust.

"Jesus Christ, Hopp—I can take this psycho out right now. One shot. We could end this."

"Negative. We don't even know if Sarah's here. And D.C. won't approve of us assassinating a sitting president without clearance."

Zeke's jaw flexed. "This guy's unhinged."

Rocha moved on. The second prisoner, an older woman, caught only a glimpse of the muzzle flash before the bullet tore through her skull. She collapsed onto the man beside her, as Mendoza tipped her chair forward. Blood spattered his cheek, clinging like war paint.

The remaining three had their hoods yanked away. Forced to stare at the mangled bodies in the dirt, they froze. Faces drained, eyes glassy, breaths shallow.

Hopper scanned them. Two older men, both shaking. Then his gaze fixed on the last figure.

A young white girl.

Sarah.

10

Hopper's pulse spiked. For the last four days, she had been nothing but a mission objective on a page—intel and photographs. Now she was real. Breathing. Terrified. In that instant, he knew he would not leave Bolivia without her. Seeing her tied up in the flesh lit a fire deep inside—his morals, his dedication. He would bring her home or die trying.

"That's her. Far right," he said.

Zeke was already relaying the intel. "Safe house, be advised: positive ID on the girl. Repeat, we have eyes on Sierra. Relay to Langley. Priority Alpha. How copy?"

The response came a moment later: "Copy that. Message relayed."

Mendoza walked alongside Rocha as he escorted the president toward his armored SUV, Rocha's expensive Italian shoes stirring dust with every step. The vehicle was parked beside the gallows, assembled the day before. The worker still stood on the platform, noose biting into his neck.

Rocha glanced up at the prisoner—eyes swollen shut, lips cracked from thirst, knees trembling after more than twelve hours upright.

"You're too soft, Teo," Rocha said. "The fear isn't sticking. Not enough of them are breaking. They've improved, but not fast enough."

Mendoza stayed silent.

Rocha climbed the gallows stairs, the wood creaking under his weight. He approached the lever, studying the gasping man before him. Without hesitation, he yanked it. The trapdoor snapped open. The prisoner dropped with a sickening jerk, his body spasming, feet swinging helplessly with no chance of finding ground.

Rocha watched long enough for the twitching to fade, then smirked. "That's how you scare them. Leave him here for the others to see. Let them know the cost of failure. Remember that, Teo."

He slid into the SUV and shut the door without a sound.

"Fuckin' monster," Zeke muttered.

Hopper kept scanning. Near the edge of the courtyard, another figure approached—a heavyset officer in a dark uniform at his side.

Hopper's chest tightened.

It was the man from the porch across the street from the safe house—the one with the pipe. He was pointing toward Roboré.

Hopper swung the directional mic. The man described the safe house in detail: the foreigners, the tactical gear, the exact location.

"Time to move. We've been burned. Let the team know."

"Copy that!" Zeke said, already transmitting. "Safe house, be advised: local asset has compromised your location. Be ready."

They packed fast. Scopes, maps, arrays—everything sealed and stowed in under two minutes.

Then they were gone, slipping into the jungle.

Silent. Swift. Racing the clock.

January 23 | 4:55 a.m. EST
Langley, Virginia

"Thanks for the update, Finn," Mindy said, hanging up the receiver at headquarters.

The building was quiet. Early mornings always brought a strange stillness here—the low hum of fluorescent lights, the faint whir of cooling fans from the server racks, the soft flicker of data streams cycling across wall-mounted monitors. Somewhere down the hall, a coffee machine sputtered once and fell silent. Most analysts and support staff hadn't arrived yet.

Mindy was pleased about that; it meant no one had seen her curled up on the couch in the break room or brushing her teeth at the sink. She was alone with the silence—and the weight of the news.

Without hesitation, she keyed in the next number.

Conley would want an update. Especially after this.

The line clicked, followed by a groggy voice. "Do we have news?"

"Yes, Director. The recon team just reported visual confirmation of Sarah. She's being held prisoner at the main compound in San Lorenzo."

She gave him the essentials first, her voice steady,

professional. But the name Sarah carried an edge.

"Physically, she looks okay. No visible injuries. But it's a dangerous place. Hopper reported that President Rocha personally executed three prisoners in front of her. Publicly. Some sort of psychological conditioning tactic."

A long pause. Then a disgusted scoff.

"This president is out of control."

Mindy nodded instinctively, though he couldn't see her. "He doesn't value the lives of his own people—let alone a kidnapped American."

Conley exhaled slowly. "Do we have IDs on the executed prisoners?"

"Locals. Possibly miners. Hopper believes the executions were meant to break the resistance of the others. A warning."

"What's the team's next move?"

"They're en route back to the safe house. Now that they've confirmed her location, they'll begin preparing for extraction. Hopper hasn't committed to a final plan yet, but they're moving quickly."

"Understood." Another pause. "I'll inform Barkley. He'll be relieved to know she's alive, even under those conditions."

"Agreed, sir. I'll stay in contact with the team and keep you updated as plans develop."

The call ended with a soft click.

Mindy remained seated, her fingers curled loosely around the edge of the desk. The news was good—Sarah was alive—but it didn't feel like a victory. Not with a sadistic warlord holding her in a camp full of armed men. Not after the murders Sarah had witnessed. Mindy imagined the gunshots echoing in that courtyard, Sarah flinching with each one.

She turned back to the operations table and opened her laptop. Status windows bloomed instantly across the screen. Her fingers moved across the trackpad, pulling up satellite overlays and terrain schematics. The map of San Lorenzo appeared on the main display: a rough top-down view with elevation lines, dirt roads, perimeter fencing. She layered in recon data, cross-referenced supply routes, tracked vehicle patterns.

The safe house glowed green. The Bolivian compound burned red.

But the drone wasn't on station yet. Delayed, likely by weather. Chile was taking heavy storms. The drone was flying in from a Navy platform off the coast. She checked the telemetry logs again. Still no uplink. That worried her.

She zoomed in on the jungle surrounding the camp. Too many blind spots. Too many places to lose contact. And the distance from the safe house on foot made retreat dangerous.

Come on. Get that bird in the sky.

She stood and crossed to the center of the ops floor, gazing up at the static feed. San Lorenzo stared back at her— still, silent, a boiling pot ready to spill over.

If the weather held the drone back much longer, the team would be forced to go in blind.

January 23 | 6:40 a.m. BOT
Roboré, Bolivia

Hopper and Zeke climbed the stairs two at a time, boots thudding on cracked concrete. Their pace was quick but measured, each step echoing faintly in the narrow stairwell. No shouts. No boots behind them. Yet.

But Hopper knew they were coming.

Bolivian forces wouldn't ignore a tip from the man across the street. Maybe they were still mobilizing, but the word was already out—he could feel it. In a place like this, information was currency. He didn't blame the man. Anyone worked to the bone would trade secrets for safety, for money, even for mercy.

Back inside the safe house, the team was already moving. Kaitlyn turned to Miguel, voice sharp. "You need to go."

Miguel blinked. "I can help—"

"No. Stay with your family. Don't come back until it's safe."

He hesitated only a second, gaze flicking to Kaitlyn, then to the rest of the team. No pride, no protest—just a man who understood the stakes. He slipped out the door and down the stairs, vanishing into the waking streets of Roboré.

For a moment, Hopper stood at the window, watching the edges of the neighborhood stir to life. A shopkeeper rolled up a metal grate, readying his store. A stray dog chased a bicycle. The ordinary rhythm of morning pressed in around him—fragile, like something that might shatter if they weren't careful. He didn't want violence spilling over into the civilians' lives.

"This isn't the place for a gunfight. Not with civvies around."

Finn, sliding a fresh mag into his rifle, gave a grim half-smile.

"Then we'd better end it before it starts."

The team went to work.

Jacks pulled extra mags and frags from a case, lining them on the floor. The sharp scent of gun oil mixed with the heavier, stale odor of the room. Finn checked the comms channel, then shoved an overturned table and a wooden chair into the hallway as a barricade. Hopper double-checked the bolt locks on the windows, the cold metal slick under his damp fingers.

Zeke posted at the southern corner window, hidden just

behind a torn curtain, rifle resting on a crate. Still, calm, his breath was slow as he scanned through the scope.

"Eyes southwest," he said. "In the tree line. Single truck. Six armed soldiers. One older guy behind the wheel."

Hopper moved beside him, raising his rifle and sighting downrange. His finger hovered over the safety.

He saw them. Jungle fatigues. The older driver wore a cap pulled low, scanning the horizon like a man who already knew.

"Plan your shots, boys," Hopper said, voice flat.

The truck slowed but didn't take the road into town. Instead, it veered off, crawling along the tree line at the southern edge. Just shy of the clearing.

Zeke tracked it. "They're stopping. Setting up in the trees. Think they're hidden."

The passenger stepped out slowly, then turned— binoculars in hand. The morning light caught the glass in a sharp flash. These soldiers didn't move like elite soldiers they had faced. They weren't deliberate or careful with their movements.

Zeke stiffened. "Boss… I think they know where we are."

Hopper didn't answer. He'd already peeled from the window, barking orders before the words even left his mouth.

"Positions at the window. No second-guessing. We take them out at the tree line before they reach town. Jacks, cover the stairwell. SAW stays quiet—you're last resort."

The three men braced rifles on the ledge. The weight of the moment settled like a held breath.

Hopper's eyes narrowed on the tree line.
"On my mark."

11

January 23 | 7:10 a.m. BOT
Roboré, Bolivia

All four team members locked in, rifles steady, nerves taut. Waiting. Summoning patience.

The early sun spilled over Roboré's rooftops, turning the southern tree line into a jagged silhouette against the haze. A military truck squatted half-concealed in the brush, its shape softened by overgrowth but still clear to trained eyes. Its presence—and its mission—were unmistakable.

Hopper adjusted his optics on the older, heavyset officer behind the wheel. The same man who'd spoken to the neighbor. Even from this distance, Hopper could tell he knew. The officer raised his hand, pointing his soldiers toward their window.

This had to be quick. Clean. No shots echoing through town. No risk to civilians. If they executed with precision, the locals might not even notice. With luck, the officer hadn't reported it up the chain yet. Maybe this was a side play—a quiet grab for influence. It would explain why such a minor element had turned up on their doorstep.

"Zeke, distance?" Finn asked, flattening against the southern window frame, rifle braced.

"Just under four hundred meters," Zeke replied, eye locked on the scope. "They're tight. Easy."

Hopper swept the area one last time. Six men. No armor. No heavy weapons. No reinforcements in sight. Their spacing was sloppy, vulnerable. Suppress and eliminate before they even realized they were in the open.

"Everyone have their targets?" Hopper asked.

"Ready," Zeke said.

"Locked," Finn added.

From deeper inside the apartment, Jacks' voice rumbled, muffled by walls. "Rear security set."

His SAW wasn't suppressed. If he had to open fire, they were already too deep.

The room tightened with silence. Breath slowed. Fingers brushed triggers. Outside, a bird lifted from the tree line, wings flashing once before vanishing into the light.

"Execute," Hopper said.

Zeke fired first. A sharp, suppressed crack. The first soldier dropped mid-step, round punching center-mass, legs folding beneath him. The second fell before the first hit the ground—a quick pair, chest then skull. He dropped flat, motionless.

Finn followed. Two precise double taps. The third and fourth soldiers crumpled into the dry grass, rifles sliding from limp hands.

The officer flinched, fumbling the gearshift. Tires spun,

kicking dust and twigs as the truck lurched into the brush and vanished.

"Truck's bugging out," Zeke called.

Hopper tracked the last straggler sprinting for cover. One squeeze. Clean hit. The man pitched forward into the dirt and didn't move again.

Then—silence. The small town of Roboré settled back into morning quiet.

"Six down. No movement," Zeke confirmed.

"Truck's gone," Finn added.

Hopper lowered his rifle, stepping back from the window. "Good work. Eyes sharp. That officer's the problem now—he'll be back, and not alone."

From the hallway, Kaitlyn appeared, carbine in hand, stance solid, face unreadable. She moved to the corner window, scanning the tree line herself.

"Clear?" she asked.

"For now," Hopper replied.

She lingered a moment. "Do we move the bodies, or wait for nightfall? What's the plan?"

"Leave them. That tree line's thick. No one's stumbling through unless they're looking for trouble. If the officer calls it in, we'll know soon enough."

Finn was already tightening his assault pack straps. "Alright. Gear up. We've got Sarah's location. No more delays."

Hopper's jaw tightened. "We move on her. Now."

No more waiting. The rescue had begun.

January 23 | 7:35 a.m. BOT
San Lorenzo, Bolivia

Captain Vargas burst into the officers' quarters, dragging an older man by the arm, lungs burning. Sweat streamed down his temples, his uniform plastered to his back from the sprint across the compound yard. His grip on the man's elbow was white-knuckled, almost desperate.

Inside, Colonel Mendoza and Rodrigo Aguilar sat at a small wooden table, sipping bitter coffee, studying a hand-drawn perimeter map of San Lorenzo. A ceiling fan spun lazily overhead, barely stirring the heavy air. Dust motes drifted through the shaft of sunlight cutting in from the open window.

Both men turned at the sudden intrusion.

"Colonel, we have a situation."

Vargas wheezed, chest heaving, fighting for composure.

Mendoza raised an eyebrow but didn't rise. This officer's stunts rarely deserved the courtesy. His silence pressed into the room—thick, expectant, dangerous.

Vargas swallowed, shifting his grip on the man at his side. His free hand twitched against his thigh.

"This man came to me with information. He said he saw foreigners in Roboré—Americans. Armed. Tactical gear. Moving into an apartment. I took six men to investigate. All six are... dead." His voice broke. "I barely made it back."

Aguilar's gaze sharpened, but he stayed silent.

Mendoza set his cup down with deliberate care, porcelain clicking against wood. "You took men without orders?" His tone was soft, but the words sliced.

Vargas faltered. "I wanted to prove my worth, sir. I thought if I brought them back in body bags—"

Crack.

Mendoza's palm slammed the table, rattling the spoon beside the coffeepot. Aguilar flinched at the sound, though his eyes never left the colonel.

"You thought?" Mendoza snapped, his voice climbing,

sharp as wire. "You acted like a fool. Six men dead—for what? A rumor? A whisper?"

Vargas dropped his gaze. "Apologies, sir."

The colonel stood, pushing his chair back with a scrape. His eyes were cold, his movements precise.

"Patrol squads clearly cannot handle this. Better soldiers will from now on."

He turned his gaze to Aguilar. The look carried weight heavier than the heat. "It's time we let the others off the leash."

Aguilar's jaw tightened—barely. He understood. Vargas did too; his breath caught. Neither spoke.

Aguilar nodded once and reached for the rifle leaning against the wall, careful with the sling on his injured arm.

As the two officers prepared to leave, Vargas yanked the informant forward.

"He knows who helped them, sir. A local gave the Americans shelter."

The old man's head stayed bowed, clothes damp with fear. His voice was a whisper. "His name is Miguel. Works the water lines. Lives two blocks from the plaza."

Mendoza stopped mid-step.

He turned, eyes locking with Aguilar's. Recognition flickered between them.

"Miguel, the water tester?"

The silence that followed stretched, filled only by the fan's lazy hum.

The old man nodded.

"Take a team," Mendoza said, voice low, even. "Find him. Alive. I'll deal with him myself."

Aguilar set the rifle back against the wall, his stare never leaving Mendoza's.

The colonel's gaze held steady, unblinking. The room

seemed to shrink, its air heavy with consequence—the officers, the informant, and the weight of what was about to unfold.

January 23 | 8:00 a.m. BOT
Roboré, Bolivia

The BREACH team moved with quiet purpose, each man prepping gear with the calm precision of soldiers who'd done this a hundred times before. Mags slid into pouches. Bolts cycled, optics wiped, rifles checked. The hint of gun oil mingled with the stale air of the safe house. Every zip, click, and scrape rang sharp in the silence. They had everything they needed—everything but Sarah.

This would be their final assault.

If they eliminated the threat and recovered Sarah Barkley, they'd move fast—out of Bolivia before Mendoza or Rocha could lock down the borders or flood the jungle with soldiers. Time was their most fragile asset now.

Hopper cinched the straps of his plate carrier, rolling his shoulders until the weight sat right. His eyes tracked the hand-sketched layout from recon: compound walls, guard rotations, fallback routes. Every detail was etched into memory.

He wanted to free the civilians forced into labor at the camp, but the mission was Sarah. They didn't have the numbers or hours to pull off a full rescue. Still, if they could bring her home with Kaitlyn's evidence, maybe someone else would finish what they'd started. After what they'd seen, walking away from Bolivia's suffering wasn't an option.

"Jacks," Hopper said, glancing up, "breaching charges ready? Looked like an old jail—iron doors."

"Locked and loaded."

Jacks patted the demo bag at his side.

Finn stood near the window, glassing the tree line through his optic. Zeke sat cross-legged on the floor, tightening torque on his scope mounts with steady care.

The compound wasn't far. They'd approach on foot, cutting through the jungle. The brush offered cover, choices. Predictability killed; terrain and direction mattered more than speed on the approach. Exfil will be another story.

They gathered once more, packs open, helmets lined on the floorboards. No speeches. No theatrics. They didn't need them. Every man knew the plan. Every man knew his role. And every man trusted the others to hold the line if things went sideways.

Kaitlyn sat nearby, quiet. When Hopper made the final call, she didn't argue.

She would stay.

Mission or not, she wasn't fit for an assault, injury aside. Keeping the safe house secure as a fallback point was the logical move. She agreed aloud, but Hopper saw the flicker in her eyes—a mix of frustration and something she left unspoken.

"I'll keep comms open. If anything shifts, I'll call it in," she said.

"Good. Keep eyes up. Don't try to be a hero."

She smiled faintly, but it didn't reach her eyes.

Hopper looked to the team. "Last chance. Anyone see something in the plan they don't like, say it now."

No one spoke. Heads shook. The silence was agreement.

Jacks clipped his ammo pouch shut. Zeke slung his rifle. Finn adjusted his straps, rolling his neck with a muted crack.

Hopper didn't believe in blind obedience. Orders mattered, but once they stepped outside the wire, experience kept men alive. Too many teams had been lost to arrogance from the top. He wouldn't let his command slide into hubris. He trusted his men, trusted their input.

"Everyone ready?"

Three nods. No last words.

They moved out single file, smooth and alert, boots tapping softly across the floorboards.

Kaitlyn lingered at the window, watching as they crossed the clearing and slipped into the jungle. Even in daylight, they moved like ghosts—heading toward a fight they all knew might not bring them back.

SECOND

BREAKING POINT

12

January 23 | 9:45 a.m. BOT
Roboré, Bolivia

Kaitlyn Thompson had finished packing. Two bags held everything essential: documents, hard drives, all the evidence they'd risked so much to gather. Unlike last time, she wasn't running. This time she had the luxury of certainty. Everything was properly packed, secured, accounted for.

The silence of the safe house pressed in, each nerve stretched taut. She couldn't sit still any longer. The team would be reaching the compound about now, maybe just arriving. She checked her watch—an hour, maybe two to spare. Enough time to say goodbye.

Miguel's house wasn't far, tucked in a quiet corner of Roboré. Just a short walk through a sleepy neighborhood. Hood up, head down, her pace steady across cracked pavement and patches of dry grass. Her ankle held well enough to mask the limp. The streets were empty—no cars, no voices, only birdsong echoing off sun-bleached walls.

Every sound seemed sharper than it should. Every corner carried threat. She turned onto Miguel's street—and froze.

The front door hung broken. Not ajar. Not careless. Splintered. Crooked on its hinges, sagging from a frame ripped apart.

Her chest tightened.

She scanned the street. No soldiers, no vehicles, no neighbors watching from behind curtains. The breeze brought only dust and the faint tang of frying oil from someone's breakfast. Should she walk away? Return to the safe house? Or push forward?

Her hand brushed the pistol Hopper had given her. She didn't draw it, but the grip steadied her. Step by step, she advanced.

Up close, the damage was unmistakable: a battering ram, deep gouges in the wood, the hinges groaning as she nudged the door wider.

Inside was chaos.

Furniture overturned, glass crunching under her boots. Drawers wrenched out, clothing and papers scattered. A coffee mug shattered across the rug. A lamp in pieces beneath a family photo knocked from the wall.

What the hell happened here?

She moved carefully, as if danger might still be lurking. Slow steps. Controlled breath. She reached the hallway. Paused.

A metallic tick broke the silence. Maybe plumbing. Maybe not. The air was hot, stale. From the corner of her eye she glimpsed the kitchen.

A bare leg on the tile. Thin. Still.

Her breath caught. The coppery scent of blood reached

her before she saw the rest.

Miguel's wife lay face down, one arm stretched toward the dining table as if she'd tried to crawl. Two gunshots to the back. Blood soaked her blouse and spread across the floor in a thick, dark pool.

Kaitlyn's hand shook as she crouched beside the body, pressing two fingers to the neck—just in case.

Nothing.

She drew back as if burned, vision blurring. Tears welled, but she forced them down. Not now. Not here.

She leaned into the hallway wall, sliding down to her haunches. Shallow breaths. Forcing control back into her body.

Her gaze shifted toward the far end of the hall. All bedroom doors closed.

Except one.

Luca's.

Her stomach turned. She didn't want to see it. Didn't need to. But she moved anyway, each step heavier. She already knew what she would find. She just prayed she was wrong.

The half-open door creaked.

From the threshold, she saw the bed. A small form beneath the covers. Motionless. A toy truck tipped on its side on the floor.

Her eyes searched for breath, for a twitch, for anything.

Nothing.

Her knees buckled. She sank outside the doorway, turning her head before she saw his face.

The silence pressed in again. The ceiling fan droned above.

She pushed herself up, wiping her sleeve across wet eyes. Miguel's room was next. Closed door. She opened it cautiously.

No blood. No body.

No struggle.

They'd taken him.

She stumbled back through the house—past the ruin of the kitchen, past the broken door. Sunlight stabbed her eyes as she emerged. She didn't look back.

She ran. Ankle screaming, lungs burning, it didn't matter.

She ran. She only needed to keep moving.

January 23 | 10:45 a.m. BOT
San Lorenzo, Bolivia

Zeke lay prone in his sniper's hide, buried in dense brush atop a ridge four hundred meters from the San Lorenzo compound. His ghillie suit blended into the terrain, just another hump of earth. From this elevation, he commanded the full view: the barracks, the infirmary, and the prison block squatting near the rear wall like a rusted afterthought.

Heat shimmered on the metal rooftops, rippling waves through his scope. Mirage could warp the shot, but the wind was minimal. No real issue adjusting.

He mounted his rifle firm against his shoulder, keyed his mic. "One, this is Four. Good position. Eyes on. Full coverage. Ready when you are."

"Copy that, Four," Hopper replied, voice steady as stone.

Below, the other three crouched behind a crumbling concrete wall ten meters from the outer gate. Their crawl through tall grass had been slow and deliberate. Now the prison sat dead ahead, across an open yard stripped of cover—broken crates, a lone tire, the shell of a collapsed shack. Too few safe options once they breached.

Daylight made everything worse. Loud, exposed,

vulnerable from every angle. But time was gone. Mendoza's men knew they were here. If Sarah was still alive, they'd move or kill her soon.

One thing worked in their favor: the compound felt half-abandoned. Little movement. Most of the guards were still hunting Kaitlyn in the jungle.

Hopper pressed his mic. "Four, we're set at the gate. What do you see?"

"Two guards in the shack. Static. One's smoking."

"Copy." Hopper glanced at Jacks. A nod. Jacks shifted his weight, ready.

"On me."

Hopper drew his pistol, crouched low. Jacks mirrored him, sidearm raised, finger tight along the frame.

They moved as one—practiced, silent.

Hopper rose just high enough above the wall to line up. His weapon steadied, the blurred figure in his sights. Two muffled shots cracked. Glass shattered. The first guard's skull burst against the far pane.

Jacks leaned in and found the second, deeper in the shack. Two quick shots. A body hit the floor with a wet thud.

"Security's down," Finn confirmed, already moving. "Let's go."

The trio stacked against the interior wall. Finn tapped Hopper's shoulder twice, and they advanced—smooth, rifles up, pistols holstered. Gravel crunched beneath boots as they hugged the building's shadow. Angles cleared. Eyes high. No words wasted.

They turned the corner—and froze.

The gallows loomed in the courtyard. A crude wooden frame from another century. Hopper had seen it already. Finn and Jacks had not.

A body hung slack, twisting in the faint breeze. A burlap

sack masked the face. Bare feet dangled above a dark stain baked into the concrete. The air thickened with the sourness of decay.

Hopper's voice dropped, heavy with regret. "We watched Rocha hang him earlier."

No reply. None needed.

Zeke's voice cut in. "Hold. Guard at the jailhouse door."

Hopper crept to the courtyard's edge. Through a gap, he spotted the sentry planted in the doorway, square in the center. No way past him unseen.

"Zeke, clean shot?"

"Wind's nothing. I've got him."

A suppressed crack. The guard pitched forward, rifle clattering, as one last squeeze sent stray rounds skipping across stone before silence reclaimed the yard.

"Clear to the prison," Zeke confirmed.

"You're slippin', Zeke," Jacks muttered.

They pushed forward, fast. Rifles never dropped. The tension wound tighter. Something was off. Too easy.

Halfway across—

"Three o'clock. Two targets clearing the corner," Zeke warned.

Two soldiers appeared from the barracks, rifles already raised. Hopper and Finn fired sharp, controlled bursts. One folded mid-stride, the other crumpled behind him.

Stillness again.

Jacks reached the prison door, gloved hand on the handle. He paused, tested the turn.

Unlocked.

A glance between them. None liked it.

Hopper nodded.

Jacks eased the door. Hopper swept in first—rifle tight, eyes scanning. Dusty light cut through high windows. The air reeked of mildew, damp concrete. Water dripped somewhere deeper, irregular. Sickly green paint peeled from the walls in curling sheets.

A desk sat near the entrance, chair tipped, like someone had abandoned post mid-shift. A coffee mug cooled beside a clipboard.

"Stack up. Clear it slow."

They advanced cell by cell.

First—occupied. An older woman crouched in the corner, face blank, hands raised.

Second—an emaciated old man, silent, eyes wide with hollow dread.

Third. Fourth. Fifth—empty.

Finn checked the sixth. Empty again.

Hopper reached the last cell. The one that mattered.

It was empty.

No blood. No struggle. Just a rope tied to the bedframe, fibers bent from strain. A thin impression still pressed into the mattress.

His rifle sagged.

Behind him, boots stilled. The team turned, waiting for what he would not want to say.

He swallowed, throat tight.

"She's not here."

The words emptied the air.

No alarms. No guards rushing. Just mildew and the sound of their own breathing.

Hopper's jaw set. "Jacks, get them out of those fuckin' cells."

13

The street-level door to the safe house creaked open. Boots ascended the stairs slowly, heavier than before. Each step dragged, shoulders slumped under the weight of gear—and mission failure.

One by one, the four members of the BREACH team entered, rounding the corner into the apartment.

No one spoke. The silence was a futile attempt to wash away the stench of their misery.

Sweat, grime, and defeat clung to them like a second skin. Zeke's jaw was locked tight. Finn's eyes stayed fixed on the floor. Jacks' gaze remained forward, unblinking. The quiet that follows disaster filled the room.

Hopper was last. He reached the top of the stairs and

paused in the main room.

Kaitlyn sat alone at the table, eyes red, hands clenched around a half-empty glass of water. Her knuckles were white. Her face pale. Not from worry—something worse.

Grief.

Hopper approached cautiously. "Kaitlyn. what's wrong?"

She looked up, lips parting as if to speak, but no sound came. Her throat worked. Her eyes shimmered. She was already breaking.

"I went to Miguel's house," she managed, voice barely above a whisper, fractured by sobs.

The other three men froze, attention snapping toward her.

"They must have found out he was helping us," she said. "They kicked in the front door. Completely wrecked the place."

Her hands gripped the edge of the table as though it alone could hold her together.

"His wife and son…" She shook her head, forcing herself to speak. "They were both dead. Shot in their own home."

The words cracked something inside her. She broke completely, shoulders shaking, tears spilling down her face.

Hopper knelt beside her. He said nothing, simply placed a steady hand on her shoulder, letting her unravel in silence. The grief came first, before anything else.

"I checked every room," she choked out. "They took Miguel. He wasn't there. Just… the bodies. Luca was still in bed. He didn't even have a chance."

The weight of it settled over the room.

Finn slid down the wall until he sat, head lowered, hands clasped tight between his knees. Jacks leaned his rifle into the corner, staring at the floor. Even Zeke, still standing, shifted as if he couldn't stay completely still.

"They'll pay for this," Hopper said, his voice edged with a promise that left no doubt. "For all of it."

Kaitlyn wiped her face with trembling hands. She felt stripped bare, exposed. But shame didn't come. These men had seen worse. They knew what loss looked like. What it cost.

She wasn't alone in it.

She drew a long breath. It shook on the way in, steadied on the way out. Fingers tightening around the glass, she looked up.

"Where's Sarah?"

Hopper hesitated. The silence that followed said more than words could.

"She wasn't there," he finally said. "They moved her. We were too late."

Kaitlyn stared hollowly. "So we lost her?"

"No." Hopper's voice hardened. "We regroup. We reassess. But no—we haven't lost her. We're not giving up. We're not leaving without her."

He scanned the team. No one spoke. They all felt it: the anger, the exhaustion, the creeping sense that the window was closing.

One by one, they began peeling off their gear in silence. Vests thudded to the floor. Gloves and rifles were set on the table. Every movement slower now, worn down by heat, fading adrenaline, and the weight of loss.

Jacks set down a ration pack. Finn passed out bottled water. Zeke switched on the fan near the window, its low hum filling the quiet.

They ate without speaking. Kaitlyn sat with them, shoulders slowly squaring. Her tears had stopped. The raw edge of grief dulled into something else.

Focus.

She didn't want to cry anymore.
She wanted answers.

January 23 | 3:00 p.m. BOT
La Paz, Bolivia

Sarah sat in the center of a stone room, ankles and wrists lashed tight to a wooden chair slick with moisture. The walls were uneven and damp, patched together with ancient mortar that flaked at the slightest vibration. No tile. No finish. Just raw, time-worn rock. The floor was cold and sticky beneath her bare feet, and the air stank of mildew and rust.

The place felt like a tomb. This wasn't a holding cell. It was a basement—old, forgotten, repurposed.

She could see little beyond the dim bulb swaying overhead on a wire, but every sound carried: water dripping, chains rattling, boots shuffling, screaming. Spanish voices spat sharp bursts of words, angry, urgent. She couldn't understand most of it, but the tone was clear.

Rage. Frustration. Pain.

From the other room came a disturbing, recognizable sound: heavy impacts against flesh, groans of someone in pain. Then sharper cries—again, and again. More impacts struck the other chamber. Sometimes muffled. Sometimes wet and gurgling. She closed her eyes and tried not to imagine it.

Impossible.

A second room sat just beyond the wall—stone like hers. A man was tied to a chair, wrists bound with leather straps, his face swollen and split from the beating. His shirt hung in tatters, ribs showing through pale skin. Blood trickled from his mouth and nose, soaking his waistband.

The old wooden table beside him was ancient and disrepair. An array of tools sat on its top.

This was no military interrogation kit. It was a butcher's bench: hammers, pliers, rusted bone saws, surgical scissors, a blowtorch, a mason's chisel. Half from a construction site, half from a slaughterhouse. The tools alone caused most to break, overcome by fear, without ever being used.

At the table's edge stood Teo Mendoza. His knuckles were bloody and swollen.

No uniform. Just a dark shirt, sleeves rolled up over thick forearms. Calm. Focused. He didn't shout. Didn't threaten. His eyes moved over the tools with deliberate curiosity, like a surgeon choosing which rib to crack first.

The man in the chair spat blood but remained silent.

Mendoza didn't ask questions.

He began with a heavy punch to the gut. Then another. The victim doubled forward. A backhand struck him, splattering blood on the floor and wall. Groans erupted from the prisoner. He likely couldn't speak even if he wanted to; his jaw was probably broken by now.

Sarah's heart pounded. Her restraints creaked as she shifted, the urge to move warring with the knowledge that stillness might keep her invisible a little longer.

Mendoza turned to the table. He grazed his hand along a row of tools before picking up a set of pliers. He weighed them in his hand, opened and closed them, testing the bite of the jaws. The pause was almost worse than what followed. He approached, grabbed the man's fingers, and clamped down on a thumbnail. No questions.

A breath. Then a sharp yank.

The nail tore free with a wet crack. The man's scream, loud and excruciating, echoed off the stone.

Another finger. Another pull. Still no questions.

Sarah flinched at each cry. Her stomach twisted, fighting the urge to vomit. She grounded herself on the floor; mental visions were worse.

Having stripped both hands, Mendoza placed down the pliers and picked up a knife. He slapped the prisoner awake as he neared passing out from the pain. He grabbed and straightened the limp arm, then made a long, deliberate cut down the inside of each forearm. Skin opened. Blood streamed. The man trembled, groaned, sagged forward.

Still Mendoza said nothing. Asked nothing. This was no interrogation. This was torture.

Eventually, the man stopped struggling.

Mendoza leaned close and whispered something only the dying man could hear. Then he drew his sidearm and fired a single round into the prisoner's chest. The shot cracked through the basement like thunder.

Silence.

Mendoza holstered his pistol, walked to the body, and lifted the head. Blood dripped from the chin. No breath. No life.

"Traitor," Mendoza scoffed.

He reached for the table and picked up a white fedora resting near the edge. With a mocking care, he placed it on the dead man's head, then let it fall forward again.

Sarah sat trembling in the next room, breath shallow, pulse so loud she was sure he would hear it.

The victim remained unknown to her. Or what he had done to deserve this treatment.

But she knew one thing—she was next.

January 23 | 4:15 p.m. EST
Langley, Virginia

Deputy Director Tom Conley stepped into the briefing room. He paused just inside the door, noting how dimly lit it was. Mindy Taylor sat alone at the table, her face buried in her hands, elbows among a scatter of folders, cables, and glowing screens. Along the wall, other analysts tapped at keyboards and spoke quietly, trying to solve a problem.

She didn't look up.

"Ms. Taylor," Conley said, moving closer, "what's wrong?"

Mindy startled at his voice, pulling her hands away. Her eyes were rimmed red, jaw tight, teeth grinding.

"Sir, sorry—I didn't hear you come in. I just got word from the team. They hit the compound. Light resistance, clean breach… but Sarah wasn't there. The place was nearly empty. They think she was moved, probably just ahead of the raid."

Conley's mouth tightened, corners drawn down as if holding back a curse. He didn't answer immediately. The disappointment on his face wasn't aimed at her or the team; it was the weight of the situation settling once again on his shoulders.

"Then we're back to square one."

Mindy gave a slight nod, shoulders shrugging briefly before straightening again.

"You may want to splash some water on your face. Congressman Barkley will be here any minute. He has something urgent to show us, but it has to be done in person."

"Understood, sir. I'll be ready."

She stood, smoothed her blouse, and left for the restroom. Conley took a seat at the head of the table, eyes drifting toward the main monitor cycling through satellite feeds, heat maps, and aerial shots of Bolivia. His mind churned over the same questions:

Where could they have taken her?

Was she still in the country?

Was she even alive?

He didn't want to voice the last aloud.

Minutes later, Mindy returned, composed, hands already moving across the keyboard. The door opened behind her; Congressman Barkley stepped in, brisk, restless. Analysts glanced up, then returned to their work.

He didn't sit.

"I got this about forty-five minutes ago," he said, setting his phone on the table. "It's a video. It's Sarah."

Mindy reached for the device, plugging it into her laptop and routing the feed to the overhead monitor. Within seconds, the video filled the screen.

Sarah appeared, tied to a wooden chair in a dark, stone-walled room. Her mouth gagged with a dirty handkerchief, her face streaked with tears and grime. She trembled, moaning softly. Fear radiated from her bloodshot, tear-filled eyes.

A man entered the frame, visible only from the waist down—dark slacks, polished shoes. In his hand, a folded newspaper: *Jornada*, Bolivia's national daily. Today's date. He let it fall to the floor.

One by one, he held up signs, dropping them after each:

STOP YOUR INVESTIGATION.

RECALL YOUR SOLDIERS.

On confirmation that they have left Bolivia, your daughter will be delivered safely to a Brazilian police station.

The last sign fell. The man stepped behind Sarah, placed a hand on her shoulder, squeezed, and dragged the barrel of a pistol along her cheek.

The screen went black.

Barkley's shoulders tightened, jaw working as if restraining something. "What do we do now?"

Conley looked to Mindy. "Tell him where we stand."

Mindy sat up straighter. "Of course."

She explained the failed raid, the empty compound, and the lack of leads. Barkley's face sagged as hope drained.

"But this video gives us something to work with," she added. "Without it, we were blind. Now—maybe not."

She returned to her laptop, overhead monitor mirroring every move. Barkley watched in tense silence as lines of code and search algorithms flickered past. She analyzed the stonework in the background, pulled archival images of Bolivian buildings and schematics, matched wall patterns, and tried to correlate lighting with sun angles in better-known cities.

Sound filters ran to isolate background noise. Nothing distinct—no voices, no machinery, no traffic. Just static and distant echoes.

Frustration flickered on Conley's face. Barkley leaned forward, hands clasped tight.

"No… no match…"

Her fingers moved faster, more images, more rejections. Then she stopped.

"Wait. This pattern—it's not common. Only one confirmed match."

She pulled up a historic photo. "Palacio Quemado in La Paz. The old Presidential Palace. Rocha's predecessor moved next door during renovations. This is from the foundation restoration work. Same material. Same pattern."

Barkley stepped closer. "You're sure?"

"I'm sure."

Conley pushed back from the table. "Time to brief the team. They're going to have a long drive."

As he walked Barkley out, the congressman's eyes lingered on Sarah's frozen, terrified face. He didn't speak, but Mindy saw it—he clung to that flicker of hope with both hands, because it was all he had left.

January 23 | 7:10 p.m. BOT
Roboré, Bolivia

"Thanks for the update. We'll make a game plan and get on recon ASAP. One out."

Hopper ended the call and waved everyone to the table. His tone was all business.

"Alright, listen up. Mindy confirmed it. Rocha's holding Sarah beneath the presidential palace, the Palacio Quemado. That means we're headed to La Paz. Full day's drive."

Finn leaned in. "Close quarters around a government stronghold. Take everything you can carry. Gear up for recon, but pack for a street fight—frags and suppressors. We don't want to get caught with our pants down."

The team nodded, already moving to prep their gear. Packs stripped to essentials—enough to stay mobile—but nothing critical was left behind. The rest went into the vehicle.

Hopper double-checked his rifle as he called over his shoulder, "Mindy's got a Predator drone overhead. She'll provide overwatch for the trip to La Paz."

Jacks looked up. "That'll help."

Across the room, Kaitlyn zipped her duffel and stowed it near the exit. She had everything she needed—but her eyes caught something strange on the monitor feed Mindy had left open: thermal outlines. Vehicles. Movement.

Suddenly, Mindy's voice came through the laptop.

"Roboré team, be advised. Four military trucks inbound,

parked inside the treeline west of your position. Multiple heat signatures deploying. This isn't a scout team. Full assault element."

"Copy that," Hopper said.

He bolted to the front window, confirming it himself. Four trucks. Soldiers piling out. Armed. Formed up. Moving with discipline.

Finn joined him. "Shit, these guys are trained—fire teams, bounding, coordinated."

"Jacks, Zeke—take the high ground. Zeke, you've got the shot. Jacks, keep their heads down with the SAW. Finn and I shift south. We'll hit them from the flank through the alley across the street and work around to the trucks."

"Copy that," Jacks said, moving into position at the window.

"Let's go," Hopper said.

He and Finn slipped out the door, cutting across the alley to a side building. The town was dark; Roboré didn't waste money on streetlights. Shadows favored them.

Zeke got behind the scope. "I've got eyes. They're using bounding overwatch—squads of four."

"They're setting up suppressive positions behind the wall across the road," Jacks said, flipping open the bipod on his MK46.

Hopper's voice came over comms. "Wait for it. Let 'em get close."

The first squad reached the stone wall across from the safe house—a crude three-foot stack of stones. Soldiers dropped to one knee, rifles propped on the ledge. Suppressive posture. Tight formation. They had line of sight to the safe house.

Zeke exhaled, counted three heartbeats, and opened fire.

The first round hit center mass. The next, a headshot. Two more soldiers dropped before the fifth even turned his head.

Return fire erupted. Two machine gunners opened up, tracers chewing into the building. Windows shattered, glass raining down on the men inside. Night air turned to thunder. Civilians ran for cover, slamming doors, praying.

Jacks opened fire, covering Zeke. The SAW barked in short, calculated bursts. But the attackers didn't break, returning coordinated fire from behind the stones.

"Contact! Multiple hostiles moving to the flanks!" Zeke shouted, flinching as splinters tore across his face, blood streaking his forehead. He hit the floor hard.

On the street, Hopper and Finn moved.

"Up and right!" Hopper called. They peeked around the corner and opened fire. Finn dropped two—one machine gunner, one rifleman. Hopper clipped another in the chest, finishing him with a second shot.

"Move!"

They pushed down the alley, sweeping corners, leap-frogging past boarded doors and rusted fences, watching for flankers. Reaching the next side alley, they headed for the open field, calling out positions and movements to over-watch.

Inside the safe house, Jacks saw Zeke bleeding. "You good?"

"Still breathing."

Zeke tossed Kaitlyn a short-barreled shotgun. "Breaching rounds. Point and shoot. Cover the stairs."

Kaitlyn nodded, taking a firing stance just inside the doorway at the top of the stairs. Hands steady. Eyes fixed.

Outside, Hopper and Finn reached the treeline behind the assault element. Only a handful of hostiles remained in the open, one last cluster around the trucks.

"Three near the trucks. One in the cab. Probably the commander," Finn said.

"Take the open field first."

With muffled shots, they dropped the three soldiers. The rest scattered for cover.

Kaitlyn heard the door creak. Boots on the stairs. She held her breath, poked her head over the top stair, and fired. The slug hit center mass. The soldier tumbled backward, thudding onto the concrete landing.

She moved cautiously forward, shotgun leveled. The second soldier kicked open the door just as she reached the top stair. He caught a slug in the face before raising his rifle and fell backward onto the sidewalk.

Silence. Kaitlyn breathed hard, shotgun still raised, cocked, waiting.

"Clear!" Zeke called over the radio.

Hopper and Finn crept toward the lead truck. No backup, no flanking squads left. Quiet—except a few moans from wounded fighters near the treeline. Finn took the passenger side. Hopper covered the driver's door.

With a sharp yank, Finn threw it open.

A man in tactical gear raised his hands.

"Please, no," he said—in Russian.

Finn froze. "Hopp—"

Hopper stared at the man, then at Finn.

"What the fuck is going on here?"

14

January 23 | 7:50 p.m. BOT
Roboré, Bolivia

Hopper and Finn climbed the stairs, rifles slung, boots crunching over shell casings and broken glass. The floor was littered with the aftermath of the battle. The fight had ended, but its chaos lingered—raw, loud amidst the stillness. Somewhere outside, a dog barked twice before going quiet. A thin draft slid through the broken windows, carrying the metallic tang of blood and the acrid bite of gunpowder and heated brass.

Kaitlyn sat just inside the living room, shoulders stiff, shotgun across her lap as if it might spring to life again. Her grip hadn't loosened since Zeke handed it to her—fingers white-knuckled, chest rising in shallow bursts. She stared past the team, past the walls, pupils tight. Her jaw twitched as if bracing for another blast. The smoke had cleared, but the fight hadn't left her; it clung to her skin like a film she couldn't scrub off.

Across the room, Jacks knelt beside Zeke on a half-splintered coffee table, pressing a gauze pad to the deep gash across the marksman's forehead. Blood still trickled along a stubborn crimson streak that refused to clot. Zeke winced but said nothing, holding still while Jacks dabbed antiseptic and taped it down with steady hands.

The room bore the scars of direct hits. Bullet holes pocked the plaster. Shredded curtains flapped limply against busted windows. Overturned furniture sat scattered across the floor, glass coating the surface like ice chips.

Finn scanned the destruction, nodding slowly. "Looks like you three threw one hell of a party in here."

Zeke smirked, bruises flickering across his face. "Could've gone sideways fast. They breached the entrance." He jerked a thumb toward Kaitlyn. "She had our backs. Dropped 'em before I even finished turning."

Jacks didn't look up. "You're lucky it's just your head that's leaking."

"No argument there."

Hopper moved to the gear table, half-crushed against a wall, setting his rifle down with a clunk. He popped the chamber, cleared it, then rechecked the sling tension. Metal clicked; nylon straps rasped under his fingers. A few magazines were scuffed and blood-slicked. He wiped them with a torn piece of curtain, the fabric catching on the feed lips.

"Check your gear," he said. "Jacks, get an ammo count when you're done playing combat nurse."

"On it," Jacks said, finishing the last strip of tape across Zeke's forehead.

"We're not staying. This place is burned. Time to roll for

La Paz."

A collective shift rippled through the team—shoulders straightening, eyes narrowing, weapons lifted. Kaitlyn blinked as the words registered. She exhaled slowly and set the shotgun beside her, fingers lingering on the grip before releasing it.

"Timing was too clean," Hopper said, slinging his rifle back over his shoulder. He pulled a compact wrap from his cargo pocket to cover the remains of the gear table.

"We also need to get on with command," he added, turning to the back of the room. "Something's off here. This isn't just a hostage op anymore."

Zeke looked up from re-securing his rifle. "What do you mean?"

"The commander we pulled from that truck—Russian. Full tactical kit. No Bolivian insignia."

Zeke's expression sharpened. "You sure?"

"I'm sure. He spoke Russian. Natural-sounding accent."

Kaitlyn's gaze lifted slightly, brow tightening. She said nothing, but the line of her mouth hardened.

Jacks straightened. "That changes things."

"Yeah," Hopper said. "Explains why this crew fought better than the last. We're not just fighting locals anymore. This was professional. Coordinated."

The weight in the room shifted. Adrenaline had carried them this far; now it hardened into something colder, more calculated. Even the air felt different, like the walls had inched closer.

"Get patched. Get packed. We move fast," Hopper said, slotting a fresh magazine into his rifle.

He pulled out his SAT phone. The screen illuminated, encryption app open. His fingers hovered, then typed:

GET DIRECTOR
IMPORTANT—MOVING TO NEXT AO.
He hit send.

They were in it now. No delay. A long road lay ahead to reach Sarah, but Hopper wasn't giving up. They had intel, they would set up, plan, and execute with precision.

No illusions. Just war.

January 23 | 8:20 p.m. EST
Langley, Virginia

Deputy Director Conley stepped into the operations briefing room and found Mindy still seated at the long table, posture rigid, eyes locked on the glowing monitor in front of her. The bluish cast from the screen painted her features pale, drawn, tired. A half-empty coffee sat at her elbow. Her shoulders were taut, as though she had been sitting in that chair for hours.

No sound but the low hum of electronics, a steady undercurrent beneath the muted murmur of voices out in the hallway. Deep somewhere in the building, an HVAC unit kicked on, sending a faint rush of air over the table. The rest of the analysts were packing up for home, but not Mindy. She would remain on overwatch for the duration of the trip to La Paz; she didn't want to leave the team without eyes in the sky.

He shut the door softly behind him. "You said the team sent an important update?" he asked, setting a fresh cup of coffee on the polished table for her.

She didn't glance up. Fingers moved over secure logs, tagged images, and streams of data. "Yes, sir. Hopper sent a secure message about twenty minutes ago. They're en route to La Paz. No specifics, just said we needed to call immediately once you arrived."

"Then let's not waste time. Get him on the line."

Mindy reached across the table to the secure SAT terminal. Her hands trembled slightly—from fatigue, caffeine, or something else; Conley couldn't tell. The green light blinked as the call encrypted and pushed out.

A second later, Hopper's voice came through the speaker. Calm. Direct. Almost too calm.

"Go for One."

Conley leaned in. "Status report?"

"Sir, we're mobile. All four team members accounted for, plus the civilian asset. No casualties on our end. The safe house was compromised again. Heavier force this time. Better tactics, tighter formation. We neutralized the threat."

Conley nodded to himself. "Understood. Anything else?"

A pause on the line. Just long enough to make Conley's eyes narrow.

"Yes, sir. This next part might raise some eyebrows."

"Go on."

"The commander overseeing the assault wasn't Bolivian," Hopper said. "Russian kit. Russian accent. Heavily equipped, body armor, clean patches. He surrendered without a fight. We let him go before heading out—couldn't take a prisoner anyway."

The room seemed to lose its ambient hum for a beat.

Conley blinked once. "Russians? You're certain?"

"Yes, sir. No Bolivian insignia. Russian comms rig. Nothing about him was local."

Conley's jaw tightened. "You think they're training and directing Bolivian units?"

"Looks that way. Could be private military. Could be direct action. Too early to say. But they're here, and they're not just observing. They're calling the shots."

Mindy finally looked up from her laptop, the edge of concern now fully visible.

Conley straightened and stepped back from the table. He wasn't one for show, yet he knew the weight of the statement. Russia wasn't a name you spoke lightly—not at Langley. Not under this administration.

He glanced toward the far wall, then back to the encrypted speaker. "Understood. Set up in La Paz. I want you dark until I say otherwise. Strictly recon. Do not engage unless fired upon. I'll move this up the chain immediately."

"Understood. One out."

The call ended. The screen dimmed. The air inside felt chillier; it shifted.

Mindy swiveled in her chair. "Do you think it's sanctioned by the Kremlin?"

Conley didn't answer right away. He grabbed his coat from the nearby hook, shrugging into it. "I think it's about to get very loud. Make the call. I want the Joint Chiefs at the Pentagon ASAP. If anyone asks why, you tell them it's Tier One urgency. No other details."

He was already moving before she could respond; the door swung shut behind him. His footsteps faded down the corridor, quick and deliberate, while behind him Mindy picked up the phone and dialed.

January 24 | 9:30 a.m. BOT
La Paz, Bolivia

The Palacio Quemado was alive with motion. The name, which translates to the "Burnt Palace," was a testament to its dramatic and often violent history. Normally a quiet place, it had been restored as the Presidential residence since Rocha took over. Most government staff worked next door. For the next few days, however, the atmosphere would be different.

Inside the grand halls of Bolivia's presidential palace, the clatter of silver trays and the sharp tap of polished shoes echoed off marble and wood. Staff moved in hurried lines between kitchens and banquet areas, arms laden with polished stemware and trays stacked with imported delicacies. The scent of wax and citrus cleaner mingled with faint notes of roasted coffee drifting from service carts. Light from towering chandeliers, polished to a hard gleam, glanced off waxed floors, making everything shine.

Tonight's summit would be the most important diplomatic event held in the capital in decades. And the palace looked the part.

Security, however, was the true show. Armed soldiers in ceremonial uniform flanked every main corridor, boots planted, rifles slung at the ready. Uniformed security guards stood at attention outside the palace doors, posture rigid despite the thin mountain air pressing into their lungs. Inside, plainclothes operators swept the halls in rotating pairs, eyes darting to every hand, every piece of equipment. No one passed without scrutiny—not even the caterers.

From a second-floor balcony, Colonel Teo Mendoza surveyed the operation below. The vantage point offered a clear view of the main floor. Dozens of workers weaved between gilded columns and velvet-lined tables, while security moved like a silent current around them. He noted the strong points: overlapping fields of vision, patrol rotations leaving no corner uncovered. His eyes lingered on chokepoints near the service entrances, filing them in his mind for extra attention. For now, the system held.

Near the west archway, he spotted Rodrigo Aguilar directing two plainclothes guards onto their next patrol route.

Aguilar's left arm remained in a sling, but the bandages didn't slow him. He barked orders in clipped, urgent Spanish, gesturing toward the service wing.

Mendoza keyed his radio. "Aguilar. Increase coverage on the path from the kitchen to the ballroom. I want double eyes on all staff. No gaps in patrols, no blind corners. And put someone on the waste exit. If something goes wrong tonight, it won't be food poisoning."

Aguilar glanced up toward the railing. "Understood, Colonel. I'll handle it personally."

Mendoza nodded to himself and continued his sweep.

Footsteps approached behind him—polished leather on marble.

"I trust your men are ready for tonight, Colonel?" came the low voice of President Rocha as he stepped to his side.

"They're prepared, Mr. President," Mendoza replied without turning. "We've rehearsed every movement. No one gets in or out without our say-so."

Rocha didn't respond immediately. He studied the floor below, hands clasped behind his back. "They'd better be. After Roboré, I have very little patience left. The Americans should've been a footnote by now. Instead, they're still breathing and closing in. Tonight can't afford distractions. No surprises. Do you understand me?"

"Yes, sir." Mendoza's jaw tightened, but his voice remained steady. "We have complete control."

Rocha's gaze followed a pair of servers moving between velvet ropes as metal detectors rolled into position. His tone softened slightly. "Tonight marks the beginning of something bigger than they realize. A partnership that will redefine the balance of power on this continent. One that doesn't flinch under the shadow of American dominance."

With a subtle nod toward the large black case one floor

below—a heavy-duty container with a crudely painted gold bat on top—he turned without another word, retreating toward his private office. His footfalls faded, swallowed by the palace's cavernous halls.

Mendoza watched him go, the weight of those words pressing in. He didn't need clarification. He knew exactly what Rocha meant—and who he meant. If he couldn't get the job done, Rocha would replace him swiftly. Turning toward the staircase, Mendoza's expression hardened as he keyed his radio again, voice rough and cold. The final security checks would be personal. No margin for error.

Tonight had to be perfect.

6:00 p.m.

The Gran Hotel Paris sat just far enough from the Palacio Quemado to stay off the radar, but close enough for a clean line of sight. Mindy had secured the team a corner suite on the top floor, facing the courtyard separating them from the palace grounds. Through the windows, muted city noise drifted in: distant horns, the indistinct murmur of traffic, and somewhere far below, the occasional burst of laughter from pedestrians. It wasn't a tall building, but tall enough for accurate recon.

From their vantage point, several of the palace's second-story windows were in direct view. Zeke had set up a full observation post: spotting scopes locked onto tripods, each feed recording to external drives. Mindy had sent over schematics of the palace and surrounding infrastructure—plumbing, electrical, every detail they might exploit.

Next to the gear table, Zeke had built himself a sniper perch. His rifle rested in a calibrated stand beside a spotting scope, current windage, distance, and elevation already dialed in. Jacks had set a small charge on the window in front of the rifle, rigged to a remote just in case he had to take a shot. Glass had a tendency to skew bullet trajectories.

On the far bed, Jacks worked through explosives and breaching kits, counting charges, checking timers, and running his fingertips over each primer to confirm they were clean.

In the other room, Kaitlyn sat cross-legged on the floor with her laptop open, portable drives and cable adapters spread around her. She'd scrubbed, sorted, and encrypted the drive containing the digital evidence, labeling each segment for the American authorities. Everything short of transmitting it. She wasn't about to risk sending anything from here—not in La Paz, not with Russian-linked hardware likely tied into the palace's security systems. Any large outbound data burst could flag their location or trigger counter-surveillance. It would wait until they were out of Bolivia. If things went sideways, it could also serve as leverage.

The door opened.

Finn stepped in, taking off his sunglasses, windbreaker zipped halfway, a coffee cup in one hand and a phone in the other. His hair was slightly wind-mussed, and there was a faint dusting of grit on his shoes from the street.

"Looks like you guys have been busy."

Zeke glanced over. "Yeah, we did all the work while you were out getting a latte."

Finn smirked and raised the cup. "Good one, too."

Hopper looked up from the scope. "What did you find?"

Finn crossed to the table and leaned over the palace map. "Southern side of the building. The kitchen entrance opens onto C. Bolivar. Staff's been going in and out steadily for over an hour. Nothing unusual until I spotted a second access point just past the service door. Small concrete staircase, recessed. Heads down. Leads below ground."

Zeke sat up straighter. "A basement?"

"Yeah. Looks like a utility or delivery entrance. Didn't stop to stare, but it matches the schematics Mindy sent. Sarah should be down there based on Mindy's video analysis."

"And security?" Hopper asked.

"Heavy. Guards posted outside. More roaming in pairs. They're locking things down—but it feels staged. Like they're bracing for something high-profile tonight."

Hopper nodded. "That tracks. We've been watching constant movement inside—staff, caterers, decorators. Looks like they're prepping for a summit or gala."

Jacks frowned. "That makes this even harder. More people, more uniforms, more eyes."

"Or fewer watching the basement," Hopper said. "Crowd upstairs could spread them thin."

Finn took a seat. "That's how I see it. If we go tonight, it has to be surgical. In and out. No margin for error."

Before anyone could respond, the SAT phone buzzed on the table.

Hopper grabbed it and stepped into the next room. "Go for One."

Conley's voice came through, frustrated, the weight behind it telling Hopper this wasn't routine. "No-go from the Joint Chiefs yet. I brought them everything—Rocha, Mendoza, the Russians. They're deliberating. Could take hours."

"We don't have hours, sir."

"I know. So here's where I bend the rules," Conley said. "If you get a shot, quick and quiet, you take it. No bloodbath. No noise. You extract the girl, you ghost. I'll take the political fallout. You're off the books until I say otherwise. Mindy's still with you, but nothing official from anyone else. Watch your six, Hopper. One mistake and we're at war."

Hopper was silent for a beat, feeling swift urgency paired with the necessity of flawlessness. The implications were clear: off the books, no safety net.

"Copy that. One out."

He rejoined the others, giving them what felt like better news than they had of late.

"We've got no green light," he said, eyes sweeping the room. "But we've got permission to act if we see an opening. Silent entry, fast exfil. Political heat lands on Conley."

Zeke let out a slow breath. "Big risk."

"So we don't fuck up," Hopper said, already checking his pistol. "Gear up. Tonight might be our only window."

15

"All right, guys. Gather up," Hopper said.

They formed fast, tension pulling the room tight around them. Lights were off—only the soft glow of a laptop screen illuminated the space. Warm air carried the stale, thick smell of sweat and a faint metallic tinge, clinging to the hotel room floor like static. The screen displayed the blueprints for the presidential palace: entrances, stairwells, electrical systems—everything they needed to know. These key details would aid in their covert entry and exit.

Hopper continued, arms crossed, stance solid.

"The director's still waiting on the Joint Chiefs. They have all the specifics and are deliberating on the next steps."

"Figures," Jacks said from where he leaned against the window frame, one hand fiddling with a zip tie. "Big bosses draggin' their asses like always."

"Pretty much. But we've got the go-ahead—if we keep this quiet and bring Sarah home." Hopper's eyes scanned the room, settling on each of them. "This is our shot. We move tonight. We get into position while Kaitlyn runs point from here."

"Put me in, Coach," Kaitlyn said with a crooked grin.

Zeke smirked. Jacks rolled his eyes. Even Finn's mouth tugged upward for half a second.

But the mood shifted quickly. The moment cracked, then reformed into something harder. More focused. Everyone dropped back into rhythm. They had to be serious, and they had to be on their game.

There was no armor, no support, no kits. Just what they could carry under civvies without drawing attention. From the outside, they looked like tourists winding down after a long day: hooded jackets, athletic pants, compact daypacks. The kind of people a security patrol wouldn't spare a second glance. They would blend—and execute.

Inside those bags, everything was calibrated for speed and silence. Suppressed pistols seated in low-profile holsters, slim entry tools wrapped in cloth to keep them quiet, flash options taped for quick pull. No frills. No dead weight.

Jacks knelt at the foot of the bed and did a final check of his sling bag, the zipper whispering shut after each compartment. Finn stood near the door, one hand on the handle, the other resting casually against the wall, posture wired, every muscle coiled, listening for any sound in the hallway. On most days, he was the patient, calm, serious one—but tonight he was anxious and tired of failure. He wanted redemption.

Zeke, hunched next to Kaitlyn, synced one of the team's tracking nodes to her interface. "Uplink's stable?"

Kaitlyn nodded. "I'm patched into the embassy relay. Got

floor schematics up so I can track you in real time." Her voice was calm, fingers tapping across the keys with steady precision. She looked up at Hopper. "I'll monitor all open frequencies. If something shifts, you'll hear it before you see it."

She was quietly content in providing support. The opportunity to contribute to the mission offered some relief from the burden she felt for causing the situation in the first place.

"Comms clean?" Hopper asked.

"As clean as they'll get without tipping the signal meter. If they're monitoring actively, they'll miss it—unless someone inside flags it manually," Zeke replied.

Hopper nodded and then turned to the others. "We leave in five. Quiet exit through the alley. Stick to the blind side of the plaza and take the west approach past the bus terminal. We won't light up until we're underground."

No one asked questions. They knew the plan. They'd gone over it in fragments since the call came in, rehearsing every element. Asking questions when needed, verbally walking through the mission one task at a time.

Hopper walked to the window and pulled the curtain back half an inch. Outside, the city was shifting into night mode. Traffic thinned. Lights glowed along streets—red neon over a bar entrance, white fluorescents in a corner market across the alley. A couple walked past on the sidewalk below, laughing softly. Normal life. Fragile, and completely unaware of what was about to move through it.

He glanced at his watch. **8:27.**

Behind him, Jacks zipped his pack closed. Zeke stood, slinging his gear over one shoulder. Finn gave a tight nod from the door. They were ready.

"This is it. No second chances. We do it quiet, we do it

right," Hopper said.

No one replied. Just quiet motion—grips checked, zippers tugged, straps settled. One by one, their expressions tightened into the calm, precise masks of professionals about to cross the line.

The door handle rotated with a soft click.

Time to move.

8:55 p.m.

Hopper and Finn strolled along the street, carefree. Laughing, loose, shoulders swaying just enough to sell the illusion. Tourists—maybe intoxicated from heavy drinking— staggered through the capital in the late hours. They moved down the sidewalk along C. Bolivar, a street named for Simón Bolívar, the man whose sword had not only won this nation its freedom from Spain but had also given it the very name it now carried.

About thirty feet behind, Zeke and Jacks played their roles just as well. Zeke pointed lazily toward a café down the block, mumbling something that made Jacks snort. No pattern. No military spacing. Just a couple of guys killing time, heading for a late-night latte.

It had to look natural. Harmless. Until the last possible second.

The palace loomed ahead, its elegant façade glowing in ivory tones beneath the streetlamps. Hopper and Finn veered across the road with a slight stagger, guiding themselves toward the far sidewalk like they were hunting for an open bar. Streetlight glare washed briefly over their faces before giving way to deeper pockets of shadow. But Hopper's eyes stayed locked on angles and shapes—on anything that didn't belong. Searching for threats.

The security presence was nonexistent along the eastern side of the building. Most of the palace guards clustered near the main gate, just out of direct sight. No rovers. No rear overwatch. Either a shift change—or possibly bait.

Could be a ruse.

Could be they know we're coming? Hopper thought.

He said nothing.

Finn took the lead at the corner, posture relaxed as he ducked his head and took a quick glance around the alley. "We're clear," he whispered.

Hopper lifted a thumb behind his back without looking. Across the street, Zeke caught it and nudged Jacks forward. The two crossed casually, never breaking stride.

A moment later, they vanished around the side of the building, slipping into the alley behind the palace. The air held a powerful odor—still smelling of cooking grease, damp stone, and food scraps left too long in bins. It attacked the nostrils, but they pushed forward.

At the far end of the alley, half-buried in shadow, a concrete stairwell dropped six feet below street level. It ended at a heavy steel basement door, recessed and unmarked. No camera. No keypad. Just an old-school lock and chipped paint.

They grouped at the bottom of the stairs.

Hopper thumbed his mic. "Eagle One, this is Badger One. Comms check."

In the hotel room, Kaitlyn adjusted the dial on her spotting scope and leaned closer to the lens. "Loud and clear, Badger One," she said, her voice crisp in his earpiece.

"Preparing to enter building now."

"Good copy. Movement along the east wall, heading your way—could be routine, could be nothing. Move quick."

"Got it. Badger One out."

No one spoke. The team drew their sidearms in quiet unison, each motion second nature. No clicks. No fumbles. Zeke's pistol dropped to a two-handed low ready. Finn shifted closer to the wall, scanning behind and above at street level. Jacks pulled his lock pick kit from a flat belt pouch and knelt at the door.

They held position without prompting. Everyone watched the angles, covering while Jacks worked. The concrete stairwell gave them cover, but once the door opened, they were committed.

He worked fast. Fingers moved with surgical calm, shoulders steady, eyes locked on the task at hand. Silence pressed in, broken only by the faint hum of the city somewhere above and the soft hiss of static in Hopper's earpiece. He could hear Kaitlyn breathing.

Then—*click*.

The sound was soft but final. The lock gave way.

Jacks eased the handle, cracked the door an inch, and leaned forward to peer into the dark beyond. He glanced back at Hopper and gave a single nod.

The threshold was clear.

"Let's move."

9:05 p.m.

Mendoza paced the halls of the Palacio Quemado, the polished wood floors groaning under his feet. His mind was a maelstrom of strategies and contingency plans, yet his eyes were drawn to the painted portraits of Bolivia's past. He paused at Simón Bolívar, "El Libertador," the man who had liberated much of South America from Spanish rule and after whom the country had been named.

A few steps later, he regarded Antonio José de Sucre, Bolívar's trusted general and Bolivia's first president, whose decisive military victories cemented the nation's independence. Further on, the intense stare of Pedro Domingo Murillo met his gaze—a symbol of revolution whose failed but pivotal uprising in La Paz now gave name to the square outside.

Finally, he looked at Andrés de Santa Cruz, whose attempts to unite Bolivia and Peru into a single confederation spoke to a legacy of ambition and turmoil. The faces on the walls were a silent reminder of the country's tumultuous history—a history of rebellion and struggle that felt all too relevant to his current predicament.

He checked in with each security chief, voice clipped and precise. Every report ratcheted his tension tighter. Patrols were in place. Camera feeds stable. No anomalies. And yet, something needled at the back of his mind—a crawl beneath the skin.

The radio on his belt chirped. Aguilar's voice came through, steady as always. "Basement secure. Returning to ground level."

"Copy that. Stay sharp."

He moved past the main atrium, where a pair of palace guards stood at parade rest near the staircase. They straightened as he passed. He didn't acknowledge them. There was no time for ceremony in his mind.

The east wing was quieter. Older. Here, the air cooled and smelled of aging books and varnished wood. It was where Rocha kept the foreign guests. Tonight, two Russian generals and their Spetsnaz detail occupied the high-security suites. Mendoza's stomach turned at the thought. Those men didn't answer to him. They didn't answer to anyone. If the Americans made it this far, there would be no coordination—just chaos and bloodshed.

And if anything happened to them…

His throat tightened. Failure here wouldn't just mean the end of his career. Rocha had made that crystal clear: *You'll be lucky if I hand you over to the Russians alive*, the president's threat echoing in his mind.

He rounded a corner and paused near the central surveillance hub. Inside, two technicians sat, faces lit by a wall of glowing monitors. They scanned the screens meticulously for anything out of the ordinary. The soft hum of the equipment filled the room. They didn't even realize he was there until he spoke.

"Anything unusual?"

One tech shook his head. "All quiet, Colonel. No movement outside the walls. Cameras show nothing suspicious."

Mendoza stared at the screens a beat too long. Street cams. Perimeter feeds. Kitchen access. The flicker of static on one camera resolved into nothing. It was all clear.

But it didn't feel right.

He tapped a knuckle against the desk. "Double the patrol frequency for the south stairwell. Rotate the sentry on camera fourteen; he looks tired."

"Yes, sir."

As he stepped back into the hallway, a dull creak echoed from somewhere deeper in the wing. He froze, every muscle tightening, ears straining.

No voices. No footsteps.

He exhaled and moved on, jaw clenched.

Up above and below, everything seemed calm.

But Mendoza knew better. Calm wasn't safety.

Calm was a trap.

A feeling of certainty washed over him. Something was coming.

9:15 p.m.

The team slipped through the door in tight formation, one behind the other. They were in the palace undetected. Four men inside a dark, wet, and silent cavern of a hallway.

A faint hum from aging lights buzzed from the walls where they hung, punctuated by the occasional flicker. The mixture of concrete and plastered stone formed the walls, worn thin where corners met the floor. Dust motes floated in the stagnant air, disturbed only by their movement, inhaled with every breath.

Hopper signaled the stack to tighten. Every step from here on was surgical.

They advanced slowly. Hopper led, pistol raised, scanning high and low.

First corner—clear.

Second—clear.

No movement. Just the sound of controlled breathing and the whisper of boots landing softly on hardened concrete with each precise step.

At the third corner, a single sentry moved mid-rotation. Muzzle-down stance, lazy pacing. Just walking the halls, with little thought or care for his assignment.

Hopper stilled. One heartbeat. Two. The hallway geometry gave them just enough shadow. The angle was tight, but workable. He raised a fist to signal halt, then pointed at Finn and toward the hallway, tapping once against his neck in the silent command: take him out quietly.

Finn nodded and moved without hesitation, tucking his pistol into his waistband.

Zeke edged forward, weapon low. With a peek around the corner, he spotted the guard with his back to the team. He ghosted across to the opposite side, ready to cover Finn if things went sideways. A quick glance back, then a nod. The marksman was ready.

Finn moved—fast, fluid, silent.

He closed the distance to the roaming guard. As he reached him, he wrapped his arm around the guard's neck, clamping down with precision. One arm held the chin in place while the other pressed his bicep into the throat, cutting blood flow to the brain. The guard tensed, struggled for a second, then slumped as the fight drained out of him.

Finn eased him down to the floor and released the limp body.

Jacks stepped in, zip-tied the wrists and ankles, then slapped duct tape over the mouth. Together, they dragged the unconscious man around the corner and tucked him near the entry door, hidden completely from view.

They regrouped. Hopper raised his hand and, with a circulating motion, signaled the others to assemble and stack up close.

They moved on, pistols tucked tight against their chests to avoid a hand grab when turning a corner, footsteps muffled by the worn concrete slab and layers of dust. Zeke crouched slightly, leading with his muzzle; Jacks turned every few steps, checking the rear.

The corridor ahead narrowed, lit only by a flickering string of mine lights on the wall that looked older than the palace itself. Every step slow and controlled. Silence was paramount. No radios, no voices—only eyes and hand signals.

Hopper's heartbeat slowed by will alone. Calm was the weapon.

They reached another turn. Then another.

Still no guards.

The quiet wasn't peaceful—it was suspended. Like the

building was holding its breath. Even the lighting seemed to dim in and out.

They rounded one last bend, and the hallway ended in a T-shaped junction. Doors lined both sides. Two staircases rose at opposite ends, one to the left, one to the right.

If Sarah was down here, she had to be in one of these rooms. This was the extent of the sublevel; no other options remained.

Hopper gestured right and tapped Zeke and Jacks. They nodded and veered off. He pointed left. He and Finn moved together, pistols raised but kept close.

First door—empty, storage.

Second on the right—nothing but broken shelves.

Second on the left held something.

A chair. Just inside the doorway.

A figure slumped in it. Male. He could tell by the close-cropped haircut and broad shoulders. Not moving, legs at an odd angle. A single bulb buzzed above, casting soft arcs of shadow across the floor. No sound. No breath. Just the shape, unmoving.

Hopper slowed. So did Finn. They inched closer, boots silent on the floor.

A white fedora sat tilted forward on the figure's head.

Hopper froze.

That hat…

It was a gut punch before his brain caught up.

He reached out, barely breathing, and lifted it away.

Miguel.

The man's face was still. His chest wasn't moving. Eyes closed. Pale skin. Dried blood at the corner of his mouth. Bruises along the jaw. Signs of torture—but no life left to fight with.

Finn stepped back instinctively, giving Hopper space. He

knew his team lead would take this hard.

Hopper stared down, hands clenched at his sides. For a moment, the dim hallway disappeared. Just him and the past, bleeding into the present.

Back to this horror scene.

Hopper lowered the hat. No words—just the slow burn of rage behind his ribs.

He nodded once to Finn. The mission wasn't over.

But someone was going to pay.

9:30 p.m.

"Colonel Mendoza. This is Aguilar, do you copy?"

Mendoza touched his earpiece and drifted toward the tall windows lining the summit room's eastern wall. Behind him, the space buzzed with layered voices and the hum of political maneuvering. Dignitaries moved from table to table under the glow of chandelier light, glasses of wine in hand, murmuring in Spanish, Russian, and Mandarin. They pitched their political wants and needs, attempting to garner support from other countries. The air was thick with cologne, sweat, and the faint whiff of expensive liquor. Every smile rehearsed, every handshake strategic, layered with hidden agendas.

His eyes shifted through the window to the courtyard below. Dark stone, empty walkways, the soft shimmer of lights along trimmed hedgerows. It looked serene, but the feeling threading through his ribs said otherwise.

"What is it, Aguilar?"

"Rear hall basement guard missed his scheduled check-in. No response on comms."

Mendoza's jaw flexed. He turned from the window and moved to the railing overlooking the summit, scanning the room without turning his head. Near the main stairwell, two palace guards stood talking too casually, rifles slung just a little too low. Unprofessional. Vulnerable. He didn't like it. He didn't see other threats.

"Understood. Make sure the prison guards are ready. Send another team down to check it out. Quietly."

"Yes, sir."

Aguilar switched channels without another word. Mendoza caught the faint echo of his voice over the secondary line.

"Team Bravo, move to the rear stairwell. Eyes sharp. Report as soon as you reach the corridor junction."

Mendoza started walking. He controlled his pace to avoid drawing attention, but his pulse ticked faster. The feeling in his gut may prove accurate.

He passed a long serving table without a glance. A Chinese liaison tracked him with a curious look, glass paused halfway to her lips. Mendoza didn't break stride.

It wasn't just a missed check-in. He knew that. Every scenario in his mind sharpened to the same point—if it was the Americans, they'd already be inside. Rocha's patience was gone. Mendoza had no goodwill left to spend.

The south wing corridor grew quieter with each step. The warm murmur of the summit faded, replaced by the cooler, emptier air of the palace's older section. Lights hummed overhead, one of them flickering in a slow, irregular pulse.

He reached the security desk near the junction. His earpiece hissed with background static.

"Team Bravo, checking in—top of the stairwell now," came the voice, slightly winded.

A pause. Then—

"... descending."

The silence stretched. Static filled the gap, a thin, steady buzz. It gnawed at his nerves; he had no patience left.

He stopped, one hand tightening around his earpiece, the other curling into a fist at his side.

But he knew.

9:35 p.m.

Hopper stepped out of the cell, jaw clenched. Miguel's body was behind him, slumped in the chair like a shadow burned into his vision. His mind raced, filling with hate and disgust. There was no time to grieve. No time for anything but the mission. He had to find Sarah—now.

He collected himself, centering his mind on what needed to be done. He gave Finn a sharp nod toward the next door. They continued the mission.

Across the hall, Zeke and Jacks cleared their third room—muzzles up, movements tight, eyes cutting through the darkness.

Another empty cell. Time was slipping.

Hopper crept to the next doorway, pistol close to his chest. He peeked through, weapon raised. A chair sat in the center of the room. A woman faced away.

Sarah?

Then it hit him.

A searing punch tore through his left shoulder, driving the breath from his lungs and dropping him like a sack of bricks, his back slamming into the hard stone wall behind him. The gunshot cracked a split second later—a deep, concussive pop that left a ringing in his skull.

His legs buckled. He collapsed back into the hallway. Shockwave stunned him. Sound distant, heartbeat loud, vision edged in white—then the cold bite of concrete beneath his back.

Finn caught him mid-fall, hauling him upright just as more gunfire erupted from the room.

Finn raised his pistol one-handed while keeping Hopper out of the line of fire.

"No! Sarah's in there."

Finn held off on firing. The risk of hitting her was too high.

Rounds tore through the plaster, splintering the doorframe behind them. Stone shards and powdered dust burst into the air, stinging exposed skin.

"Contact!" Finn shouted, dragging Hopper back. Muzzle flashes flared inside the room, fast and brutal.

Zeke and Jacks were already moving, sprinting toward the gunfire. They caught sight of Finn hauling Hopper down the corridor, blood slicking the floor in a dark smear. Finn waved them off, signaling retreat.

Jacks and Zeke pivoted instantly, falling back toward the junction while covering their angles. Two quick suppressive shots hammered into the doorframe, forcing hesitation from the enemy.

Finn gripped Hopper under his good arm, pulling him upright. Together, they staggered toward the corner.

The comms crackled.

"Badger One, lots of movement upstairs," Kaitlyn warned. "Soldiers running for the basement stairs. You need to move now."

Then—boots. Dozens of them. Pounding down the stairwell.

Three silhouettes burst into view at the base of the steps, rifles already raised.

"Down!" Finn shouted.

Gunfire shredded the corridor. Bullets punched into the walls, sending stone splinters whipping through the air like shrapnel. The roar filled the confined space, deafening, the air tasting of hot metal and pulverized dust.

Hopper and Finn dove around the corner just as another burst ripped past, snapping the air. A wall of noise and heat rose.

Jacks and Zeke held the corners, firing toward the stairs. One soldier dropped, but more descended behind the first three. The team regrouped in a crouch just beyond the corner.

"We gotta move!" Hopper said, one hand clamped over his shoulder. Blood pulsed through his sleeve in waves.

Finn yanked open the trauma kit, slapped a QuickClot patch over the exit wound, and cinched a wrap tight. His hands moved fast, face locked in focus. "Through and through. Still bleeding heavily."

Zeke fired a few more rounds from the corner.

A new sound: controlled automatic fire from the opposite stairwell. Rounds chewed through the wall behind Jacks. One caught him.

Jacks grunted, stumbling. A round punched clean through his thigh, spinning him sideways.

"Shit!" he said, teeth clenched. "I'm good, keep going!"

He limped into formation, upright, still firing. Controlled, deliberate shots. The team retreated, Jacks and Zeke providing cover fire when needed.

They fell back through another hallway, boots slipping slightly on the blood-wet floor. Hopper's vision wavered, but he kept moving. Just barely.

They ducked into a shallow alcove for cover.

"Status?" Hopper said through gritted teeth.

"Wounds packed for now. Jacks took one in the leg— through muscle, not arterial. We can move," Finn said, breathing hard, hands red.

Zeke leaned into the wall, bracing with one hand, pistol

locked in the other. He peeked the corner, fired two fast shots, then pulled back as more rounds tore chunks from the frame beside him.

He released the magazine, dropping it to the floor and sliding a new one in. Then he saw them. Shapes advancing through the chaos. Not Bolivian. Not even close.

Black uniforms. Tactical gloves. Crimson berets.

Zeke froze for a beat, gut tightening.

Their movement was clean. Synchronized. Advancing without fear. He'd seen that kind of movement before.

"Boss!" he shouted over the gunfire. "Spetsnaz are here!"

16

January 24 | 9:38 p.m. BOT
La Paz, Bolivia

"Spetsnaz are coming? Shit, we have to get out of here now, boss! Those guys don't fuck around," Jacks said, stumbling into position. Blood soaked through the torn fabric above his knee, each step leaving a darker blotch on the concrete. He leaned against the wall, breathing hard, scanning behind them.

Hopper groaned, his hand clamped tight over the gunshot wound in his shoulder. Warm blood oozed between his fingers, soaking through his shirt. The clotting patch had failed. He could hardly move his arm. Pain pulsed in sync with his heartbeat—hot, stabbing, dizzying. Still, he forced his voice steady.

"Time to move. We need to get back to the hotel."

Finn and Jacks hauled him up, one under each arm, bodies straining under the added weight. Hopper gritted his teeth against the pain, boots dragging. Every breath hitched with every jolt. Behind them, Zeke stayed in the rear, calm and lethal. He fired two shots, controlled and precise, conserving ammo.

Concrete chipped and sparked under incoming fire. Zeke shifted left, tracking movement, then pivoted and sprinted after the team.

"Go!"

They exploded through the basement door and pounded up the stairs, boots thudding on the concrete steps. At the top, the cool night hit them like a slap. Alley shadows stretched long under the streetlights. The hum of La Paz returned. Distant horns, a burst of laughter, someone shouting across the street. As if the chaos below hadn't happened.

"Zeke, help me with this!" Finn shouted, gripping the edge of a heavy steel dumpster.

Zeke slammed his shoulder into it. Together they shoved with everything they had. Rusted wheels screeched. The metal groaned across the pavement. It teetered, then dropped, crashing into the stairwell.

Gunfire erupted immediately below. Bullets hammered the underside of the bin, tearing into the steel with explosive force.

"Down!" They ducked as rounds tore through the edges of the doorway, curling the metal outward like flower petals.

"Alley across the street! Move!" Hopper shouted, voice strained.

They bolted across C. Bolivar. Neon signs flickered around them—restaurants, bodegas, a hotel front. Horns blared. Cars swerved. Pedestrians screamed and scrambled at the sound of gunfire. A taxi clipped Finn's heel as it swerved away, skidding into another vehicle.

Jacks trailed behind, each step a war of endurance. Blood ran down his leg, soaking into his boot. He nearly stumbled, but Zeke grabbed his belt and yanked him forward. No time to stop.

Halfway through the alley, a **BOOM** ripped through the air. The dumpster exploded upward in a fireball. Garbage, smoke, and burning debris rained down. The blast slammed into them like a shockwave, sending Jacks to his knees. Asphalt tore into his skin. Zeke helped him up.

Out of the smoke came Spetsnaz and Bolivian soldiers, fighting side by side. They moved through passing traffic.

Crimson berets. Black body armor. Predators.

Muzzle flashes split the smoke like firecrackers. Gunfire lit up the night, ripping through glass storefronts, shredding signs, thudding into walls. Civilians screamed and hit the ground. A delivery truck jackknifed into a light pole. The enemy didn't care.

The team dove behind a row of dumpsters lining the alley. Bullets tore into the metal. Sparks flew. Pings ricocheted like angry hornets.

Zeke dropped low, grunted, and started dragging the rearmost bin with him, inch by inch. His shoulders screamed from the effort. It weighed a ton, but the wheels turned better on this one. It shielded the team's retreat. Finn stayed tight, still hauling Hopper, pistol ready in his off-hand. Outnumbered, outgunned—they wished they had their rifles.

"Almost there," Finn said. Sweat poured down his face, mixing with grime. He glanced back. The Spetsnaz were crossing the street.

Behind them, a Bolivian soldier dropped to one knee. A thump. The hollow *bloop* of a grenade launcher.

The round hit Zeke's dumpster with a massive *CLANG*.

The explosion was deafening.

The blast hurled Zeke backward in a storm of flame, garbage, and twisted metal. He slammed onto the pavement hard, motionless.

"Zeke!" Finn skidded beside him, choking on smoke and dust. He dropped low, checking for blood, for a pulse. Zeke's chest rose—shallow, but rising.

He slapped him hard. "Zeke! Come on, wake up!"

Zeke blinked. "I'm up…I'm up…"

"Then move your ass!"

Finn hauled him upright. Zeke's legs stumbled into motion, dazed but functional. The flaming, smoking wreck of the dumpster behind them offered momentary cover.

They reached the next alley intersection. A left turn should provide more cover and set them on a path back to the hotel.

"Clear?" Hopper asked, panting.

"Shit," Jacks said.

"What is it?"

Jacks pointed. A twenty-foot brick wall blocked the alley. Solid red stone. No ladders. No drainpipes. No way to climb, no way to safety.

"Fuck! That wasn't on the map," Hopper groaned.

"We'll have to double back," Jacks said, limping, already turning.

"No time," Zeke snapped. "Bolivians are advancing through the fire."

Rounds struck the wall beside them, chipping bricks, sending dust into Zeke's eyes. He swore and shoved Finn to the ground just as another burst hit.

"We need somewhere to Alamo from!" Zeke shouted.

He slammed in his final mag and chambered a round. "Last mag!"

He pulled a flashbang from his belt and tossed it toward

the flames.

CRACK.

The alley lit white. Screams followed from Bolivians moving ahead of the Spetsnaz. The Russians let the locals take the brunt of the carnage.

Then—another grenade streaked through the alley.

It sailed high, hitting the upper story of a building. The explosion threw a cloud of brick dust, forcing the team to cover their heads. Without tactical gear, they were naked and vulnerable.

Finn spotted civilians across the intersection, hunched behind a car. He flashed a silent hand signal: Go the other way. Now.

Finn tossed his own flashbang and fell back.

They collapsed behind a dented delivery van. The side panels scorched and covered in brick dust. The windshield spidered with cracks. But it was something.

Zeke leaned against it, shoulders heaving. Jacks collapsed beside him, hands gripping his pistol. Hopper dropped to one knee, arm limp, shoulder still bleeding through the patch.

"Hopp! Give me a mag!"

The injured team leader struggled to free the pistol mag from his belt, tossing it to his marksman once he finally managed.

For a moment, none of them moved. This was it. This alley might be where it ends.

Hopper looked at each of them. Bloodied, battered, soot and brick dust covering faces and shoulders. They'd made it this far together. Part of him wished it weren't the end—that they could have pushed further, finished what they started. But now, with barely any ammo and nowhere to run, he knew it was grim. They'd come as far as they could.

One by one, they looked at Hopper and nodded,

acknowledging the gravity of the situation. They would fight until there was no fight left. Unspoken, but understood.

Hopper reached for his radio transmitter, hand shaking. Static squelched.

With utter disappointment he said, "Eagle One…Badger One, we might not make it out of this. Use the secure uplink to reach command. Get yourself extracted and get that evidence in the right hands. Badger One out."

He let go of the button. The radio light dimmed.

Far off, but closing fast—boots on pavement. Another shout. Another burst of gunfire. Closer.

He looked up at his men.

"We hold here," he said. Resigned. Resolute.

"We stand our ground. No matter what comes around that corner."

The silence between them was sharp.

Zeke checked his mag. Three rounds plus the one from Hopper. He swapped for the fresh mag. Jacks adjusted his grip. Finn exhaled once, slow.

Smoke drifted toward them. Orange firelight twisted it into strange shapes. Shadows danced at the alley mouth.

The enemy was coming.

And they had no way out.

17

January 24 | 10:00 p.m. BOT
La Paz, Bolivia

Zeke leaned out from behind the battered van, one eye barely exposed. The alley smelled of dust and burning garbage—a stale mix that clung to his nostrils. From the corner, four Bolivian soldiers moved into view, rifles raised, boots scraping the pavement in a slow, methodical sweep. The narrow space trapped every footstep, every breath. There was no other cover nearby. The Bolivians scanned left and right. They knew exactly where the team was holed up. This was it.

Zeke's pulse quickened. Muscles tensed, waiting for the right moment. His finger hovered lightly above the trigger, ready.

Four shots rang out.

Bodies dropped with thuds onto the asphalt.

Zeke blinked, stunned for a moment. The quiet after the

chaos hung in the air. He peeked around the van again. Then he saw them. Two civilians, standing behind the fallen soldiers, pistols raised, eyes scanning down the alley toward the flaming dumpster. Not just civilians. That much was clear.

The same pair Finn had waved off earlier.

"Let's go!" one shouted, urgency cutting through the smoke.

"Guardian angels, boys," Zeke said, shifting his weight, muscles aching from the tension coiled tight in his body.

The team pushed off from cover, limping forward. Zeke dragged Jacks along, his leg still bleeding. Finn kept Hopper steady as the man struggled to stay upright, blood soaking through his left sleeve. His arm was effectively useless now, but he moved with determination, jaw clenched against the pain.

The Spetsnaz unit opened fire. The civilian rescuers turned, returning fire with precision. Two of the Spetsnaz dropped from direct hits.

"Keep moving! Black SUV, two hundred yards!"

The team crossed the alley intersection. Zeke paused long enough to fire a few one-handed shots. Recoil rocked his arm, but he forced it. He wasn't sure how much longer he could keep carrying Jacks. Chest tight with every breath.

He pulled a smoke grenade from Jacks' belt and flung it behind them. Thick gray clouds filled the alley, masking their retreat. The scent of burning rubber and metal stung his nose as they scrambled forward, moving southwest.

The six of them reached the SUV as another burst of automatic fire chewed through the brick at the intersection. They dove in a scramble of limbs, weapons, and blood. The back seat was cramped, but all four piled in. They had to escape. Fast.

The man in the front passenger seat turned, grinning. His

accent was unmistakably British. "Well, well. You Americans are always blowing shit up no matter where you go, aren't you?"

"Hey, Harry Potter," Jacks grunted from the back, climbing into the cargo compartment and pressing a bloody wad of gauze to his thigh, "technically, they were blowing us up. Get it right."

The Brit chuckled. "Fair enough, mate. Name's Sully. Wheelman is Dano. Former S.A.S. We were scouting the palace perimeter for a client when we walked into that little war zone."

Hopper extended a shaky hand. "Hopper. The Texas asshole in the back is Jacks. Finn's our medic. Baby face back there is Zeke. Thanks for the save."

"No trouble," Sully said—just before a taillight exploded into shards of plastic and glass. A fresh barrage lit up the rear of the vehicle. Low visibility, but the muzzle flashes from the corner were clear.

"They're right behind us!" Zeke shouted, returning fire with the last of his magazine. Fingers numb from recoil. "Punch it!"

"Hold on!" Dano slammed the SUV into gear. Tires screamed as rounds thudded into the rear bumper. He jerked the wheel, drifting out of the alley and weaving between late-night traffic. Horns blared. Pedestrians scattered, faces flashing past.

Both Brits rolled down their windows, grabbed smoke grenades from the door storage, and casually dropped them. The alley vanished in a thick curtain of smoke.

Inside, tension pressed down. Hopper clenched his jaw, sweat mixing with grime as the SUV jolted over potholes. Finn dug into the med kit the Brits had in the back, tearing open a packet of clotting agent and pressing it hard into

Hopper's shoulder.

"Through and through. Might work better than the patch. Clean exit. You'll live, but you'll need blood back at the hotel."

Jacks wasn't as lucky. His thigh wound was ragged, a small chunk missing. Still bleeding despite the compression bandage. He bit down on gauze, eyes tight, body wracked as Finn pressed a dressing in place.

Zeke slumped back, coughing soot. Body battered, bruised, ears ringing. He rubbed his face, trying to clear the haze, but fatigue settled in, heavy as lead.

As Dano tore through the streets, white and blue lights appeared ahead—La Paz municipal police. Patrol pickups and motorcycles flooded intersections, sirens blaring. Too little, too late.

"Police are sweeping in," Sully said, eyes scanning the road. "Let's not get stuck in their net."

Once they put distance between themselves and the palace, Dano took a winding path through the city, checking mirrors twice. Streets felt different now, like they weren't just escaping gunfire but a storm already closing in.

When the SUV finally slowed, Sully looked back at Hopper. "So, as I was saying before we were so rudely interrupted—pop star client, big performance tomorrow night for some presidential event. We were doing recon. But after what we just saw, I'm going to strongly suggest she get the hell out of Bolivia."

"Smart move," Jacks said, voice hoarse.

Hopper nodded, thoughts flickering to their mission, to Sarah. "We snuck into the palace basement. They're holding an American prisoner—a teenage girl, daughter of a congressman."

Sully met Dano's eyes. No words needed. The decision was mutual.

"Not worth it," Sully said. "This country's boiling over. No performance is worth the risk."

Eventually, they circled enough to feel safe from a tail. Hopper gave Sully the hotel address and radioed ahead. Kaitlyn's voice crackled back.

"Copy, Badger One. Standing by with med kits. Get your asses back here."

They parked a couple of blocks from the hotel and walked the rest of the way. Each step a test. Hopper leaned on Finn, every movement sharp with pain. Blood loss had him near collapse. Jacks dragged his leg but stayed alert. Zeke and Dano covered the rear, eyes scanning every shadow. No sign of surveillance.

Sully slowed as they approached the building.

"You're staying this close to the palace?"

"Close enough for recon. Quick deployment," Zeke said, quiet but confident. "So close that no one will suspect it."

"Ballsy," Dano said, shaking his head, admiration and disbelief in his tone.

They reached their floor. Hopper keyed the radio.

"Eagle One, Badger One. Entering the nest, plus two guests."

"Copy that, Badger One."

The door opened. Warm light spilled out. They were home. For now.

10:35 p.m.

"You lost them?"

Colonel Mendoza's voice thundered down the corridor.

"How in God's name is that possible?"

His soldiers froze, eyes downcast, backs pressed against

the cracked plaster walls as if distance could soften the impact of his wrath. He barked rapidly in Spanish to keep the Russians from catching every word, but his fury transcended language. Even without translation, it was obvious: heads were about to roll.

"They were bleeding, limping, cornered! And you let them vanish into the city?"

One of the senior officers stepped forward, voice trembling as he tried to explain, but Mendoza cut him off with a sharp wave of his hand. The sound of boots shifting on the marble floor filled the silence that followed.

"It doesn't matter anymore. Take as many men as you need. Lock down every street, every exit. Tear the city apart if you have to. Find them. If the Russians walk away from this deal, the President won't just fire me. He'll have all our heads. Understood?"

"*Sí, Colonel.*"

The soldier replied quickly before spinning on his heel and rushing off to rally more men. Orders echoed through the corridor moments later, the building coming alive with frantic movement.

Mendoza exhaled through clenched teeth and stepped out onto the narrow balcony overlooking the darkened city below. A stiff wind funneled between the buildings, carrying the distant wail of sirens and the faint smell of smoke from the palace district. He leaned over the wrought-iron railing, knuckles white, jaw grinding as failure echoed in his ears. His mind replayed the last radio calls—each one another nail in the coffin of a plan gone wrong. A plan he had been sure was airtight.

How did this happen? How did they get inside unnoticed?

A quiet presence approached. Mendoza glanced to his side and found himself face-to-face with Dimitri Petrov.

The Spetsnaz team leader was massive—in both height and breadth. Broad-shouldered, bearded like a Siberian bear. He moved with the heavy, deliberate steps of a man who had never needed to raise his voice to command respect. His shadow stretched unnaturally long in the dim balcony light.

"I have information," Petrov said, his English rough, thick with a Russian accent. "You will want to hear."

Mendoza straightened, cautious. "What sort of information?"

"The Americans did not escape alone. They had help. Extracted by a vehicle before we could close in." Petrov's eyes narrowed with recognition. "A vehicle I recognize. It belongs to two British contractors—private security for the singer at tomorrow's event."

Mendoza's lips curled in disgust. "Of course. The British."

He let the words hang, considering the new angle. His mind quickly began fitting the pieces together—how the foreigners might have slipped through the net, and how he could turn this to his advantage. Then his gaze locked on Petrov. "Can you and your men deal with them? Quickly."

Petrov's head tilted slightly, almost a predator's nod. "It will be done."

Without another word, he turned and disappeared into the shadows of the corridor, footsteps fading like a distant storm.

Mendoza watched him go, the cool air biting harder now. For the first time in days, a flicker of relief crept into his chest. The Russians didn't bluff—not like his own men.

But as he stood there, fingers tightening on the iron railing, he knew relief was a dangerous thing in a war not yet won. And wars like this rarely gave second chances.

18

January 24 | 11:45 p.m. BOT
La Paz, Bolivia

The hotel room looked less like a place to sleep and more like a field hospital after a firefight. Gauze wrappers and stained cloths littered the floor in uneven piles. The air reeked of antiseptic and blood, sharp enough to sting the nose. A single lamp flickered in the corner, throwing uneven light across the walls, while the muffled hum of traffic and wailing sirens from the streets below leaked through the thin glass.

The altitude pressed on them all, making every breath shallow and ragged, as if even recovery here demanded extra effort. Hopper leaned against the window frame, one shoulder bandaged tight, his reflection a pale outline in the dark glass. Pain radiated from the bullet wound with each heartbeat, a dull, hot throb that never let him forget how close it had come. His arm would require as much rest as he could provide to be useful later. He forced himself to keep watch anyway—eyes on the city, posture rigid—because doing nothing felt like surrender.

In the main room, Jacks sat slouched in a chair, his leg stretched out stiff in front of him. Sweat streaked his temples, and his knuckles were white against the armrest where he gripped hard enough to dent the padding. Finn knelt close, curved needle and thread in hand, stitching the hole in Jacks' thigh with steady precision.

"They got you good. Lucky it didn't hit you dead on," Finn mumbled with thread in his mouth, eyes narrowed in concentration. He tugged the thread through and wiped a smear of blood with the corner of a rag. "You're gonna have a good chunk missing, but at least it didn't break your leg."

"Comforting," Jacks said through clenched teeth, jaw muscles tight. "Still hurts like hell." He exhaled hard as another stitch pulled taut, the sound closer to a growl than a sigh.

Hopper shifted against the window, pain flaring as he adjusted his stance. The dressing at his shoulder was fresh, but the wound burned beneath the gauze with a pulse of heat every time his heart kicked. Moving his arm sent white sparks across his vision, a reminder of how limited he really was. He hated that helpless feeling, hated standing still while the others worked, but tonight his body had won the argument.

Across the room, Kaitlyn sat cross-legged on one of the unmade beds, her back resting against the wall. For the first time in weeks, she wasn't running. She wasn't hiding in the jungle or flinching at every sound in the dark. The presence of the team—their voices, their steady movements—gave the room a strange sense of safety, however temporary. It almost felt normal, though the ache of exhaustion and her ankle still sat deep in her bones.

Sully had pulled a chair around to face her, elbows resting

on his knees, while Dano leaned against the dresser, arms folded, watching the other's work, taking in their determination to push forward. The banter between the Brits was familiar to Kaitlyn. She listened in, a faint smile tugging at her lips despite everything, reminding her of home.

"What will you do about your pop star?" she asked.

The question drew a sharp grin from Sully, who shot Dano a sidelong glance.

Sully's grin faded into something more thoughtful as he leaned back in his chair. "Dano, mate, I think it's time you headed over to the hotel. Get the rest of the team up to speed and send Sabrina home in a hurry. I'll stay here with the guys and figure out the plan. Come back once she's on her way to the airport."

Dano nodded slowly, his face tightening with the same calculation Hopper often wore. "Good idea. Can't exactly call them either. Not after the night we just had. If they're tapped into cell towers, everyone becomes a target."

"Exactly," Sully said. "Best she hears it face-to-face. No panic. No leaks."

Dano straightened, pushing off the dresser to grab his bag. The movement caught Hopper's eye near the window. He turned, his expression sharpened by pain and fatigue but still all command.

"Dano."

The Brit looked up. Hopper crossed the room and pressed a folded slip of paper into his hand. On it, an address and a short numeric code written in Hopper's tight scrawl.

"What's this?"

"CIA safe house," Hopper said. "It's got an armory. On your way back, grab everything you can from there. We'll need it."

Dano's brow furrowed as he studied the paper. He knew

what it meant for Hopper to share that kind of resource. An asset that wasn't meant to leave Agency hands. He tucked it carefully into a side pocket and met Hopper's eyes with a slow nod.

"Understood."

From across the room, Zeke glanced up from where he was sorting gear, his expression unreadable, though his sharp gaze lingered on the exchange. After what these men did for the team, the risk they had taken, it didn't surprise him that Hopper had gained some trust in the men.

Dano turned to Kaitlyn and gave her a gentle smile, softening the edge of the moment. "Don't let these bloody Yanks get you shot, yeah?"

She smirked back. "No promises."

Dano gave a short wave before slipping out the door, the latch clicking shut behind him. The room quieted again.

Kaitlyn watched him go, the sound of his boots fading down the hallway, then turned back toward Hopper. He'd stepped away from the window now, his posture uneven, one hand braced against the edge of the table. His face was pale, drawn—pain riding him in more ways than one. She tilted her head slightly, sensing the shift.

"What is it?" she asked.

Hopper hesitated. He looked at the SAT phone on the table, then at the folded map beside it, as if searching for the right words in anything but her eyes. Finally, he motioned her closer.

"I didn't get the chance earlier," he said, voice lower than before. "We found Miguel. His body anyway."

Kaitlyn froze. "What?"

"We found him in one of the basement cells at the palace." Hopper's jaw flexed, the words coming out clipped, restrained.

Her breath caught. For a moment, she just stared at him, waiting for him to take it back, to say she'd misheard. But his expression was flat, unchanging. She swallowed hard, the weight of the news dropping into her chest like a stone.

"I'm sorry. I know you two were close," he said.

She sat down slowly at the table, as though her knees had given out. Her hands trembled in her lap, and she blinked rapidly, but the tears still came—silent at first, then tracing slow, uneven paths down her cheeks.

"He was kind to me," she whispered, her voice raw.

Silence hung between them, broken only by the faint rustle of wrappers and Finn's steady voice as he coached Jacks through another stitch across the room. Hopper stayed near, steady but distant, giving her the space to grieve while forcing himself not to show too much of his own.

After a long moment, Hopper pushed himself upright, the motion stiff, his hand pressed against the bandaged shoulder as though to hold himself together. He glanced at Kaitlyn once more, her grief cutting deeper than he'd admit, then turned toward the others.

Finn tied off the last stitch in Jacks' leg, muttering a satisfied, "That'll hold."

Zeke continued his quiet ritual of checking magazines, the click of metal-on-metal steady, grounding. For a moment, the team almost looked whole again. Though they felt defeated, they weren't finished. Not until they got Sarah home.

"Get some rest," Hopper said finally, his voice low but carrying. "Heal up. We've got a lot of shit to figure out tomorrow."

He didn't add what pressed in the back of his mind—that tomorrow felt like it was already rushing at them too fast, that the enemy would move while they slept. Every second they spent patching wounds was another second Sarah slipped further out of reach.

But none of that would help them now. All he could do was keep standing, keep leading, even if his body screamed otherwise. He leaned once more against the window frame, eyes on the dark city below, and forced himself to hold steady.

That was his way of leading his men.

January 25 | 2:00 a.m. BOT
La Paz, Bolivia

Five identical high-end black SUVs idled in front of the hotel, engines low and steady. After a quick rain shower, their headlights washed pale beams across the wet pavement, reflecting in oily streaks. Inside, the last of the pop star's entourage shuffled out to the vehicles, carrying suitcases and dragging rolling bags behind them. Most of the staff were bleary-eyed and silent, luggage wheels clattering faintly against the curb from lack of wakefulness and control of their limbs.

Dano stood at the edge of the sidewalk, arms folded, watching the operation unfold with a soldier's detachment, ensuring all staff members were accounted for. He'd got the singer and her full staff packed and ready to go in under two hours. No drama. No complications. A clean extraction, so far. The kind he preferred—precise and efficient.

The plan was simple. No announcement to the Bolivian authorities. No press. Just a quiet departure in the middle of the night, and a waiting private jet, fueled up on the tarmac, far from the eyes of any government personnel.

The last staffer slid into the back seat of the rearmost SUV. Dano gave the door a firm tap with his knuckles, signaling the drivers to depart. Moments later, the convoy rolled out, taillights glowing like coals as they disappeared into the sleeping city.

He exhaled, tension bleeding from his shoulders. That part of the night was over.

Dano turned and started walking, hands in his jacket pockets. The air was cool. Thin. Every breath came shallow, a reminder that La Paz sat higher than any city had a right to. Even trained lungs work harder here. The city around him felt like it was holding its breath—only the distant grind of a late-night bus and a muffled horn breaking the silence on his walk.

He pulled out a phone and dialed.

Sully picked up on the second ring.

"Package away safely. Heading to gather gear and head back to the nest shortly," Dano said.

Sully's voice crackled faintly, then the line went dead. That was enough. They didn't need chatter. Especially not tonight.

He slipped the phone away and veered off the main sidewalk, cutting through a narrow passage between buildings. The alley was dark and damp, slick with the recent rain. A single yellow bulb flickered above a rusted side door half-way down, buzzing faintly like an insect caught in a glass.

Dano liked alleys. They were quiet, predictable. No crowds. No cameras. They offered good shortcuts and easy ways to disappear.

The CIA safe house was only a few blocks away. Safer this way.

He moved at a steady, casual pace, boots barely making a sound. Every motion was instinctive. Former British Special Air Service—the training that drilled silence into your bones. Surveillance, counter-surveillance, vanishing into shadows. It was muscle memory now.

Somewhere off to his right, something scurried low, knocking over a stack of bottles, likely a rodent. He slowed, tilting his head, scanning low, then the rooftops out of habit. A faint hum of an air conditioner in the distance, the whisper of rainwater dripping from a gutter—minor sounds everywhere. No obvious threats. Still, they put a fine edge on his senses.

He moved on, eyes shifting between shadowed doorways and the narrow strip of sky above. His fingers brushed the inside of his jacket, reassuring himself that his sidearm was there and ready. His pace stayed measured, every step cautious, but giving no appearance other than casual.

At the alley's end, he slowed even more. A pale rectangle of light cut across the pavement from a streetlamp beyond. A little further stood the service door. A keypad hidden in the recessed frame—this is the clandestine entry point to the CIA safe house.

Reaching into his pocket, he pulled the slip of paper Hopper had given him. He checked the address and code and then slid it back. Twenty paces. Nothing to it.

For the first time that night, he allowed himself a hint of satisfaction. He'd helped save a group of Americans from certain death, secured his high-profile client and got her out of the country, and pulled it all off without incident. Not bad for one night's work.

He stepped forward, crossing the strip of lamplight.

Something shifted in the dark.

The scrape was subtle, just ahead and to the left—a heel dragging once across damp concrete. Dano's head turned, eyes narrowing, scanning the deeper shadow where a wall jutted out. His right hand shifted in his pocket, gripping his pistol.

A shape detached from the wall.

The movement was too fast to counter. He caught the glint of metal, then the rifle butt slammed across his temple from the other side. A distraction, and he fell for it. Bone jolted, pain detonating in a burst of white light behind his eyes. His knees buckled as his balance vanished from the sudden blow to the head. He tasted copper.

The second impact never even registered.

Lights out.

Everything went black.

6:00 a.m.

The hotel room was quiet. A weak morning light filtered through the curtained windows, casting pale lines across the floor and across the clutter they'd left behind the night before. Empty water bottles, torn gauze wrappers, a smear of dried blood on the edge of the sink. The smell of antiseptic still clung to the air, sharp against the staleness of sweat and damp clothes.

Outside, a distant truck engine groaned somewhere below, then faded. A wall clock ticked faintly. Every sound seemed amplified in the stillness.

The team sat clustered around the table in the main room, heads low, bodies bruised, bandages stark against their skin. The rest was much needed. Hopper's shoulder still burned under the wrap, every throb reminding him he wasn't moving at full strength, but he regained some movement of the limb. Jacks shifted in his chair, rubbing his thigh, the leg stiff and uncooperative. Kaitlyn sat with her arms folded tightly, eyes distant, jaw set in a way that made her look far older than she should. Even Sully was uncharacteristically still, his fingers drumming once against the table, then stopping.

No one spoke. They had slept, just not enough. They were all still tired and achy.

It felt less like a strategy session and more like a silent group therapy circle. Each of them lost in their own wounds, waiting for someone else to break the silence.

Finally, Jacks leaned forward, his Texan accent and gritty voice breaking the air.

"So... where do we go from here, boss?"

Hopper didn't answer right away. He stood and began pacing slowly across the room, favoring his injured shoulder. His face was tight, focused, clearly contemplating. He could feel the pressure building—not just from Bolivian forces or Rocha. Something bigger.

"Our first move has to be figuring out why the Russians are involved," he said. "We get that piece, maybe we get leverage. Or at least some clue about what we're up against."

Finn sat up straighter. "I don't think it's about oil. They've got more than enough of their own. And if Rocha's running slave labor out of those mines, maybe there's something deeper underground—rare earth metals, maybe. Weapons-grade minerals. Something valuable."

"Could be. Something money can't buy, or that Russia can't be seen buying publicly anyway," Hopper said.

Zeke scratched his scruffy beard, thinking. "What if it started as a partnership, and then the Russians took it over? Rocha thinks he's still in charge, but they're just letting him play king."

"Hostile takeover," Finn said. "Classic Kremlin move."

He leaned forward now, tone low. "Only other angle I can see is military—like Cuba, back in the day."

Hopper raised an eyebrow. "Missile silos?"

"Not necessarily. But think about it. Back then, Russia wanted launch sites closer to U.S. soil—fast strike options.

Today, missiles can hit anywhere. But boots on the ground? That's different. What if they're staging something? Troops. Armor. Air assets. If they've got a foothold here, they're within spitting distance of Mexico and the southern American border."

Kaitlyn finally spoke, her voice quiet but steady. "And if Rocha's letting them do it, it means he's already sold the country out from under his own people."

The room was still again. No one dismissed the idea. Not anymore. They sat with that for a while, the weight of it pressing down, heavy as the morning light. No matter which of those thoughts was correct, the international implications were massive.

Then Jacks moved toward Sully and asked him quietly. "Hey. You heard from Dano?"

Sully checked his watch. "Not yet. He should've been back by now."

He pulled out his phone and tried calling. Straight to voicemail. He tried again. Still nothing. His jaw tightened. Worry crept in. He stepped away from the table and tried another number, pacing near the window. Hopper's eyes followed him, reading the tension in his shoulders, and the concern etched on his face.

When Sully came back, his voice was nervous. "Something's wrong."

Zeke looked up from his laptop, eyes narrowing. "Boss... I've got something. Intel report just hit the feed. Says the Bolivians detained a foreign operative overnight."

Hopper moved to Zeke's side and leaned over the encrypted laptop. He read in silence. Then he looked up at Sully.

"You're not gonna like this. They're saying it's a British spy."

Sully was already moving. He leaned in, scanned the report himself. He read it twice, hoping it was wrong. Hoping it was anyone else.

Kaitlyn had gone pale. She moved without a word to the small TV mounted on the wall and flicked it on. Static hissed for a second before a local Bolivian news station appeared on the screen. She flipped to a second channel. Then a third.

There it was.

A breaking news banner ran across the bottom:

Espía británico capturado. British spy captured.

The reporter's voice was too fast to follow, Spanish pouring over grainy live footage of a bridge in La Paz. Early morning light. A crowd gathered in the vicinity. Police tape flapped in the wind around the scene. Officers pushed people back to control the area.

The camera panned—and froze.

Hanging from the center of the bridge, in a torn shirt and bloodied slacks, was a man. It was Dano. His face battered. His arms hung limp. Around his neck, pulled tight, was a noose of coarse yellow rope. His body swayed in the wind high above the ground.

The caption at the bottom shifted:

Ejecutado al amanecer. Executed at dawn.

Kaitlyn's hand flew to her mouth. Sully stepped back from the TV as if something had physically hit him, fists clenched so tight the veins in his forearms stood out. Turning in anger, he launched his fist through the drywall with a painful grunt, not because of the pain in his hand. Dano was his best friend. Jacks muttered a low curse under his breath, and Finn just shook his head slowly, disbelief cutting through his exhaustion. Zeke reached forward and closed the laptop without looking, as if shutting down one screen would make the other vanish.

No one spoke.

The image held there, unflinching. It was a message. A warning intended for them.

The silence in the room thickened into something heavier than grief.

Hopper's eyes stayed on the screen, the morning light catching the edge of his bandage. He removed his arm from the sling and began working it with slight movements. There was no walking this back. No negotiation.

The war had begun.

19

The team sat hunched around the table, gear scattered in loose piles beside them. The silence wasn't tactical. It was emotional—a kind of heaviness none of them had the words to break. Outside, muted city noise bled faintly through the windows, but fazed none of them.

After the news report on television, there had been little discussion.

There had been a few murmured condolences to Sully, a handful of quiet reflections on Dano, but mostly there was just the weight. It lingered in the air like smoke from a dead fire.

The SAT phone rested in the center of the table, black and still. A few minutes earlier, Mindy had called to warn them that updated tasking was inbound from the Joint Chiefs. Hopper welcomed it. They all did. Anything to shake loose the grief. They needed direction, purpose.

The team hadn't finished in Bolivia. Sarah was still out there—still depending on them.

But the tension in the room had shifted. Hopper noticed the signs. Jacks was fidgeting with the straps on his vest, snapping and unsnapping his gear pouches. Zeke kept drumming his fingers on the table, his eyes unfocused. Kaitlyn stared at nothing, her hands clasped in her lap as if she were holding on to something invisible.

The phone rang.

Every head lifted. Hopper reached out, answered the call, and hit speaker.

"This is One. You're on with the full team."

Deputy Director Conley's voice came through, clear but tight, as if he was already bracing for their reaction. "Status check. Are you Oscar Charlie?"

It had been a beat since their last official sitrep. Hopper understood the request.

"We're operationally capable, sir. Took some hits, but still in the fight. One of the British soldiers who rescued us was publicly executed this morning. Russians confirmed on the ground and hostile."

"Understood," Conley said. The clipped delivery wasn't cold; urgency pressed it flat. "You have updated orders. Your team is still tasked with recovering Sarah, but she's been moved to a secondary priority. The prime directive is intel recovery of the Russian presence. Comms, docs, drives—anything that explains what the hell they're doing in Bolivia."

There was a pause.

"So she's not the primary objective anymore?" Jacks scoffed.

"She's still a priority," Conley replied, more carefully now. "But the situation's changed. With a Russian footprint this close to U.S. soil, the Joint Chiefs want answers. Fast. The kind of answers only your team can get."

Hopper felt the words like grit in his teeth. Every instinct pushed against the shift, but orders were orders. He forced the resistance down, kept his voice even.

"Copy that."

Everyone could hear the strain in Conley's voice. This wasn't his decision. He was just relaying the shift from the top.

No one argued. They didn't need to. The mission hadn't changed in their minds. They would get Sarah out. And find out why the hell Moscow was staking ground in South America.

Hopper reached over and ended the call. The phone stayed on the table, like a quiet trigger waiting to be pulled.

Jacks exhaled hard. "Well. Guess that's our fire lit."

Finn stood and pulled a tube from his pack, unrolling a worn blueprint of the Presidential Palace. He spread it flat across the table, the paper edges curling from years of use.

"Let's work the problem."

The team crowded in, eyes scanning the layout. Hopper leaned over the edge, shoulder stiff but eyes sharp.

"Back entrance is a no-go," Zeke said. "They'll have that sealed tighter than Jacks' ass wound after last time."

"Front's suicide," Finn added. "Too many checkpoints. Too many eyeballs."

They circled the options, trading quick, quiet assessments.

Zeke tapped the roofline on the schematics. "What about here? Rocha's office is on the top floor, right? If we can get to the roof—"

"No ladders. No fire escape. That side's bare," Finn

countered, his finger tracing the approach routes.

"True. But this building behind it. Government office, six floors. Close enough for a rope drop. We get up there, rappel onto the palace roof, punch in through the roof access door, and bypass the ground floor entirely."

Hopper nodded slowly. "That puts us right outside Rocha's office."

"For the concert tonight, they'll be watching Rocha like a hawk. But the office itself? Probably unguarded," Sully added.

"And I always have party favors just in case," Jacks said, a faint smirk breaking the tension.

"Did we pack climbing gear?" Hopper asked.

Jacks' smirk widened. "For a trip through the jungle? Hell yes."

"Alright. That's the route. We move after dark, when the palace is crowded for the concert. Get in, split up. One team searches for intel in the office; the other finds a way to the basement. We get Sarah, pull anything valuable we can from Rocha's office, and we get out."

The team started moving with purpose. Jacks gathered gear. Zeke prepped his rifle and rechecked his optics. They wouldn't be going in empty-handed this time.

Kaitlyn quietly helped Sully sort spare magazines and flashbangs from a pile of unclaimed kit.

Sully didn't speak. He clipped a knife to his belt and checked the slide on his sidearm. His face was unreadable, but his movements were deliberate, every check and adjustment just a little harder than it needed to be. His eyes burned, fixed on a target only he could see.

He wasn't just prepping for an op.

He was hunting—revenge for Dano.

January 26 | 1:04 a.m. BOT
La Paz, Bolivia

The team was silent as they piled into Sully's SUV. The big black vehicle sat heavy on its shocks, reinforced but quiet, with enough space to hold the full team, Kaitlyn, and if everything went according to plan—Sarah. There would be room for hard drives, documents, anything else they could rip from Rocha's office before vanishing and getting the hell out of this country.

No one said a word as the doors shut with soft, deliberate clicks.

Limo-tinted windows turned the outside world into shadow play. Only the occasional glare of light from passing streetlamps cut through the dark, washing pale streaks across their gear and faces. The low hum of the engine blended with the whisper of tires over rain-slick streets. A steady rhythm beneath the weight of impending struggle.

Hopper sat in the front passenger seat, eyes scanning the passing intersections. This could be their last chance to extract Sarah before being overrun. If that happens, it's all over.

The city slid by in brief, dimly lit frames—wet pavement, shuttered shops, darkened windows. Hopper remained vigilant, alert, but the weight in his chest was heavier than the body armor. This was it. No more dry runs. No more recon. He rotated his shoulder to get used to the pain.

He didn't like it.

Not the mission. Not the odds. Not the silence. And especially not the fact that Kaitlyn was in the back seat, wedged between Jacks and Zeke, riding toward one of the most dangerous locations in the country.

She didn't belong on a raid. Not like this.

Over the past few days, she'd proven to him that she

could hold her ground, adapt under pressure, survive what most civilians never would. But bringing someone he'd once pulled out of a firefight back into the teeth of another? It went against every instinct he had. This wasn't protocol. This wasn't how it was supposed to go.

But neither was this mission.

Kaitlyn's presence was purely logistics. The goal was to grab Sarah, recover whatever intel they could, and exfil in one motion. No doubling back. That meant she had to be there. The less time they spent on the street, the better. They would need every second to get out of the city and into Chile. Cleaner that way. Safer.

At least, that was the idea.

He glimpsed her reflection in the window. Her posture was steady, hands resting lightly on her thighs, but her eyes fixed forward. Calm but alert. Like someone bracing for a storm they couldn't see yet, but knew was coming.

In the back, Finn adjusted a suppressor, threading it onto the barrel of his carbine. The metallic click muted by the soft interior of the SUV. Zeke double-checked his magazines, running a thumb over each one before sliding it back into place. Jacks gave a silent nod toward Kaitlyn and passed her a pair of compact ear protection inserts, which she accepted without a word.

They weren't talking, but they were ready. Each man locked into his own rhythm, years of training distilled into quiet, deliberate movements and pre-battle rituals. Each had their own way of preparing to step into the fire.

The SUV turned onto a narrower road, cutting through a quiet business district. The buildings here were dull concrete structures, their façades streaked with years of rain and neglect. There was not a soul on the sidewalk. There was not a light in the windows. The air smelled faintly of wet concrete and oil.

Up ahead, a soft mist had fallen, scattering the glow from the streetlamps into hazy halos. Droplets pattered lightly against the windshield, the wipers sweeping them aside in slow, steady arcs.

They were close now. The government office building they planned to use for roof access was only a few blocks away. They would enter the building quietly, make their way to the roof, then rappel next door for a rooftop insertion of the Presidential Palace. One step at a time. Neighboring building first.

Sully drove like a man used to moving through danger with elegance. Slow, steady, no sudden shifts. Just one more shadow in a city that had grown used to ghosts.

Hopper glanced over at Sully. Their eyes met for a moment. No words needed. Everything had been said.

This was the last calm. The last quiet breath before they breached the storm.

And somewhere ahead in the dark, the storm was already awake.

January 26 | 12:32 a.m. EST
Langley, Virginia

Deputy Director Conley snapped the brass buckles shut on his leather briefcase. The soft click carried farther than it should have in his vacant office. For a moment, he stood there, hand resting on the handle, eyes unfocused, glaring out the window. He trusted the team implicitly; they had proven themselves worthy of that trust. But this mission had been anything but clean—too many setbacks, too many unknowns still hanging in the air like a single shadow in an alley. Loose ends that could unravel everything if tugged from the wrong angle.

He pushed the thought aside. There was nothing left to do from here except wait—and Conley had never been good at waiting. The team had to retrieve intel from the palace before anyone could make tactical decisions or form strategies. There was little understanding in the moment, and that's what they needed most.

The corridor outside was empty, lit in sterile strips by overhead lights. His polished shoes struck a steady cadence on the tile, each step echoing faintly off walls lined with framed mission commendations for the director and classified boards of potential future operations. Deep somewhere in the building, a copier cycled down with a mechanical whir, followed by a hollow silence.

He slowed as he passed the open doorway to the main briefing room. The lights were still on.

Mindy sat alone at the far end of the table, bathed in the soft blue-white glow of her laptop, a white halo highlighting her blond hair from the fixture above. Dozens of windows filled the screen: real-time satellite sweeps over La Paz, encrypted comms traffic scrolling in green code, logistics updates ticking in the corner. She was coordinating with Navy ships in the area, searching for a suitable exfil platform for the team once they retrieved Sarah. The low hum of electronics wrapped the room in a cocoon of quiet vigilance.

Conley lingered in the doorway. "Let me know if anything comes up. You're sure you don't need me to stay?"

Mindy glanced up, posture straight, expression calm but eyes sharp. "I'm fine, Director. I've got this. Besides, you've got a late meeting with the brass anyway. Everything here is under control."

"I can get one of the overnight analysts over here so you can take a break and head home?"

Her fingers hovered over the keys for half a beat before resuming their steady rhythm. "Not a chance. I'm not leaving them out there with backup that doesn't know them."

He hesitated. Not because he doubted her—he didn't—but because something about the quiet felt fragile, like glass underfoot. Still, he gave a small nod.

"Alright. Keep me posted."

As he turned toward the exit, Mindy leaned closer to the screen, her glasses catching the light. The reflection in the lenses was a constellation of data feeds, each one a thread in a web she couldn't afford to let slip. A single satellite window updated with a new sweep, coordinates shifting by fractions of a degree. She exhaled once, quietly, and kept working. The hum of the room swallowed the moment.

Outside the doorway, Conley's footsteps faded into the corridor.

The building seemed even quieter now. All had left long ago, but Mindy remained. She hadn't been assigned to the team for long, but she felt a responsibility to do everything in her power to keep them informed, to keep them safe. This was *her* mission as well, just from a different angle.

January 26 | 1:48 a.m. BOT
La Paz, Bolivia

The team crouched low on the rooftop of the government office building, their silhouettes dissolving into the dark. From here, the Presidential Palace was a lit jewel in the night, its floodlit façade casting pale gold across the courtyard. A chilly wind rolled over the roof, thin and biting at La Paz's altitude, carrying faint notes of exhaust and the distant echo of music from the concert below. The air felt sharp in the lungs, a chill that settled in the bones if you stayed still too long.

Getting this far had been smooth, unnervingly so. They had slipped into the office building through a service entrance, passed two half-asleep janitors who never looked up, and reached the roof without raising a whisper. No government employees, no security. An unguarded building, likely due to the security needs next door.

Zero footprint so far.

Just how Hopper liked it. And yet, something about the ease gnawed at him.

Zeke adjusted the focus on his spotting scope, elbows braced on the ledge, scanning below. Figures in tuxedos and evening gowns drifted toward a row of waiting limousines, their movements sluggish, half-dulled by champagne and the late hour. Last-minute conversations before leaving the event.

"Palace is clearing out, boss," Zeke said. "VIPs are heading out."

Hopper crouched beside him, eyes narrowing. The concert had been their best distraction—he wasn't about to waste the tail end of it. "We move while their eyes are still on the guests."

He signaled to Jacks.

Jacks pulled the compact grappling gun from his pack—a modified M320 launcher, its barrel widened for a four-pronged steel hook. A CO_2 canister mounted beneath propelled the projectile. He moved to the ledge in a low crouch, weapon tight to his body, scanning once before bracing on the edge. His breathing slowed. Aim crucial. The target: a telecom tower bolted to the palace roof. Solid steel, interlaced beams, a perfect anchor for the crossing.

The hook launched with a muffled thump, trailing a length of black rope. The team watched as the projectile bit clean between two beams, metal scraping as the prongs locked in place at an angled joint. Jacks reeled in slack with slow, steady pulls. No rattle. All quiet.

"Anchor set," Zeke confirmed, kneeling to secure his end of the line to a steel mount above the stairwell housing. He cinched the knot and gave the line a sharp test pull. It held firm.

Harness buckles clicked. Carabiners locked. Gloves tugged snug.

One by one, they maneuvered across, high above the alleyway. Bodies tight against the rope, weapons slung across their chests. Boots whispered on the line, the descent quiet except for the faint hiss of rope through metal as carabiners bore their weight. Zeke landed first, dropping to one knee, rifle up, scanning. Finn followed, tapping Zeke's shoulder as he passed to take the next sector. Each arrival rippled through the roof, the team slotting into position without a word.

Jacks came last, rolling off the line in a kneeling position. Now, five shadows occupied the palace roof, spread in a defensive arc.

All quiet.

Hopper's eyes swept the perimeter. No patrols. Just the hum of rooftop air conditioning units. The place felt... hollow.

"Finn, on me."

They glided across the roof toward a long, glass pyramid skylight. Below, the atrium glowed with warm light. Chandeliers threw soft halos over polished marble. Guests lingered, but most were funneling toward the front doors. Uniformed guards lined the hallways, their gazes fixed outward, more concerned with high-profile departures than the emptying palace interior.

"Almost empty," Finn said.

"This is our window," Hopper replied. "Intel second. Sarah first."

No one questioned it.

Jacks moved to the stairwell door. He crouched low and set to work with his tools. The metallic click of the last pin was barely audible over the background hum. The door eased open, hinges silent.

They stacked up in the shadows. Even injured, Hopper went first. His shoulder ached unrelentingly, but he pushed through. Finn, Zeke, Jacks, and Sully followed, bringing up the rear.

Five shadows slipped inside, vanishing into the dark spine of the palace. The door closed behind them without a sound.

Somewhere below, a faint echo of footsteps broke the stillness. Hopper froze mid-step, hand raised—a silent command for the team to hold.

The quiet felt suddenly thinner.

20

The team huddled in the shadows just outside the heavy metal fire door at the base of the rooftop stairwell. Their breathing was slow and controlled, hearts beating in rhythm with the mission's silence. According to the blueprints Mindy had fed them, this door opened onto a high-level office corridor. On one side was Rocha's office; on the other, an administrative chamber. The hallway consisted of two floor sections, one on either side of an opening to the floor below in the center.

It was a kill box. They would be completely exposed the moment the door opened.

Hopper crouched low, shifting his weight carefully, distributing it across the balls of his feet to minimize noise. The air inside the stairwell was cool and dry, carrying the faint scent of varnished wood from the offices beyond. His gloved hand reached forward. With glacial patience, he turned the handle and cracked the door just enough to see the scenario beyond.

A lone palace guard paced along the left side of the corridor, rifle slung lazily over one shoulder. His footsteps thudded softly against the polished marble, echoing faintly in the otherwise still hallway. The light was soft, provided by antique wall sconces, but bright enough to make movement obvious.

Hopper held still. He had no visual on the right side; the door's angle blocked it. There could easily be another sentry outside Rocha's office. The risk was clear, but it was a risk that had to be taken.

He eased the door closed and turned to his men. No words—hand signals only.

One guard. Left side. I'll handle him. Zeke, cover right.

If there were another guard posted opposite, Hopper couldn't risk exposing his back without support. Every precaution mattered now. No more mistakes.

Zeke gave a tight nod, slinging his rifle to his back in favor of his suppressed pistol. Sully shouldered his borrowed carbine and took position directly behind, ready to cover the corridor's far end. The team moved like a seasoned unit—smooth, silent, practiced.

Hopper cracked the door again and watched through the gap as the guard reached the end of his pacing pattern, closest to the team, and turned. Timing was everything. The moment the guard began walking back toward the grand staircase hall, Hopper slipped through the door and into the corridor like a shadow sliding off the wall.

Zeke leaned out behind him, sidearm raised, clearing the blind corner on the right. Nothing. No guards, just the closed door to Rocha's office. The risk paid off.

Hopper moved low, almost gliding across the floor, boots whispering over the marble. Light on his toes, ninja-like.

Sully provided overwatch above Zeke, keeping the fire door propped open with his hip, rifle steadied downrange in case an unexpected soldier stepped into the far end of the corridor.

Hopper closed in on the patrolling guard. The man walked unaware, weight shifting rhythmically from step to step. Hopper drew his knife from the upside-down sheath on the shoulder strap of his chest plate, keeping the blade tight against his body to avoid any glint.

He moved with the silence of a shadow, each step placed with the practiced ease of a hunter. The guard, lost in the monotonous rhythm of his patrol, never heard him.

Five steps out.

Three.

One.

Hopper rose to a full stance and, in a single, fluid motion, the former SEAL was on him. His left arm snaked around the man's neck, hand clamping down over his mouth with the force of a vise—a preemptive strike that choked off any chance of a cry escaping. As he pulled the man back into his own body, feeling the guard's weight against his chest, his right hand moved, a dark extension of his arm. The knife, a glint of muted steel, found its mark. It wasn't a slash or a theatrical jab, but a swift, clean thrust into the soft tissue of the neck, severing the carotid and silencing the body's protest before it could react. The guard's weight went dead against him, a lifeless sack of bone and muscle. A clean kill.

Hopper eased the body down, tucking it flat behind a decorative column. A thin smear of blood marred the baseboard, but it was otherwise invisible in the forgiving light.

Zeke advanced, confirming the corridor was still clear. He

gave a quick nod, and Sully moved through the threshold. Finn and Jacks followed, rifles pressed to their shoulders, every footstep smooth and deliberate.

They were out in the open. Vulnerable.

Hopper motioned across to Finn. They moved together—simultaneous breach.

Hopper's trio crossed to the office opposite Rocha's suite. The door opened, the men entering, weapons sweeping the corners. Finn and Jacks peeled into Rocha's office. The doors opened in sync.

Inside Rocha's office, Finn hugged the left wall. Jacks pushed right, eyes tracking corners as their barrels led the way. The room was spacious, lined with bookshelves and a polished antique desk. A marble bust of Bolívar loomed in the corner. Elegant, audacious, Rocha had a clear style that loomed over his countrymen.

Clear.

They pressed forward into the inner office through an arched entry. Still no contact.

Finn keyed his mic. "Rocha's suite is clear. Beginning SSE."

The sensitive site exploitation began fast—grabbing files, drives, and documents, dropping them into collection bags.

Across the hall, Hopper's team moved quickly. The layout mirrored Rocha's suite. Zeke and Sully cleared the corners. Hopper was about to call it clear when Zeke froze in the back room's threshold.

"Boss, you're not gonna believe this."

Hopper approached his partners and stepped through the arch, stopping cold.

Sarah Barkley.

Tied to a wooden chair in the center of the back room, wrists bound to the armrests, ankles lashed together. Her head was down, hair matted and tangled, a gag pulled tight across her mouth. Her breathing was shallow but steady.

She was alive.

Zeke exhaled slowly. "After the last breach attempt, they must've moved her. Probably figured nobody would get this far upstairs through all the soldiers."

"Muppets," Sully muttered.

Hopper crouched, taking a knee. He placed two fingers under her chin and raised her head gently, looking into her eyes. "Sarah. We're American. Your father sent us. We're here to take you home."

Her eyes locked on his. Even gagged, her breath caught. Relief broke through in a sudden rush. Brows arched, tears welling and spilling down flushed cheeks, wetting the cloth in her mouth.

"We've got you," Hopper said.

He reached for his mic. "Package located. Jackpot. I repeat, Jackpot."

Zeke was already cutting the ropes, fibers parting with quiet snaps.

Finn's voice came over the comms. "SSE almost complete. We'll exfil when you're clear."

Hopper looked back toward the hallway.

They came in silently. They intended to leave the same way.

But he could feel it—the quiet wouldn't last. They had to get moving.

21

The office of President Alejandro Rocha smelled of cigar smoke and polished wood, the air still heavy from whatever late-night meeting had ended hours ago. Thick curtains blocked the city lights, leaving only the pale glow of a desk lamp to spill over the lacquered floor and across the sprawling red oak desk. The hum of an air vent was the only constant sound, low and steady, like background static.

Finn and Zeke moved with the efficiency of a seasoned smash-and-grab team.

Zeke yanked open the top drawer of a tall filing cabinet, the rails squealing just enough to make his jaw clench. Manila folders jammed so tightly they bowed at the edges. He swept an arm through them, scooping stacks into his open pack—stamped binders, thick envelopes marked *Privado*, even sealed plastic pouches with embossed government seals. The sharp scent of old paper mixed with the metallic scent of the cabinet's frame hit his senses and steadied him.

Finn crouched low at the side cabinet, rifling through its contents. The brass handles were cold against his fingertips. "Bingo," he said, pulling out two rugged external hard drives. He added an encrypted tablet, the matte casing slick with dust, and shoved it deep into his bag. The weight of the gear shifted against his shoulder as the pack filled.

They weren't here to read anything. This was an extraction—data, hardware, whatever Rocha didn't want falling into the wrong hands. Langley could piece it together later. That was their wheelhouse.

Zeke moved to the desk, its surface a cluttered spread of papers, pens, and a half-empty tumbler of scotch. The liquor's smoky aroma mixed with the lingering cigar haze. He unhooked the laptop from its docking station, yanked the charging cable from the wall with a muted snap, and shoved both into his pack. His eyes flicked to the door out of instinct. Still clear.

The comms earpiece crackled in Finn's ear. Hopper's voice came through, low but urgent.

"Zeke, Sully's inbound to relieve you. You're heading topside. Get word to command from the roof, then secure our exit to the alley. Quiet and fast."

"Roger that, boss. Moving."

Zeke zipped his pack, the sound loud in the stillness, and slung it over his shoulder. He gave Finn a curt nod—no handshake, no parting words—just a look that said *Don't get dead.*

Then he was moving, boots whispering over the large rug as he threaded through the office toward the rear stairwell. The air felt cooler by the door, a faint draft slipping under the frame. His hand closed around the lever. A soft click echoed from somewhere deeper in the building. Zeke froze at the threshold, head tilting, ears straining. Nothing but the low hum of the vent.

He pushed through the door and started up the narrow steps, taking them two at a time.

Time was burning. They had to get off the "X."

January 26 | 1:59 a.m. EST
Langley, Virginia

The briefing room glowed with the cold light of monitors, the overheads dimmed long ago to keep eyes sharp on the feeds. Rows of dormant workstations sat in silence, their chairs aligned with military precision. The air carried the bitter aroma of a coffeepot that had shut off down the hall, faint but clinging. The muted hiss of the open comms channel reminded Mindy that a single fragile thread connected Langley to Bolivia.

She sat at the main console, elbows braced on the edge, eyes locked on the thermal feed from a Reaper drone circling above La Paz. For the past hour, her world had been reduced to a stark black-and-white overlay of the presidential palace and the surrounding city blocks. Heat signatures, vehicle patterns, the occasional bird flashing across the frame in a brief flare of warmth—this was all she had.

Her gaze traced the perimeter for the hundredth time. Still no unusual troop shifts. No sharp radio bursts. No infrared spikes that screamed hostile overwatch. The palace perimeter remained steady, cars idling in neat rows outside, chauffeurs waiting to shuttle important guests back to hotels or airports.

Earlier, she'd tracked the team's heat signatures as they crossed rooftops—five distinct shapes moving with deliberate precision. But thirty minutes ago, they'd slipped inside the palace. Since then, the rooftop had shown nothing but empty tiles cooling steadily in the night air, the heat bleeding away in soft gradients.

Her stomach tightened.

In her experience, silence wasn't comfort—it was warning. And warnings always came before the storm.

Her fingers tapped the console as the drone's gimbal swept on automatic arcs. She followed every pass as if willing the lens to uncover something, anything. A vent glowed faintly as it expelled warm air. A guard traced his patrol through the courtyard. But the rooftop stayed stubbornly empty.

Then—movement.

At last.

The roof access door cracked open. A rectangle of warmth flared against the cold rooftop. Mindy had the drone pilot zoom tighter, thermal sharpening on the lone figure crouched low. Even at this distance, she recognized the deliberate posture: weight balanced, head scanning, steps calculated. Operator discipline. One of hers.

The figure dug into a pack and pulled free a small object. It lit hot for a second in the thermal, then cooled—likely a comms device.

The shrill ring of the briefing room phone made her flinch. She snatched the receiver before the second ring.

"Go for command."

Static, then a voice—familiar, calm but undercut with adrenaline.

"Command, this is Four. Jackpot secured. Team prepping for exfil. Party will be team plus three guests."

Mindy sat straighter, knuckles whitening on the handset.

"Copy. Exfil platform notified. Coordinates pushed to ATAK. Eyes overhead good for one hour—bird needs fuel after that."

"Understood. Four out."

The line cut with a hard click.

Mindy exhaled, her shoulders loosening only then. Her jaw unclenched, leaving her cheeks sore. On the main screen, she watched Zeke tuck the device away and fade into the rooftop shadows, already hunting the next threat.

A quiet smile ghosted her lips. They were alive. They had Sarah. Relief surged but stopped short of celebration. The hardest stretch was still ahead. The palace was far from empty.

Now came the real fight: getting out unseen. And after that, the long trek to the coast.

When the drone had to peel away, they'd be on their own.

January 26 | 3:05 a.m. BOT
La Paz, Bolivia

Hopper and Jacks waited in the roof access stairwell, eyes fixed on the open corridor beyond. The polished tile lay still and silent, dim sconces casting uneven shadows down the hall.

Sarah crouched just behind them, pressed against the wall, flinching at every faint groan of the old building. The muffled thump of bass from the after-party far below barely reached this high, blending with the steady hum of ventilation through the ducts. Zeke was already on the roof, hands moving fast to rig their line for descent. The plan was simple: rappel down the rear face of the palace, pile into the waiting SUV, and vanish into La Paz before anyone knew better.

Hopper tapped his comms. "Finn, status?"

"Charges are armed. Out the door in one mike."

"Copy. Hallway still clear."

Inside Rocha's office, Finn knelt at the ornate desk, pressing adhesive charges into place behind heavy cabinets. The sharp, oily tang of plastic explosive stung his nose. Sully shadowed him, rifle steady, eyes locked on the door.

Once they stepped out, chaos would follow. The blasts would rip through the palace, drawing every guard and agent into a frenzy—long enough for the team to slip the net.

Finn secured the final charge, gave it a quick once-over, and nodded. Together, he and Sully moved to the door. Finn cracked it open, scanning both ways.

From the stairwell, Hopper caught sight of them and signaled.

They broke low and fast, boots whispering across tile. Jacks covered with his rifle until they slipped past, then eased the door shut.

Three men headed for the roof. Finn stayed behind, the one-man anchor to cover their exit and light the fuse.

"Jacks, Sully—watch the courtyard," Hopper ordered as they emerged onto the roof. "Zeke, status with Sarah?"

"Almost there," Zeke replied. He knelt, cinching the harness tight around her frame. Sarah trembled, knuckles white as she clutched the anchor points.

"You're gonna hold on here and here," he said, placing her hands against the rig just below his shoulders. "Wrap your legs, lock your grip, and don't let go unless I say."

Sarah nodded, eyes wide, muscles rigid with adrenaline. Days of terror had left her raw, but resolve still flickered behind her stare.

Hopper clipped into the rappel line first. The cord was

anchored to a chimney base and a steel vent stack, tied off twice for redundancy. He gave it two hard tugs.

"Going down to cover."

He stepped onto the ledge and leaned back. Gravity seized him, boots braced against the brick as he controlled the slide. Every ten feet, he kicked off to keep the pace steady. Night air cut cold across his face. The alley rose quick. Seconds later, he landed with a muted thud, sidearm sweeping left, then right. Empty—though shouts echoed faintly from beyond the palace walls.

He unclipped and took up a defensive position. "Alley secure. Send her."

On the roof, Zeke hooked onto the line. Sarah clung to him, arms clamped around his torso, legs shaky as they wrapped his hips.

"You're good. We're almost out," Zeke murmured, steady and low.

He eased back, letting the rope take their combined weight. Step by step, they slid down. Halfway, Sarah's hand slipped from his harness, and she gasped.

"I got you," Zeke grunted, locking her tighter against him with one arm.

The rope scraped rough against the brick, tearing fabric and skin along his back. Pain flashed, but he held, guiding them the rest of the way.

Hopper caught Sarah as Zeke landed, easing her upright and unclipping the harness. Her knees buckled, but she was still standing.

"Get her in the SUV," Hopper ordered, nodding to the idling vehicle tucked beside a dumpster. Exhaust curled in the cold night as the engine purred. He shouldered his rifle and covered the alley mouth.

Sully and Jacks followed, rappelling fast. Jacks hit hard, ankle twisting as he landed.

"You good?" Hopper called.

"Yeah," Jacks gritted out. "Just tweaked it. I'll walk it off."

Hopper pulled the SAT phone from Zeke's vest and dialed. Mindy answered on the first ring.

"Command, this is One. Package secure. Team exfil underway."

His eyes stayed locked on the shadowed mouth of the alley. Somewhere beyond, the city stirred—about to wake into chaos.

3:19 a.m.

Teo Mendoza stood at the east wing of the palace, overseeing the departure of the last guests. It dragged on too long for his liking. His security detail had the exits under control, with Spetsnaz operators still stationed throughout the building. The event had run without a hitch, but Mendoza wanted the halls cleared. Ending the night without incident would cement his worth to President Rocha.

He glanced at his second-in-command, Rodrigo Aguilar, and flashed a smug grin—half confidence, half mockery. The Americans hadn't dared a second attempt. They were hiding in defeat.

Then his earpiece crackled.

"Presidential office guard is not at his post," came a tense voice.

Mendoza's smile vanished. He turned to Aguilar. "Take two men. Check it. Now."

Aguilar nodded and grabbed the two nearest guards. All three moved at speed, tailored suits cut to hide the holsters at their ribs. Their polished shoes slapped against marble as they mounted the grand staircase. The air still carried the heavy traces of champagne and brandy from the gala, now sour in the quiet.

At the landing, the soldier who had radioed stood rigid, rifle leveled down the corridor toward the president's suite. Aguilar passed him, pointing across the hall.

"Hold this position. If anyone slips past us, drop them."

The corridor ahead was darker than the floors below. Sconces sat farther apart, leaving longer shadows. Aguilar scanned every flicker. Then he saw the missing guard— slumped behind a pillar, eyes vacant, throat punctured. A black smear of blood streaked the baseboard. Aguilar crouched, pressed two fingers to the man's neck. Nothing. He looked back at his men and gave a sharp shake of his head.

His pulse quickened. The girl couldn't have gotten past the palace's lower levels, and the Americans couldn't have breached this deep without raising alarms. But the corpse on the floor didn't care about logic.

One guard eased the next office door open. Aguilar entered first, pistol raised one-handed, his other arm bound in a sling. The air still held the smell of the girl's fear, the trace of a prisoner who had once been here.

The chair was empty.

Cut restraints coiled on the floor like discarded snakes.

Aguilar's arm dropped. His jaw locked tight.

"Mierda."

He holstered the pistol and raised his radio with visible reluctance.

"This is Aguilar. The prisoner has escaped."

Static buzzed before Mendoza's voice tore through, furious.

"She what?"

"She's gone. The restraints are on the floor."

"Get to the president's office. She must be in there!"

Aguilar turned, signaling the others forward. They crossed the hall quickly. The soldier at the end shook his head—no movement. He marched to cover the door as Aguilar shoved inside.

The three men swept the office—behind the desk, the curtains, every corner. Nothing. No girl. No intruders.

And then—

Click.

The blast hit like a thunderclap. A wall of white-orange fire roared out of the rear office, heat slamming into them with the force of a wrecking ball. The shockwave stole the breath from Aguilar's lungs. Glass and shrapnel tore through the room, hurling the men backward toward the doorway. Their clothes ignited, limbs jerking as the fire ate through them.

The concussion wave tore down the hall. The posted soldier had no chance—lifted off his feet and thrown over the railing in the center of the corridor. He crashed into the atrium below, his skull cracking on the herringbone floor less than ten feet from Mendoza. Blood spread fast, pooling around his head.

The remaining guests screamed.

Back in the stairwell, Finn slipped the detonator into his pocket and bolted for the roof. He slammed through the door, clipped into the rappel line, and swung over the ledge. Boots skimmed brick as he dropped fast, the night air ripping past him.

Below, the team was already loading into the SUV. Hopper waved him on.

Finn landed running. He was halfway to the vehicle when the crack of breaking glass cut the air. Gunfire spat from a second-floor window, muzzle flashes competing with the glow of flames licking from the destroyed office.

Hopper spun, rifle up, firing back in tight bursts. Each shot wrenched at his injured shoulder, recoil pumping fire into the wound.

Rounds skipped off pavement near Finn, stone chips stinging his legs. He drove forward, lungs burning.

Jacks braced on the SUV's running board, machine gun rattling in a storm of fire, brass clattering across the wet alley.

Zeke leaned across the cab, yanking the passenger door open.

"Move!"

Finn dove headfirst into the seat, slammed the door, and rolled up. Hopper and Jacks piled in after him.

"Go, go, go!"

The SUV screamed down the alley, tires shrieking.

They cleared the corner when the sunroof shattered inward. Glass sprayed the cabin, followed by more rounds hammering the roof.

A sharp cry cut through the chaos.

Kaitlyn screamed.

"Shit! Kaitlyn's hit!"

22

The team made a quick stop—just long enough for Finn to swap places with Sully. Finn slid into the rear seat beside Kaitlyn, who sat slumped in the middle between him and Hopper, her face pale but composed, focused despite the pain. Blood had soaked through the sleeve of her jacket. The bullet had struck high in the right shoulder, a clean pass-through, which was fortunate, though the wound remained serious and dangerous.

Jacks crouched in the far back, where Sarah huddled small beneath a blanket pulled tightly around her. Hopper wanted the big gun at the rear, covering their six in case anyone tailed them. Sully shifted up front into the passenger seat. Zeke stayed at the wheel, steering them west out of La Paz, his eyes glued to the mirrors with calm, surgical precision, scanning every set of headlights and every alley they passed, searching for the threat he knew was out there.

The scent of fresh blood mingled with the faint chemical sting of the med kit as Finn snapped it open. The low rumble of the engine vibrated up through the floorboards, while the steady drone of the tires against asphalt filled the silence that lived between clipped words.

Finn tore a glove pack open with his teeth and pulled them on, his movements quick, deliberate, clinical. He skipped the comfort talk.

"Need you to hold still for me, love," he said.

Kaitlyn winced as he peeled away her jacket. Her breathing came shallow and fast, every inhale sharp, but she nodded once, jaw clamped tight.

"I'm fine," she lied.

"You're not. But you will be."

He worked fast—sterilizing the wound, then drawing a dose of local anesthetic from Sully's kit. Her lips pressed into a thin line as he pressed gauze against both entry and exit points. Blood seeped through immediately, spreading crimson across the pads.

"Through-and-through," he muttered to himself. "No shattered bones. Lucky."

"I prefer skilled," she said, managing a taut smile.

He didn't answer. His concentration stayed on his hands as he packed the wound and bound her shoulder tight with a compression bandage. Every bump in the road jolted the SUV, drawing another wince from her. He finished by taping her arm against her torso, fashioning a rough sling.

"You're patched for now. Don't try anything heroic with that arm."

"Too late," she whispered.

Outside, the city was stirring awake. Streetlights still

carved yellow pools in the dark, but early signs of life crept in—delivery trucks idling curbside, the day's papers dumped in stacks, a lone vendor unlocking his metal stall. The air outside looked cold and still, but inside the SUV the heat of too many bodies and the taut, choking tension made it feel thick and suffocating.

No one allowed themselves to relax. The streets behind them remained empty, but every turn of the wheel came with that familiar itch between the shoulder blades, the instinct of operators who knew eyes were on them. No sirens. No flashing lights. But that didn't mean the hunt wasn't closing in.

They had linked up with Mindy shortly after the rescue. She had worked every angle she could inside Langley to secure an exit. Her solution: the USS *Porter*, an Arleigh-Burke-class destroyer, ordered to loiter off the Chilean coast just long enough to pull them out.

It wasn't perfect. Nothing about this op had been perfect.

Driving west to the Pacific would take close to eight hours—if nothing stopped them, if no one intercepted them. The *Porter* would ease in toward the coast near sundown, her silhouette hidden by nightfall. But she couldn't linger for too long. An American warship off a neutral coast was a provocation, and every extra hour carried the risk of a diplomatic explosion—or worse.

Bolivia had already ignored borders. With Russian jets prowling the skies and air options erased from the board, the *Porter's* captain wasn't going to risk an engagement. The time-table was locked. The team had to make it.

"Two hundred eighty klicks to the Chilean border, boss," Zeke reported, eyes still flicking to the mirrors.

"Roger," Hopper said from the rear seat, his gaze fixed on the dark city receding behind them.

The SUV rolled on through La Paz, threading intersections and neighborhoods still wrapped in predawn hush. Yet the tension never let up. Any cross street could hide a convoy. Any green light could be the one that turned red at the worst moment. Each minute on the road was one more minute for the enemy to close in.

The only way out was still hours—and every danger away.

4:03 a.m.

Colonel Mendoza made his way toward the ruined presidential office after locking Rocha inside the reinforced safe room. As he approached the corridor, scorch marks clawed across the walls surrounding the doorway, streaks of black radiating outward like the blast's own signature. He stepped inside and took stock of the devastation. That's when he saw him on the floor.

He knelt beside the charred remains of his second-in-command.

Rodrigo Aguilar had never been the most disciplined officer. He was brash, reckless at times, too eager to prove himself. But he had been loyal—fiercely, unquestioningly loyal. And now he was gone, reduced to a blackened husk barely recognizable, his body curled just inside the shattered threshold like a child burned in its bed.

The entire office was gutted. Splintered marble from pillars once gleaming lay scattered in jagged heaps, their polished faces cracked and dulled by heat. Broken glass crunched underfoot. Scorched wood and twisted rebar sprawled across the carpet. Fires still burned in pockets where the sprinklers had failed, flickering orange against walls stained an oily black. The once-luxurious office reeked of burnt leather and paper, layered with acrid smoke and the faint copper musk of blood.

Mendoza whispered a prayer under his breath. His fist curled tight at his side. With his other hand, he reached down and pressed Aguilar's half-melted eyelids shut, the skin still soft with lingering heat.

He stayed crouched for a long moment, the flames licking at his uniform, the smoke searing his lungs. He forced himself to remain still, to master the rage boiling under his ribs. Pride and humiliation tore at him in equal measure. How had this happened under his command? How had the Americans slipped past his men, taken the girl, and left only ruin behind?

When he finally rose, it was with squared shoulders, clenched teeth, and eyes that no longer blinked.

"Colonel Mendoza, sir!" a voice called from the hall.

He turned. A young communications officer stood rigid at attention, face pale in the flicker of firelight, smoke curling between them like a veil.

"What is it?" Mendoza asked, stepping out from the ruined doorway.

"Sir, a street patrol just reported the Americans. Black SUV, multiple bullet holes. They're heading west toward Route 4."

Mendoza surged forward, seizing the young man by the collar and slamming him into the wall with one hand. His knuckles dug into the fabric, grip iron-tight as he leaned close, eyes burning into the soldier's.

"Lock it down," he growled. "The entire city. Notify every checkpoint. I want them ready. Box them in."

"Yes, sir!"

"And send the Russians," Mendoza added, voice dropping into a cold, deliberate register that froze the air between them. "I want blood in the streets."

He held the officer's gaze for a heartbeat longer, letting the weight of the order burrow into him, before releasing with a shove. The soldier snapped a salute, breathless, and bolted down the corridor, already shouting into his radio.

Mendoza stood alone in the hall, flames snapping and crackling behind him, smoke drifting around his shoulders like a funeral shroud.

The Americans would pay—and when they did, there would be nothing left to bury.

4:28 a.m.

Every team member kept their focus locked on the windows as the SUV crept through the city.

Finn had Kaitlyn's shoulder patched, and she leaned quietly against the seat between him and Hopper, her face pale and drawn from blood loss. She was conscious, but only barely, her eyes glassy and drained.

Civilians were scarce at this hour. Most of La Paz still slept, save for early laborers, but the eastern horizon was beginning to pale. Hopper figured the slaves in the mining towns were already bent to their work—no sunrise reprieve under this regime. Rocha brutalized his own people, and once Kaitlyn's evidence, coupled with the team's intel, reached Langley, maybe it would force someone's hand before the damage became irreversible.

Hopper leaned forward and placed a steady hand on Zeke's shoulder.

"Take it nice and slow. City limit checkpoint ahead."

"Got it, boss," Zeke murmured.

Traffic thinned but up ahead red taillights shimmered in a thin, crawling line. Vehicles slowed to a bottleneck at the checkpoint. Hopper's neck prickled. The Bolivians wouldn't let them just drive off with Sarah—not after the palace explosion, not when she was leverage.

Sully narrowed his eyes through the windshield. "I count four. All Bolivian. No Russians. Maybe word hasn't hit yet."

That was something. But not enough.

"Lock it in, boys," Hopper said quietly. "With these bullet holes and our uniforms, we're not sneaking through anything. Quick and quiet."

They edged forward—third in line now. The SUV's tinted glass kept them shrouded in the predawn dark, offering a sliver of advantage.

"Finn, you and me." Hopper checked the chamber of his sidearm. Finn mirrored him.

Second in line.

Up ahead, one soldier leaned over the driver's side, hand resting on the roof, speaking low to the civilian. Another hovered on the passenger side, rifle slung but ready. A third crouched low, rolling a mirror on a pole beneath the chassis—standard explosive check. That precaution likely hadn't been in place last week. Word from the palace must have filtered down.

The last soldier stood planted square in front, machine gun strapped across his chest. Older, harder, the way he shifted his weight said he was ready to use it.

This was their moment.

"Time to move," Hopper said, cracking his door.

He and Finn slipped out together, shadows in the predawn gloom. Their jungle camo looked almost black, blending them into the background. Pistols came up smooth, silent.

Finn took the driver's side soldier. A muted crack, and the man folded with a clean headshot. Hopper mirrored the move on the passenger side. Both men shifted and fired again at the soldier crouched with the mirror. Their wires crossed—two shots, one target. One round hit the neck, the other drilled the skull. It didn't matter. He was down.

That left the machine gunner.

He caught the muffled fire, eyes snapping wide as the last body fell. He swung wide, weapon rising toward Hopper. Hopper pivoted, trying to level his pistol, but he was half a second too slow—the barrel was already climbing.

Then—two sharp suppressed pops.

The gunner jerked, chest jumping twice, head snapping back in a mist of red. He toppled lifeless to the pavement.

Hopper turned. Sully's pistol was braced against the lowered passenger window, steadied between the mirror and doorframe. His face didn't change.

Hopper gave him a silent nod. Gratitude. Respect.

The civilian vehicle ahead peeled away, tires squealing.

Sully pushed his door open, joining Finn without a word. Hopper covered them, pistol ready, his wounded shoulder biting but steady. Finn and Sully dragged the four bodies off the asphalt, hauling them behind a low concrete divider. No finesse—just speed. They yanked branches and roadside debris over the corpses, disguising uniforms and rifles. It wouldn't last long, but it would buy minutes.

The three operators climbed back into the SUV, doors slamming in unison.

"Let's get the fuck out of here before anyone checks this post," Hopper muttered.

"Roger that," Zeke said, already rolling them forward. "About ninety klicks to the highway turnoff. Call it an hour and a half."

And just like that, they were through—slipping west, shadows chasing them as the night surrendered to dawn.

4:42 a.m.

Cold air leaked through the cracked window as Colonel Mendoza climbed into the front passenger seat of the lead armored vehicle, his boots clanking against the steel floor. The chill didn't touch him—only the fury tightening in his gut. He slammed the door hard enough to rattle the frame, jaw rigid, eyes locked forward. Without glancing at the driver, he made a tight circular gesture with two fingers.

"Move out."

The convoy roared to life in a chain reaction—six vehicles staggered for overlapping fields of fire. Two China Tiger APCs with mounted PKMs flanked the formation, while a Russian-made BTR sealed the rear like a steel wall. Between them, three Engesa EE-25 cargo trucks carried soldiers standing in the open beds, rifles braced, breath steaming in the frigid predawn air. They were ready for a fight, though not all were truly prepared.

Fog ghosted across La Paz's streets, sodium streetlamps spilling amber streaks across wet pavement. The city itself felt uneasy, as if it knew something violent was moving through its veins.

Radios squawked across multiple channels—checkpoints calling in, orders relayed and updated in clipped tones, every voice taut with urgency.

The dash radio crackled.

"Colonel Mendoza?"

He snatched the handset in a sharp motion. "Go for Mendoza."

"Sir, all checkpoints report no contact, except the unit at Colegio Jorge Cabrera. We've lost comms with them."

Mendoza didn't hesitate. "They broke through. Wait for orders. I'll get back to you."

His eyes dropped to the map spread across his lap, scanning for the enemy's likely route.

Static hissed as he spoke again, each word sharpened to a point. "Contact the Russians. I want them ready at the border. Call the outpost at Patacamaya. I want roadblocks at every highway intersection. If they breach that, they'll aim for Puesto de Control. Tell Petrov to be ready."

"Understood, sir."

He tossed the handset onto the dash; plastic clattered against steel. Twisting in his seat, he fixed on the communications officer in the back. The young man sat hunched over a glowing laptop, green-blue light flickering across his face as icons shifted on a satellite map—blue for friendlies, yellow for checkpoints, red for suspected enemy movement.

"Get me a helicopter," Mendoza ordered, his tone like an icy blade. "Ten minutes. I want an Mi-17 with door guns and full fuel."

The officer nodded without looking up, fingers flying over the keyboard. "Yes, sir. Gunship will be on standby."

From the open bed of the second truck, a Bolivian sergeant barked over the engine noise: "Weapons check! Eyes open!" A soldier slammed a fresh drum into the PKM, the metallic click swallowed by the convoy's rumble. They looked ready for battle, though most were here out of fear of torture or death, not loyalty.

On a Russian frequency, a guttural voice came through calm and confident: "Forward elements in position. Border lockdown in progress. We will intercept."

Mendoza leaned back, armor plates cold against his shoulders. His face was carved in shadow, eyes locked on the black ribbon of road unspooling ahead. He flexed his fists, joints cracking. They had killed his men, torched the palace, stolen his leverage. Every second they remained ahead wasn't just defiance—it was personal. It was an insult, a wound to his pride and a threat to his survival.

He would hunt them to the border, to the mountains, to the coast, into the jungle if that's where they fled. The convoy would smash through barricades, bleed the roads if necessary. And if the chase carried them into hell itself, Mendoza would be waiting at the gates.

6:15 a.m.

Morning light crept over the horizon, minute by minute.

Official sunrise was still moments away, but the first amber glow had already spilled across the eastern hills. It bathed the highway in a soft haze that, for most people, meant safety. For covert operators, it meant exposure. No shadows to vanish into. No cover overhead. Daylight stripped you bare.

The SUV rolled steadily along Highway 1, tires humming against the asphalt. Traffic remained sparse this early. An old farm truck lumbered by in the opposite lane, and a lone motorbike faded into the distance. The roads hadn't fully awakened—but they soon would.

Ahead lay the mid-sized city of Patacamaya. To locals, it was home. To outsiders, just a forgettable pit stop between Bolivia and Chile. To the BREACH team, it was the next choke point. Once they cleared the center of town, they'd cut right onto Highway 4. That road stretched straight to the Chilean border—a clean shot, hopefully fast, hopefully quiet.

But Hopper didn't trust hope.

It was still more than two hours from the turnoff to reach the border. Two hours in hostile territory. Two hours for

Mendoza to close the gap. Two hours for something—anything—to go wrong.

Inside the SUV, the air pressed close with fatigue. Zeke drove, shoulders tight, eyes flicking from mirrors to blind spots to the road ahead. Sully rode shotgun, rifle braced between his knees, pistol resting on his lap, scanning rooftops and side streets even at speed.

In the second row, Finn sat left, Kaitlyn in the middle, her injured arm tightly bandaged and immobilized, Hopper on the right. Every breath tugged at Hopper's ribs, the dull throb of his shoulder wound pulsing with each heartbeat. His rifle lay across his lap, safety off, one hand gripping the stock, the other ready to steady the barrel.

In the rear cargo space, Jacks and Sarah sat among their stripped-down gear. Jacks kept his leg stretched stiff, ankle and thigh both wrapped, bandages dulling the pain just enough. Sarah sat beside him, pale but steady, wide eyes fixed on each passing vehicle as though every one could mean danger.

They were down to a couple of magazines each—if that. Most had been burned back in La Paz, trading rounds from the second floor of the palace. Food and water nearly gone. None of them had slept more than a handful of hours in days. They were running on grit, muscle memory, and adrenaline.

And they weren't clear yet.

Between Jacks and Sarah, half-buried under blood-stained packs, rested the only thing that made this gauntlet worth it: Kaitlyn's files and the hard drives pulled from Rocha's office. Evidence of the regime's crimes. Hopefully, proof of Russian involvement—and answers to why.

Everything that mattered was in that bundle.

And if they didn't get it out of Bolivia, it would all vanish—buried, denied, erased.

January 26 | 5:19 a.m. EST
Langley, Virginia

Deputy Director Conley stepped into the briefing room inside the BREACH building at CIA Headquarters. Muted chatter drifted in from the hallway—extra analysts had been pulled in to reinforce Mindy's efforts. The sound gave him a measure of relief. At least she wasn't carrying the weight of this alone anymore. She had been grinding for days, keeping the team alive from thousands of miles away.

At the main table, she sat hunched over her laptop, fingers hammering the keys in sharp bursts. A half-empty coffee cup sat at her elbow, long gone cold. Her hair was slightly mussed, a loose strand falling across her face as she rubbed her eyes and forced herself back into focus. The dark smudges beneath her eyes hadn't faded since the night before. She probably hadn't slept at all. Her dedication to the mission—and to the team—was unshakable, but Conley worried about the toll it was taking.

He slid into the chair across from her, careful not to break her rhythm.

"You alright to keep going, Ms. Taylor? I can pull in another analyst if you need a break."

She shook her head without hesitation. "I'm okay, Director. Managed a quick nap during the last leg of the team's exfil. I'm good."

He gave a slow nod but didn't push. She wouldn't quit until she collapsed. He knew that type well.

"Very well. Where do they stand now?"

Her eyes stayed locked on the screen. "I've got them on satellite. Drone coverage had to be recalled for fuel, so I lost that angle. But I still have their GPS tracking. It's just slower. They're reaching Patacamaya now, about to make their final turn onto Highway 4. If everything holds, it's a straight run to the Chilean border."

"Good. We need them all home—sooner, not later."

Mindy's fingers faltered, then stilled. Her shoulders tightened.

"Damn it…" she muttered under her breath. "Another Bolivian checkpoint just populated. Full military presence. Dug in."

She lifted her head, urgency in her voice. "If they don't spot it in time—"

Conley's jaw hardened.

"Then make damn sure they do."

January 26 | 6:20 a.m. BOT
Patacamaya, Bolivia

The SAT phone in Hopper's chest rig vibrated with a low, insistent buzz. He tapped the receiver and brought it to his ear.

"Ease it down, Zeke. Mindy's calling. Could be something up ahead."

Zeke lifted his foot slightly, bleeding off speed without making it obvious. The SUV rolled on at a casual pace, the city just beginning to stir with the first hints of morning.

Hopper listened, jaw tightening as Mindy's voice came through. His brow furrowed.

"Another checkpoint."

He dropped the phone into his lap and flipped open the ATAK terminal strapped across his vest. The screen flared against the dim interior, a satellite overlay snapping to their position in real time. The roundabout up ahead pulsed red— the choke point.

"Got a plan, boss?" Zeke asked, eyes glued to the road.

The roundabout loomed, less than five hundred meters out.

"Next alley on the right, then sharp left. Parallel back street. Should rejoin the highway two hundred meters south of the checkpoint."

"Copy."

Zeke swung them into the alley. Tires crunched over loose gravel. The SUV dipped, swallowed by a narrow corridor boxed in by tall apartment blocks. Shadows closed around them. Rusted dumpsters lined the walls like improvised barricades, guarding concrete that had seen better decades.

Weapons came up without a word. Every window looked like a firing port. Every doorframe a potential muzzle flash. Nothing moved—only the low hum of the engine and the steady grind of tires over grit.

The alley bent left. The passage widened, though it still felt claustrophobic. Ahead, rows of long-haul trucks stretched in uneven lines, local freight drivers catching sleep near the border. Diesel and stale cigarettes hung in the air. A choke of dumpsters forced a tighter turn, but the path remained clear.

"There's the highway," Sully said from shotgun.

No entry ramp. Just scrub brush and a strip of dirt separating them from pavement.

"Send it."

Zeke didn't hesitate. He punched through, the SUV bouncing hard over the dirt strip before jolting onto the asphalt. He merged clean, pacing traffic like another commuter catching a shortcut.

The vehicle leveled out.

PING!

A sharp metallic crack split the morning.

Then—***CRASH***—the rear windshield shattered inward, glass detonating across the cargo bay.

Jacks lunged sideways, wrapping Sarah with his arms and dragging her low as shards sprayed like razors.

"Down!" he barked, forcing her head below the seat.

Kaitlyn ducked. Sully spun, weapon coming up. Hopper twisted in his seat, eyes raking the rooftops flashing past. Somewhere out there, a scope had locked onto them.

Wind roared through the gaping rear glass, whipping hair and rattling gear. The SUV pushed faster, but they were exposed—open game. They had to get south, get to the border.

Jacks shoved Sarah flat, then yanked his MK46 up into the shattered frame. Braced against the ragged metal, he scanned for the shooter.

"Truck rear. Jacks, go loud," Hopper ordered.

23

January 26 | 6:20 a.m. BOT
Patacamaya, Bolivia

Jacks squinted through his optic. A hundred meters back, a pickup truck tore after them—an improvised technical with a mounted PKM machine gun bolted into the bed. The Russian 7.62mm beast spat fire as a soldier braced behind it, spraying rounds wildly up the highway.

"Technical!" Jacks roared, squeezing the trigger.

The MK46 in the SUV's rear came alive, its brutal chatter drowning the engine with a hammering stream of suppressive fire. The cabin pulsed with noise and concussion, ears ringing as muzzle flashes lit the interior in strobing bursts.

Zeke stomped the accelerator, jerking the wheel left to throw off the gunner's aim. The SUV swerved, tires squealing as enemy rounds shredded the lane they'd just vacated. Asphalt geysered behind them. The violent maneuvers rattled

Jacks' sight picture, making the return fire feel impossible.

"Hold steady—steady!" he barked, frustration boiling. Firing from a moving vehicle at another moving vehicle felt like trying to swat a fly from the back of a roller coaster. His bursts finally chewed into the oncoming truck's front end— punching through headlights, grill, and radiator. Plastic shards and twisted metal spun off in a spray, but the gunner held firm, brass cascading around him as he raked the highway with wild, punishing arcs.

The technical's next burst stitched across the SUV's rear quarter panel. The driver's-side taillight exploded; the hatch caved with jagged dents.

"They're closing!" Sully shouted, eyes on the side mirror.

"Last mag!" Jacks yelled, racking back the slide, hooking it on his pouch, and slamming the final belt into place.

Finn and Hopper rolled their windows down together, torsos leaning into the wind as they aimed rifles outward. They fired in tight rhythm—controlled, deliberate shots meant to disable—but the dance between speeding vehicles left every round a gamble.

Jacks reacquired the gunner, led him just ahead, and unleashed a long burst of fire. Rounds slammed into the soldier's chest. His body jolted, then dropped like dead weight into the bed.

"Gunner down! I'm Winchester!" Jacks shouted, weapon dry, his hands momentarily empty.

The truck didn't stop.

The passenger scrambled out the window, clawing his way into the bed. His hand closed on the PKM's grip—

"Shit," Hopper muttered. Half out the window, he fired twice. Both rounds punched center mass. The man staggered backward, painting the tailgate in blood before crumpling across the corpse of his predecessor.

At the same instant, Finn's shot tore through the technical's fractured windshield and drilled the driver. He sagged over the wheel.

The truck wobbled, veered right, and slowed. Smoke bled from the hood as momentum carried it off to the shoulder.

"Stop the car," Hopper ordered.

Zeke braked hard, pulling them onto the gravel. The SUV skidded to a halt, tires spitting dust.

"What are we doing?" he asked, tense.

"We're almost dry. We need ammo."

Doors flew open. The team spilled out, rifles sweeping arcs. Hopper and Sully advanced along the passenger side; Jacks and Finn ghosted up the driver's side. Jacks ran pistol now, the empty MK46 slung dead weight against his chest.

Zeke held position, engine running, Kaitlyn and Sarah sheltered inside in case they had to break fast.

Hopper peered through the passenger window. The man inside was folded against the seat, unmoving.

"Clear."

"Clear," Sully confirmed from the bed.

Jacks edged closer to the driver's door. A pistol suddenly snapped up from behind shattered glass—aimed square at his face.

Instinct fired before thought. Two shots. Both punched into the man's chest. Blood misted across the dash. The pistol dropped with a metallic clatter.

Jacks lowered his weapon, breath steady.

"*Real clear.*"

They tore through the wreck, pulling what they could: two AK-47s, six spare mags, and a pair of grenades. Not much—but more than nothing.

No time to linger. They piled back into the SUV, doors slamming as Zeke floored it. Tires spat gravel, the vehicle surging back onto the highway.

The border was still hours ahead.

But at least now, they weren't empty-handed.

7:55 a.m.

It was nearly impossible for Colonel Mendoza to hear the co-pilot over the pounding rotors of the Mi-17 helicopter. The aging Soviet-era gunship screamed as it clawed through the thin morning air, every rattle and knock in the fuselage betraying its decades of service. Even the internal comms were antiquated—long before noise-canceling headsets became standard in modern airframes. The static and distortion grated at his ears almost as much as his rising fury.

The co-pilot twisted in his seat to face him, voice raised.

"Colonel Mendoza, we haven't been able to raise the checkpoint team at Patacamaya. Ten minutes—no answer."

Mendoza's brow hardened. Not unexpected. The Americans had proven far more capable than anyone anticipated. They had broken ambushes, fought through fire teams, even survived Spetsnaz pursuit. These were not mere soldiers—they were a covert strike unit. Elite. Dangerous. And still alive.

The rural outposts had never been meant to stop them outright. They were speed bumps, meant to buy the Russians time—time to dig in at the border and trap them before they reached Chile. If by some chance Petrov's men faltered, Mendoza would finish the job from the air. He would be the last line. And if fate allowed, he would be the one to end them personally.

The floor thrummed beneath his boots, each vibration of the old turbine feeding his impatience. The cabin stank of fuel, oil, and metal fatigue. Turbulence slapped the hull, jarring his grip on the armrest. He wanted control. He wanted blood.

"Patch me through to the Spetsnaz at the border," he snapped.

The co-pilot turned back to the console, flicking switches and twisting a dial. Static flared, then broke into a crackling connection. He gave Mendoza a quick thumbs-up.

A deep voice answered, thick with a Russian accent.

"Petrov, here."

"Commander Petrov, the Americans broke Patacamaya. The border is next. Have your men ready—they'll reach you within the hour."

"Understood. We are ready."

Mendoza leaned back, jaw clenched as the Mi-17 shuddered in the crosswind. He looked out the window at the jagged ridgelines streaking past. His mountains. His soil. His country. And now foreigners dared carve a path through it.

They would not leave Bolivia alive.

If Petrov failed—Mendoza would not.

January 26 | 8:30 a.m. BOT
Jancoaque, Bolivia

Zeke eased the SUV off Highway 4, the tires scattering loose gravel as they rolled into the barren lot of a warehouse the size of an aircraft hangar. The building sat stranded in the middle of nowhere, its corrugated walls dulled and scarred from decades of wind and grit, every window sealed with rusted panels. A mile beyond, the Chilean border cut a harsh line across the horizon—razor wire glinting under the morning sun, guard towers jagged like teeth along the fence.

A few shipping warehouses and the skeletal border booths stood nearby. Otherwise, it was abandoned, or at least it wanted to look that way.

Hopper's gut tightened, a cold knot that refused to release. This was as close to safety as they'd been since free-falling into Bolivia, but here, safety was nothing more than an illusion. Borders were chokepoints, funnels where even the best-laid plans came to die.

They had been on the run for hours. Every bone in his body ached. The bullet wound in his shoulder throbbed, hot and merciless, and the grit in his teeth was from more than just dust. Beside him, Finn's jaw ground slowly, his knuckles pale against the rifle stock. Kaitlyn sat between them, her hair plastered to her face with sweat and dried blood, her eyes drifting toward the border as if she could will them across. Jacks hadn't spoken in twenty minutes; he only shifted his weight against the rear cargo floor beside Sarah. His breathing was steady, controlled, every motion stiff with the wound in his leg.

The warehouse lot stretched out like a wasteland of cracked asphalt and weeds. A gutted semi-trailer lay on its side near the far wall, its rusted frame casting a jagged silhouette against the building. Beyond it, faint dust plumes marked the slow crawl of a patrol truck along the fence line. The occupants couldn't be seen, but their presence was close enough to remind them this border wasn't abandoned at all.

Hopper swept the area through the SUV's tinted windows, his senses sharpened despite exhaustion dragging at his body. The engine idled softly, but the quiet pressed in like a weight—thick, charged, the kind of silence that lived just before a lightning strike.

"Everyone stay sharp," he said at last, his voice steady. "This is the endgame. They'll throw everything they've got at us before that border. Count on it."

The words landed heavy. Zeke checked his mirrors, his grip unflinching on the wheel. Finn gave a single nod. Kaitlyn caught Hopper's eyes and returned the faintest nod. Blood loss was taking its toll, but she was still in the fight. Not the type to give in—the jungle had already proven that much.

Hopper let his gaze drift past the warehouse to the shimmer of heat rising over the border road. Freedom was less than a mile away, but between here and there stretched a strip of asphalt where everything could still unravel.

In the heat haze, he thought he saw shapes—watchers crouched low, weapons ready, waiting for them to commit.

His gut had been right before. And it hadn't stopped twisting since sunrise.

The last hurdle stood in front of them.

And he could feel the trap coiled, waiting to spring.

24

"I'm only seeing Chilean border guards," Hopper said, his eyes tracking the line of tan uniforms clustered at the checkpoint. A handful leaned against a concrete barrier, rifles slung, looking bored in the morning heat beginning to rise. One kept glancing toward the hills. Another adjusted the radio on his vest.

"Makes me nervous."

"There's no way they just let us waltz into Chile," Zeke replied from behind the wheel, his tone calm but edged. His gaze stayed locked on the road. "But you're gonna have to make a call soon, Boss. Twelve hours and two hundred and ten klicks to the rendezvous with the ship. Not sure this ride will survive it. We might be walking the last stretch."

Hopper lowered his head, rubbing grit from his brow. His

shoulder pulsed with pain, each throb reminding him they had no luxury of time. He exhaled through his nose, eyes narrowing toward the horizon.

"You're right."

From the back, Jacks broke the silence. "I figure we've got two options. One—full blitz across the border, punch through, and pray these sons of bitches don't follow us into Chile. Two—ditch the wheels, head into the hills, miss the boat, and walk our asses back to the States."

The SUV went quiet.

One by one, heads turned toward Jacks with varying degrees of irritation. Finn's eyes narrowed. Kaitlyn arched a brow, unimpressed. Zeke didn't even bother looking. Jacks just shrugged, half-smirking like he already knew the answer.

Am I wrong?

Hopper sat for a beat, weighing the words, then made his call.

"Frags to Sully and Finn."

Zeke passed his last grenade to Sully. Hopper pulled one from his vest, the cool metal pressing into his palm before handing it over. Jacks dug out the two he'd lifted off the truck in Patacamaya, the dull rattle in the cramped SUV a reminder of just how little ordnance remained.

That was all they had.

"No blue on blue," Hopper said. "We do not engage the border guards. No exceptions."

His gaze locked on Finn and Sully. "You two run rear security. If the Bolivians are lying low and we're boxed in— or they try to run us off the road—you toss those frags out the windows. One left, one right. Last resort only. Mendoza's got something waiting for us here. Count on it."

Both men nodded, eyes scanning the desolate lot.

"Alright," Hopper continued, drawing in a slow breath.

His focus shifted back to the border road. A faint dust plume curled just beyond the fence—too far to identify, but close enough to stir unease.

"Here we go..."

8:40 a.m.

Commander Petrov had his men set at the border. Two weathered buildings flanked the dusty road leading toward the Chilean guard stations—one on each side, their walls pitted from years of neglect. Between the structures and the checkpoint, Russian soldiers crouched low in the alleys, swallowed by shadow and hidden from the view of anyone approaching along the highway.

A battered BTR-80 idled behind the eastern building, its diesel engine rumbling, turret already locked on the road. The steel barrel shifted in tiny increments, adjusting under the operator's steady hand.

Petrov raised his binoculars and scanned the approach. The advantage was theirs. The Americans had no idea what lay ahead.

The air was brittle with heat, every breath dry in his throat. Waves of distortion shimmered off the asphalt, but not enough to hide what he saw: the black SUV pulling off Highway 4 into the shipping lot. Even through the haze, the vehicle was unmistakable—its frame riddled with bullet scars, a survivor limping toward what it thought was freedom.

A thin smile tugged at Petrov's lips. Russian pride ran close to arrogance, sharpened through decades of training and blood. The Americans were skilled—resourceful even. But skill bred confidence, and confidence made them predictable. They would not cross this border.

He lowered the binoculars, watching the SUV idle in the

lot. Dust swirled around it like smoke off a dying fire. It was only a matter of time before the vehicle rolled forward toward the choke point.

"Enemy vehicle sighted," Petrov said into the radio. His tone was calm, almost bored. "Move into position. Hold fast. Await my command."

Behind him, his men checked magazines, racked bolts, and shifted gear with the efficiency of soldiers who had done this too many times to count. Silence, except for the metallic rhythm of preparation.

"They think they can cross without consequence," Petrov muttered, more to himself than to them. His jaw tightened. "They are wrong."

The SUV rumbled forward from the lot, angling toward the border road. Petrov's fingers curled around the transmit button. He waited just long enough to feel the weight of control settle in his chest.

"Now."

8:41 a.m.

Zeke jammed the SUV into gear and yanked it out of the shipping lot, nose pointed straight at the border. This was their only shot at making the rendezvous with the *Porter*. Dangerous as hell, but hesitation would cost them the window. If they didn't move now, they were done.

No time left. This was it.

"Punch it!" Jacks barked from the rear, his Texas drawl slicing through the tension.

Zeke slammed the accelerator. The engine roared, RPMs climbing as the SUV tore forward, tires clawing across cracked asphalt. He shifted, pushing the vehicle toward the border in a reckless surge.

Ahead, Chilean border guards snapped to attention, weapons raised, tracking the oncoming SUV. Zeke caught the flash of muzzles angling toward them but, for now, no shots came.

They're not going to just let us roll through, he thought grimly. *Not at this speed.*

"Right side! Russians in the alley!" Sully shouted.

Figures emerged from the shadows, darting out from the edge of the warehouse—the last possible choke point before the border.

Hopper dropped his window and leveled the AK-47, the steel weight steady against his shoulder. He squeezed the trigger. The rifle chattered a punishing rhythm, muzzle flashes ripping daylight from the morning air. Enemy soldiers collapsed in the alley, cut down one after another.

The rattle of gunfire had the Chilean guards twitching, fingers poised on triggers. This wasn't the sleepy border shift they'd expected.

And while every eye fixed on the right alley, the left came alive.

A lone Spetsnaz soldier stepped clear, dropping to one knee. RPG hoisted, tube steady, he tracked the SUV like a predator waiting for the strike.

With a concussive roar, the rocket leapt free. A shockwave and a column of smoke trailed back as the projectile streaked toward them.

The explosion hit just ahead of the rear tire. Asphalt erupted, fire and debris punching upward as the SUV catapulted into the air.

The world turned sideways, then upside down.

Time fractured into snapshots—shards of glass spinning like glitter, heat searing the cabin, steel screeching as the frame twisted. The vehicle rolled violently, gravity a blur.

Then—impact.

The SUV slammed down hard on Chilean soil, skidding upside down across the pavement with a banshee's scream. It smashed against the border post building, finally grinding to a stop. Smoke curled from beneath the wreck. Fire licked at the undercarriage.

"Everyone good?" Finn croaked, coughing through smoke.

"Jacks' head's bleeding bad!" Sarah cried, panic raw in her voice.

"I'm fine!" Jacks growled, blood running down his face. "But we gotta move! Car's on fire!"

He kicked out the shattered side window.

The team spilled free—bruised, battered, but alive— scrambling around the building's corner to cover.

Hopper's eyes locked on the SAT phone, half-melted and crushed near the wreck's engine bay. He snatched it up, then hurled it into the fire with a curse. "Fuck. There goes any hope of calling command."

Zeke risked a glance around the corner. Flames consumed the SUV, thick smoke curling skyward. The Chilean border guards stood frozen, weapons raised, but still not firing—watching.

"They're holding their line," Zeke said, voice low. "Time to disappear."

"Head for the hills," Hopper ordered, shaking off the blast ringing in his skull. "Fast."

They bolted, seven figures breaking into a desperate sprint toward the distant ridgelines. The fire's smoke cloaked them, the towering border post shielding their dash just enough. Maybe—just maybe—it would be enough to slip away before the enemy regrouped.

9:10 a.m.

Daylight flickered as Petrov clawed back to consciousness with a guttural grunt, face-down in the dust, ears shrieking, lungs locked. The explosion had crushed his skull inward with brutal pressure. Pain tore through his right shoulder. He reached instinctively, dragging his palm across sticky warmth and pulling it back slick with blood. Two gunshot wounds, high near the collarbone. The acrid stench of scorched flesh filled his nostrils—his own flesh. He could smell himself cooking. The rocket had been fired in the wrong direction for their position. Bad timing. Fatal timing.

The sky glared white-hot overhead. His vision swam, colors smeared, sound muffled into warped echoes of distant shouting. Slowly, his mind crawled free from the fog.

With a groan, he rolled onto his back and fumbled at the pouch on his chest rig. Bloodied fingers dug until they found the packet of clotting agent. He tore it open with his teeth and dumped the powder into both wounds. His body jolted, jaw clenched tight, an unnatural groan leaking through gritted teeth. It was pain, yes—but also pure frustration. Then the syringe. Morphine laced with stimulant. He stabbed it deep into his thigh and squeezed the plunger. Heat flared, then clarity surged. The fog lifted.

Blinking against the glare, he forced himself upright and scanned the carnage. His men lay sprawled in broken heaps where they'd fallen, blood pooling beneath them, soaking into dirt and blacktop. Across the road, four surviving Spetsnaz clashed with Chilean border guards—Spanish and Russian shouted over one another, rifles raised, nerves stretched taut to breaking.

Petrov had no time for language barriers.

He staggered forward, snatched a discarded rifle from a

corpse, and stalked toward the road. The AK-47 settled into his grip like an extension of his own arm. With one sharp motion, he pulled the bolt. The metallic snap cracked loud through the thick silence. A brass casing flashed inside the chamber. The bolt slammed forward with a heavy *clack*. Locked. Ready.

The sun scorched down. His body throbbed. But rage burned hotter.

Rounding the alley corner, he closed on the standoff: four Spetsnaz locked against four Chilean guards. Warnings barked. Threats spat back. Fingers itched on triggers. Time stretched thin.

Petrov raised his rifle.

He didn't speak. Didn't warn. Didn't hesitate. There was nothing left to care about.

Crack-crack.
Crack-crack.
Crack-crack.
Crack-crack.

Each Chilean border guard took two precise rounds center-mass, collapsing to the sunbaked asphalt in spasms of blood and twitching limbs. The Spetsnaz froze, stunned, then pivoted to him. His face showed no remorse—just sweat, fury, and the ruthless clarity of command. He jerked his chin toward the flipped, burning SUV across the line. The order was silent, but unmistakable.

The Spetsnaz moved.

Two swung wide left, flanking around the blazing wreck. The other two advanced tight along the right-hand wall, rifles up, intent on finishing the Americans. Petrov anchored behind them, setting into overwatch, rifle steady despite the molten agony still chewing through his shoulder. His mind was razor-sharp now.

He tracked their movements as they crept toward the smoking husk where the Americans had vanished. Any second, he expected resistance. A burst of fire. A shadow moving. Something.

Instead, one soldier turned back, confusion etched across his soot-streaked face.

"They're gone. It's empty," he called in Russian.

Petrov's jaw locked. His temple pulsed with a steady, hammering beat.

Smoke curled skyward. The wind carried heat and ash. Blood darkened to rust on the asphalt, drying fast beneath the merciless sun.

THIRD

OPERATION BRAVO SIERRA

25

January 26 | 3:20 p.m. CLT
Chilean Countryside

The sound came first—a whisper, the faint rustle of gravel beneath boots.

Then came the door. Kicked open, splintering apart as it gave way.

Hopper watched it swing wide, breaking in his mind the same way it had years ago. A small village in Afghanistan. A raid like the dozen they'd run before. But this one carried a sharp edge of anxiety, the sting of frustration. Intel had been thin, orders pushed down hard. Not how he operated, but he hadn't been given a choice.

No gunfire. No shouting. Just three steps inside—then the world went white.

He remembered the pressure wave lifting him clean off the ground, the endless ringing in his ears, that fleeting,

traitorous sense of weightlessness—before the crunch of
reality smashed him into a wall. The air thick with blood,
scorched earth, and the crude tang of cheap explosives. Only
he and Finn had made it out. Another teammate had been
alive when they pulled a stone slab off his chest. But not for
long.

His hands twitched. His jaw locked. Breath hitched,
trapped in his throat.

"Hopper?"

The word cut through. He blinked, dragging himself
back. Finn's gaze was steady on him, brows drawn in concern.
The sun scorched the back of his neck; the wind blew dry and
thin. Chilean countryside unfolded again—hills, rusted
buildings, and the constant ache in his ribs since the blast at
the border.

He inhaled slow, shoving the memory back into its cage.
"What's her status?"

Finn glanced at Kaitlyn, then back. "Weak. Lost too
much blood. Supplies are gone—no meds left to fight infection, no painkillers. She's stable for now, but barely holding."

Hopper nodded, that grim heaviness settling deeper. He
watched her where she sat propped against a trailer wall, skin
pale, breaths shallow. Sarah stayed close, sharing bites from
the last MRE between them. Kaitlyn caught him looking and,
somehow, managed a half-smile.

Six hours of brutal hiking had worn them thin. The heat
and elevation had punished every step, the pace relentless.
After skirting a lake, they'd reached this rundown scatter of
barns and warehouses—barely a speck on the map, but better
than open ground.

Zeke was limping hard. His knee had taken a hit when the
SUV flipped; now it was swollen, angry. Jacks' scalp wound
had stopped bleeding, but the field dressing was crusted red,

wrapped tight around his head. Finn's hands shook faintly, nerves raw from working nonstop since the firefight. Sully's breathing came shallow, each inhale a reminder of cracked ribs. He hadn't complained once, but Hopper could read the pain in his every move.

Time bled out of them as quickly as the fluids.

The USS *Porter* would reach the coast of Arica in under five hours. If they missed extraction, there'd be no second chance. No captain would risk 270 sailors and a billion-dollar ship for four operators and three civilians.

"Keep her moving," Hopper ordered. His voice was steady, firm. "She'll get the medical she needs on the ship. But we have to make it there."

Finn gave a clipped nod and bent back to his kit, cobbling together whatever he could to buy them more time.

Across the lot, Zeke and Jacks crouched beneath the dashboard of a battered pickup, fumbling to hot-wire it. Not something they'd done before, but training had covered the basics. Walking was no longer an option—the terrain too rough, the distance too far, the injuries too severe. Kaitlyn could hardly stand, and Jacks looked one misstep from collapsing outright.

Hopper drew a long breath, let it out slow, and scanned what remained of his team.

Alive. For now.

But if they didn't move soon, they wouldn't stay that way.

January 26 | 2:25 p.m. EST
Langley, Virginia

Conley sat rigid at the BREACH briefing table, the weight of the crisis pressing into his shoulders. Across from him,

Congressman Barkley tapped a pen against the polished wood in a staccato rhythm that betrayed his nerves.

Between them lingered the issue neither man could ignore: the evidence Kaitlyn Thompson had secured. They didn't yet know its exact contents—or how powerful it might be in shifting the balance for the Bolivian people.

"What do we realistically expect from Kaitlyn's intel?" Conley asked, voice low, deliberate.

"Enough to push the administration toward cutting financial support for President Rocha's regime," Barkley replied, his tone sharp despite the tension. "At least, that's what I gathered from her over the phone."

Conley sighed, rubbing his temples with two fingers. "If the evidence confirms war crimes or systemic human rights abuses—and ties them directly to Rocha's orders—we could justify a strong response. But the geopolitical landscape is volatile. Cutting aid outright could destabilize the region, and that may end up hurting civilians even more."

From the far side of the room, Mindy Taylor finally broke her silence. "There's also the matter of international law. If Kaitlyn's evidence is solid, it could justify proceedings before an international court."

Barkley frowned. "The International Court of Justice only hears disputes between states, doesn't it? Not individual cases?"

"Correct," Mindy said. "For war crimes or crimes against humanity, the venue would be the International Criminal Court. But here's the complication: the ICC needs either state party consent or a U.N. Security Council referral. And with Russia holding veto power…" she let the point hang in the air.

Conley nodded grimly. "So the ICC path is unlikely. But diplomatically? We could still leverage the intel—pressure allied nations, apply targeted sanctions, rally public opinion. It becomes a game of influence rather than prosecution."

"Domestically, the fallout could be just as severe," Mindy added. "If this evidence leaks, or if it's mishandled, we could compromise ongoing covert operations, maybe even fracture diplomatic ties we can't afford to lose."

The room fell silent, the air thick with calculation. All three pairs of eyes drifted to the secure phone in the center of the table.

"Any updates from the team, Ms. Taylor?" Conley finally asked.

Mindy shook her head. "No, sir. I've tried reaching them, but no response."

"Are we still tracking them on satellite?"

"Negative. We lost coverage. The last feed I had wasn't ours—I can't redirect it."

Conley's jaw tightened. He hated it. The team was isolated, deep in hostile territory, and until they reached the coast, no one could reach them.

"Keep trying, Ms. Taylor," he said quietly, the weight of command in his tone. "Everything you can."

January 26 | 3:40 p.m. CLT
Chilean Countryside

Four Spetsnaz operatives stood at the edge of a small, rippling lake. For hours they had followed a trail of boot prints leading from the smoldering wreckage at the border, up into the hills. The path had not been difficult to trace. Seven sets of prints, uniform in stride and pressed deep into the soil, stood out like scars on the untouched terrain. No other travelers had passed through these parts in recent days, and the silence of the wilderness confirmed it. They were closing in. They were on the right track.

But now, the trail ended. At the water's edge.

One soldier crouched low beside the waterline and motioned sharply for his commander. Petrov approached, his steps heavy, his arm still stiff from the wound burning beneath his uniform.

"The trail ends here, sir," the soldier reported, gesturing to the last clear imprint in the sand before it vanished beneath the shallows. The tracks led straight into the lake.

Petrov narrowed his eyes, scanning the shoreline with care. The wind carried the mingled scent of pine and damp earth. Across the water, the land rose sharply into hills scattered with dry brush and pale stone. Their prey was exhausted and hurt. The likelihood of swimming across this lake and then scaling the jagged cliff faces beyond was minimal in his mind.

"They didn't swim across," Petrov said with certainty. "Too risky, too much effort in their state. They walked into the water to mask their direction. Follow the shoreline. Watch for signs of where they came out again."

The men moved without hesitation, continuing along the shoreline at a steady, hunting pace. Rifles stayed low, muzzles forward, eyes raking the rocks and reeds for the faintest clue. They scrutinized every snapped twig, every scuffed stone, every unnatural ripple in the mud. The trail might have disappeared into water, but the Americans had left just enough evidence to stay within reach.

Petrov followed at a short distance, slipping his encrypted phone from a vest pocket. A sharp pull shot through his shoulder as he lifted it to his ear, the injury flaring hot. The pain fueled his anger—anger at the Americans, at their resistance, at his own wound.

"I have them," he said flatly into the receiver. "The trail is fresh. They're heading south. We'll catch them before they reach the coast."

He ended the call with a snap and slid the phone back into his vest. Then he moved forward again. One step. Then another.

Boots crunched on the hard desert terrain ahead of him. In his mind, he was already gaining ground on the injured group. His men wouldn't stop. Not until they closed the distance. Not until the chase was finished. Not until the Americans were dead.

4:38 p.m.

The engine coughed to life with a rattling shudder. Smoke belched from the tailpipe, thick and black as long-used oil. The truck was smaller than the SUV and twice its age in rust, but it would have to do. Two people would be forced to ride in the bed. They had no other option.

Hopper turned at the sound of the struggling vehicle, his eyes narrowing, then gave a small nod of approval. At last, they had a chance.

Zeke tapped the accelerator, listening as the engine sputtered, whined, and finally settled into a low, uneven idle. The exhaust was cracked, rattling loud enough to wake the next valley over, but the wheels turned—and that was all that mattered now.

"Load up. Time to move," Hopper called, urgency sharpening the edge of his voice.

The team didn't need to be told twice. They hurried toward the truck, shoulders tight with fatigue, every joint and muscle aching with motion. Kaitlyn leaned heavily on Sarah for balance as they eased her into the cramped back seat. Sully followed, one arm pressed against his side. Jacks climbed into the bed with deliberate slowness. Finn came last, shutting the door behind Sarah, his eyes already scanning the ridgelines above them.

The sun beat down on the rusted hood, baking the metal. The air reeked of exhaust, hot rubber, and the acrid bite of burning wires.

Zeke pressed the gas. The truck jerked forward with a metallic groan, rolling at a labored pace, its busted exhaust roaring like a chainsaw. No stealth. No grace. Just stubborn, hindered motion.

Three and a half hours. That was all the time they had left.

If they made good time—and nothing else went wrong—they might reach the coast just as the USS *Porter* came into range. But without the SAT phone, there would be no way to contact anyone. No backup plan. No last-minute audible.

And this mission hadn't given them a single smooth stretch yet. The thought settled in with each of them, heavy as the heat.

January 26 | 8:08 p.m. CLT
Arica, Chile

The battered truck limped through the city streets of Arica, engine sputtering, frame groaning beneath the weight of seven occupants. Fading sunlight stretched long shadows across cracked asphalt and worn concrete. At last, they had reached the coast. Ahead, the Pacific glittered in molten shades of orange and red, its light spilling beyond rows of shipping containers and narrow alleys.

Arica's coastal port was a blessing they had hardly dared to hope for. The air, heavy with salt and diesel, was a welcome reprieve from the choking dust of the interior. The harbor throbbed with the rhythm of commerce—cranes swinging, cables clanging, containers stacked in chaotic grids. It was the perfect camouflage for the USS *Porter*: no display of force, just another vessel ghosting along the shipping lanes, shepherding a suspect freighter. Amid the tangle of ropes and rusted steel, there were no patrols, no alarms—just one final sprint between survival and the sea.

Zeke coaxed the truck forward, though its battered chassis could manage little more than a crawl. Overloaded, ancient, every bump made it groan as though the road itself might tear it in half. Still, it rolled.

"One more turn," Hopper said, his tone tight but edged with hope. "We hit the waterfront, reach the beach, and wait for the boat."

They rounded the corner.

The road erupted. A line of gunfire chewed into the asphalt ahead, ripping rock and dust into a blinding curtain. Zeke slammed the brakes as the world vanished in grit.

"What the fuck?" he shouted, squinting through the windshield.

As the haze began to clear, he punched the accelerator. Staying still meant death.

"Helo on the left!" Sully barked, pointing through the dust cloud.

Out of the gloom, a green-and-black Mi-17 helicopter swept across the skyline, banking low. Its side door yawned open, and the PKM roared to life. Tracer fire raked the street, tearing the road apart.

Zeke floored it toward the beach.

In the back, Jacks drove a boot into the rear window.

Once. Twice. The third strike sent the entire pane and frame tumbling free. He yanked it out and flung it onto the road.

"Gun! Now!"

Sully shoved a rifle into his hands. Jacks steadied himself on one knee, braced against the roof, breathing deep to kill the tremor in his arms. The Mi-17 flared again—broadside. Perfect for the gunner.

Tracer rounds screamed overhead as Jacks lined the sight. Not the pilot. Not at this range. The gunner, maybe.

He fired. Bursts shook through his shoulders.

Miss.

Miss again.

Then—impact.

The helicopter jolted, smoke hissing from its rotor mast. Jacks had punched holes through the magnesium alloy skin, rupturing a gearbox lubrication line. Pressure dropped; the overheated shaft belched gray smoke from the rotor head like steam from a boiling kettle.

The Mi-17 yawed right, wounded but alive, drifting away in an uneven spiral.

"We're stopping here!" Zeke yelled, wrenching the truck onto the sand.

The vehicle coughed its last breath and rolled to a dead halt near jagged rocks jutting from the beach.

"This'll do," Hopper snapped. "Out. Behind cover. Move!"

They scrambled. Kaitlyn stumbled; Finn caught her arm. Sully pressed his ribs, pale with pain. Sarah, dazed, kept moving. Their bodies were wrecked, lungs raw, but desperation dragged them forward.

The beach was a funnel: cliffs hemming them tight, no way out but into the surf. The ocean had always been the goal. Now it was their only hope.

They crouched behind the rocks, the sound of the surf hammering in rhythm with their breath. Offshore, no sign of the *Porter*. No way to call. Just faith. Just time running out.

Hopper scanned the sky. The Mi-17 was spiraling down, trailing smoke in controlled descent. Not the crash he wanted. Damn it.

"They'll be here any second," he muttered.

Then, louder: "Everyone in the water! We don't have time to wait. Swim out, far as you can. Quick breaths, then dive. Stay under. Follow my men."

Sarah froze. "We'll be sitting ducks out there!"

"Stay under," Hopper repeated, eyes hard.

"They'll still shoot us!" she cried, panic clawing her throat.

Zeke gripped her shoulder. Calm, steady. "Bullets don't travel through water like in the movies. You're safer down there than up here. Just stick close."

Tears streaked her face as she nodded and ran for the surf with the others.

Hopper lingered. Crouched behind the rocks, he checked his pistol. Magazine—empty. He racked the slide. One round chambered. That was it. He would make it count.

Forty meters out, his team clawed through the waves, strokes sluggish with injury and exhaustion. Their forms flickered in the dying light—barely shapes, but still moving.

Figures appeared at the road's edge. Five of them.

Four riflemen fanned wide. One lifted an RPG. And behind them, calm, deliberate, hands clasped behind his back—Mendoza.

Hopper's jaw locked.

Gunfire ripped across the water. Muzzle flashes stuttered like lightning. Bullets chewed the waves, spraying plumes around the struggling silhouettes.

Then—another sound.

The deep metallic roar of a RHIB engine. Hopper knew it instantly.

Moments later, the sea erupted with the thunder of a minigun. Orange fire streaked across the surf as the USS *Porter*'s RHIB unleashed fury. Tracers carved into the sand, shredding men and rock alike. Two Spetsnaz crumpled instantly, cut in half. The others fled—but the shore became an inferno.

The RHIB's bow rose and fell, cutting through the waves, spitting light and death.

Petrov scrambled for cover. RPG in hand, he flipped the sight up, tracking the rescue boat. He had a clean line.

He raised it—

CRACK.

A single gunshot.

Petrov's skull snapped sideways in a burst of mist and matter. Blood and bone sprayed across Mendoza's face, hot and metallic, mingling with the salt air. Petrov collapsed to the wet sand.

Hopper's pistol locked back with a hollow click. Empty.

He didn't pause.

He surged forward, teeth bared, pistol clutched like a hammer.

Mendoza's eyes widened as Hopper closed the distance, weapon rising—

Hopper hurled the pistol, steel flashing in the firelight, and roared:

"Motherfucker!"

26

The empty pistol struck Mendoza square in the face, a bone-jarring blow that snapped his head sideways. It wasn't much, but it was enough. Hopper launched forward—a snarling blur--and slammed into him, driving them both down into the wet sand with a punishing, crushing tackle.

Both men rolled in the churned surf, thrashing, kicking up water and grit as small waves crashed over them.

Still on their knees, Mendoza landed the first clean hit—a brutal fist across Hopper's jaw. A blinding flash of white exploded behind Hopper's eyes, sending him tumbling sideways and landing with a hard splash on his back. Dazed, he scrambled up again.

His legs trembled. No food. No rest. No real sleep for days. The wound in his shoulder throbbed like a second heart, blood soaking through his uniform, saltwater burning the cut into a fiery brand. His body was failing.

But he didn't stop.

They charged toward each other.

Mendoza swung. Hopper ducked low and countered with a gut punch that blasted the air from Mendoza's lungs, folding him forward. The colonel snarled and lunged, one hand clamping Hopper's throat while the other drove his thumb deep into the bloody shoulder wound.

Hopper bucked and thrashed, teeth clenched, every nerve a white-hot scream. The world dissolved into pain.

He snapped forward and smashed his forehead into Mendoza's nose with a sickening crunch. Bone shifted with a wet crack.

Mendoza reeled back, staggering, one hand clutching his mangled face. Blood gushed from both nostrils. Not all of it belonged to his fallen Russian comrade anymore.

"*¡Hijo de puta!*" Mendoza roared. A snarl of pure rage twisted his features as he ripped the blade from the sheath on his belt.

Hopper swayed where he stood. Pain. Fatigue. Blood loss. His tank was empty. Each ragged breath was a desperate gasp as darkness crept at the edges of his vision.

Mendoza lunged.

The first thrust came in a blur, grazing Hopper's ribs. The second bit deep across his forearm, a jolt of white-hot agony tearing through skin and muscle. His hand spasmed open, fingers refusing to close. For a moment, he thought the arm was gone. Blood streamed down, dripping from his fingertips into the sand.

Mendoza flipped the knife in his grip and raised it overhead for a final, savage blow.

Hopper moved on instinct. His right hand snared

Mendoza's wrist, while his left forearm jammed against the elbow, wrenching it the wrong way.

A sickening pop. Mendoza's scream—raw, primal—split the night.

Hopper ripped the blade free from his hand.

No hesitation.

He drove it into Mendoza's chest with a brutal thrust. Then again. Then shoved it hard into the man's forehead, burying it hilt-deep. This wasn't vengeance anymore. It was survival. It was war.

Mendoza collapsed instantly, eyes wide and glassy, dead before he hit the sand.

Hopper stood for half a second—then dropped.

Pain. Exhaustion. Blood loss. Everything caught up. He lay in the surf as waves hammered him with cold salt and grit.

On all fours, coughing, gasping, he dragged himself toward the sea.

The water. The boat. The team. Sarah.

He had to make it.

He slid into the surf and kicked weakly, letting the current take him. Each stroke was agony. Shapes danced before his eyes—waves, shadows, voices. He blinked away blood and salt, fighting to stay conscious.

Beyond the breakers, the rescue boat floated, silhouetted against the dark horizon. The team stood stock-still aboard—Finn, Zeke, Jacks, Sully, Kaitlyn, Sarah—all scanning the shoreline.

Nothing.

Minutes passed.

Sarah's breath hitched, a choked sob. What if he hadn't made it?

Then—movement. Just a ripple at first.

Hopper surfaced, barely above the water.

Finn saw him first. "There! Nine o'clock!"

The team surged to the edge. Finn reached out as Hopper paddled the last few feet—bringing it full circle, just as he had pulled him from the rubble before. They seized his limbs and gear straps, hauling him aboard.

Hopper flopped onto the deck, chest heaving, gaze fixed on the stars. He let out a long, ragged sigh.

He didn't have to fight anymore.

Sarah grabbed Kaitlyn, hugging her tight. Relief poured through them.

The BREACH team—bloodied, battered, bruised— shared quiet nods. Nothing needed to be said. Relief was enough.

It was over.

The boat tore into the dark, carving a line across the sea toward salvation.

27

Pacific Ocean (Off Peruvian Coast)

The steady thrum of the engines vibrated beneath the deck, a constant undertone as the USS *Porter* cut through the Pacific. Safe. Homebound.

Hopper sat in a folding chair inside the medical bay, shirtless, his shoulder and ribs freshly bandaged. A nurse taped down the last strip while the ship's doctor scribbled notes onto a clipboard.

"You're lucky," the doc said. "That cut on your forearm missed the artery by a quarter inch. A little more and you wouldn't have made it off that beach."

Hopper didn't answer. He only nodded, the adrenaline finally ebbing, leaving behind a numbing fatigue.

In the passageway outside, Sully leaned against a bulkhead, staring through a small porthole.

"How you feeling, mate?" Sully asked.

"I'll be all right."

"You sure? You took a hell of a beating."

"Surprisingly, I'm very sure. I've had the shakes for months," Hopper said, lifting his hand. "Shakes are gone, for now. Maybe I just needed a fight I really believed in. Gonna see the doc when we get home, but I feel better about it."

"Glad to hear it, Hopper."

"You good?" Hopper asked.

Sully turned, eyes shadowed. "No. But I will be."

The low vibration of the ship filled the silence. Then Sully added, "I keep thinking about Dano."

Hopper didn't speak.

"He had plans, mate. For some godawful reason, he wanted to move to the States. Said he'd buy a cabin in Wyoming. Spend every damn day fishing when this was all over."

Hopper nodded slowly, feeling the weight of it. "He deserved better."

"Yeah. He did."

They stood without speaking, grief a shared weight that needed no explanation.

Around the ship, the rest of the team had spread out—resting, rehydrating, decompressing. Zeke sat cross-legged on the hangar deck, earbuds in, head leaned back against a stack of crates. Jacks was passed out on a cot, boots still on, snoring like a chainsaw. Finn leaned on the railing of the port-side deck, cup of lukewarm coffee in hand, staring out at the endless waves.

Kaitlyn stood beside Sarah in the crew lounge. Both wrapped in gray Navy blankets. Sarah was talking now, quietly—more than she had in days. Kaitlyn just listened.

Hopper leaned against a bulkhead, the faint hum of the

engines a familiar vibration through his boots, echoing his years with the Teams. He wasn't quite ready to leave this ship, though he suspected he was the only one who felt that way.

The destroyer's executive officer approached—a tall man with a permanent five-o'clock shadow and a weary gaze, a folder tucked under his arm. He skipped small talk.

"You and your boys are a priority, Hopper," the XO said, voice a low rumble. "A Sea King will be on deck at 0800 tomorrow morning. It'll take you to the airfield in Lima. A C-17 will be waiting to get you stateside."

Hopper nodded, sharp and brief. "Roger that, sir."

"You did good work," the XO added, tone softening. "Get some rest."

***

Later that afternoon, the team gathered in the officers' mess for a hot meal—real food, not rations. Plates of chicken and rice made the rounds, and for the first time in days, there was laughter. Tired. Muted. But real.

"Who's got the best scar?" Jacks asked, lifting his shirt to reveal a stitched gash across his side.

Finn snorted. "Please. That's a paper cut. Hopper's out here auditioning for *Rambo IV*."

Kaitlyn gave a dry smile. "Don't tempt him. He'll actually grow the hair and vanish into the woods."

Even Sarah chuckled.

Hopper raised his cup—half water, half stale coffee. "To Dano," he said. "To those who didn't come home. And to those who did."

They lifted their drinks.

"To the Breach," Zeke said.

"To the Breach," the others echoed.

For a moment, everything stilled. Just five battered operatives, a journalist, and a rescued girl. All scarred, their survival written in the way they held their cups, in the tired lines around their eyes.

Tomorrow would bring questions. Politics. Fallout.

But tonight was calm.

And for the first time in a long time, that was enough.

28

January 29 | 2:15 p.m. EST
Arlington, Virginia

The rear ramp of the cargo plane lowered slowly, revealing the blinding glare of the sun on the tarmac at Ronald Reagan International Airport. At the bottom of the ramp stood Congressman Barkley—eyes bloodshot, jaw tight, fists clenched at his sides. The moment he saw his daughter step into the light, his composure cracked. Tears welled, unrestrained.

Sarah bolted forward. She sprinted down the ramp and leapt into his arms. He caught her with a grunt, wrapping her in an unrelenting embrace. She clung to him like letting go might make him vanish all over again. The familiar scent of his aftershave was a lifeline after weeks of dust, sweat, and blood.

"Dad…" she choked out, her voice muffled against his

shoulder. "I missed you so much."

"I'm so glad you're home safe," he whispered, voice thick with emotion. He pressed his cheek to her hair and held her tighter. "I thought I'd never see you again."

"I love you, Daddy."

Behind them, the team descended the ramp. Battered and bruised. Limping and sore. But alive—and home. Watching Sarah reunited with her father gave them a deeper sense of accomplishment. For a moment, all the blood, the pain, and the loss felt worth it. Even the bruises seemed lighter.

Still holding Sarah close, Barkley looked toward the team. His eyes locked on Hopper, full of gratitude and disbelief.

"Thank you," he said, his voice breaking. "How can I ever repay you?"

"You're welcome, sir," Hopper said, giving a small, weary nod. "Just do what you can for the Bolivian people. They don't deserve that bullshit."

Barkley nodded, blinking through another wave of tears, as the team continued forward.

Trailing at the back, Jacks muttered his own parting shot.

"And don't forget to give that bastard Rocha a good ol' American ass-whooping."

A faint, shared chuckle passed among the team—just enough to ease the weight of the moment.

They moved toward a waiting van, unmarked, parked near the edge of the runway. Kaitlyn Thompson and Rick Sullivan followed, hauling multiple bags of evidence gathered from the Presidential Palace. The bags were loaded in the back before the doors slammed shut.

As the van rolled away from the tarmac, heading toward headquarters, Hopper sat in the rear seat, gazing out the window.

Pride settled quietly in his chest. The mission had been

brutal—a gauntlet. But they had stood their ground. And they had come out on top.

He looked at the faces of his team. One by one, the guys returned his glance with quiet nods. That was their language—the agreement, the respect, the thanks.

They were heading straight for debriefing.

No medals. No fanfare. Just the ride home.

January 29 | 5:25 p.m. EST
Langley, Virginia

The debrief had stretched past the hour mark inside a secure conference room buried deep in CIA headquarters. The space was quiet but charged, lined with open tablets, thick dossiers, and mugs of coffee long since abandoned to cold rings on the table. The air was filtered, clinical, and unsettling in its sterility after weeks breathing the humid rot of the jungle.

Deputy Director Conley sat at the head of the table, brow furrowed as he flipped through the latest report. His expression shifted from skepticism to something closer to disbelief.

"You sent all this from the *Porter*?" he asked, looking up at Kaitlyn.

She gave a weary nod. "Everything I had. Names, dates, transcripts, location data, photos. The prisoner debriefs confirmed Mendoza's chain of command. One even heard Rocha giving orders directly."

Conley let out a sharp breath. "Jesus... This is enough to choke off every dollar of aid. State's going to rip through this like wolves."

Kaitlyn didn't move, didn't soften. She wasn't here for praise. The adrenaline had bled away hours ago, leaving only the ache of exhaustion and the dull ringing of memory. Across from her, Hopper sat stiffly, a compression bandage cinched tight around his ribs. Every slight shift drew a wince. His body looked like a casualty map. Finn, stitches bisecting his brow, quietly scrolled through satellite images from San Lorenzo, tagging details the analysts had missed.

The team looked like hell, but they were alive.

"We lost good people," Hopper said at last. His voice was gravel ground down by days without rest. "But we brought this home. All of it. And the world needs to see it."

Conley closed the file with deliberate care. "They will. The President will be briefed directly. Rocha's shield is gone. He'll face international pressure—possibly arrest. But don't expect speed. Politics doesn't move like justice should."

"Will the ICJ actually act? Or is this just leverage for the State Department?" Kaitlyn asked.

"They'll move if the evidence is ironclad. And this?" Conley tapped the file. "This is about as damning as it gets. But don't mistake 'damning' for fast."

The silence that followed was long and heavy. Victory didn't erase weight—it only redistributed it.

Hopper finally broke it. "One more thing, Director. If we're going to keep running ops like this, we're done with garbage SAT phones. I want full JTAC comms for every operator. No more dropped signals, no more losing a phone and being blind. We either get proper kit, or next time we bury people because of budget cuts."

Conley gave one short nod. "Done. Mindy—make it happen."

The men exchanged the smallest of nods, unspoken recognition. They had done their job. Against all odds, they had pulled Sarah Barkley out of hell and dismantled the network that held her there. But survival came at a cost. The mission had left its fingerprints on all of them—burn scars invisible but permanent.

Hopper's eyes fell to the table. Wedged between two reports lay a bloodstained photo: a still frame from San Lorenzo. Locals being shoved into a mass grave. Everything they'd endured pressed down again, but his mind stuck on one image—Miguel's face, defiant until the end.

BREACH would push on. Because that's what they did. Bloodied, battered, raw, and relentless. They carried scars no one would ever see—wore them like armor, buried them like landmines.

The world didn't get quieter. It only got meaner.

EPILOGUE

3 Months later...
April 29 | 2:45 p.m. EST
Langley, Virginia

Mindy dropped a thick file stamped **"ZMEY-03"** onto Deputy Director Conley's red oak desk with a dull, bone-deep thud.

Conley leaned forward, his expression sharpening as he flipped through the contents. High-resolution satellite images of a large warehouse in Istanbul, CCTV photos of Turkish smugglers with their names below, Balkan smuggler routes, Russian blueprints scribbled over with dense Cyrillic notes. Intercepted transmissions—faint, distorted, but brimming with urgency and menace.

"This is what we pulled from Rocha's office," Mindy said, her voice steady but low. She slid a finger across a page that displayed a compact device, no larger than a suitcase. The caption in bold read: *Portable Nuclear Device Prototype—ZMEY Series.*

Conley's jaw tightened. He pressed a fist against the desk, knuckles whitening as the weight of it sank in.

"They're building a weapon," he muttered. "Small enough to smuggle anywhere in the world."

Mindy didn't flinch. Her gaze was level, uncompromising.

"And it's not just a design. The intel suggests Russians are already moving prototypes to the Balkans, to smuggle to our neck of thew woods. That's why they were in Bolivia—to secure a path to sneak a nuke in the U.S."

Silence settled like a storm front. Conley rose from his chair and crossed to the window. The Washington skyline shimmered in late-afternoon light—monuments and marble facades glowing with borrowed peace. Ordinary lives carried on below, unaware of the ticking shadow coiled at their foundations.

For a long moment, he said nothing. When his voice finally came, it was low, absolute.

"Activate the team."

THANK YOU

For giving my story your time. If you could take a few minutes, an honest review on Amazon, GoodReads and/or the online retailer you purchased it from would be greatly appreciated.

SIGN UP FOR MY NEWSLETTER

For updates, new releases and general info.

www.EdwardGray.ca

ABOUT THE AUTHOR

EDWARD GRAY

Edward Gray is a Canadian author and self-employed, hardworking family man with a passion for storytelling, strategy, and all things action-packed. B.R.E.A.C.H. is his debut novel, born from a love of military thrillers and a desire to create something gritty, realistic, and impossible to put down.

When he's not writing, Edward can usually be found in the garden or spending time with his family—whether that's chasing their goats with his daughter or simply enjoying a quiet moment at home. He's a proud husband and father and credits his family as his greatest source of support and inspiration on this journey.

B.R.E.A.C.H. is the first in. a new series that dives deep into covert operations, international threats, and the team willing to risk everything to stop them.

Stay tuned for the sequel "November Rain"

ACKNOWLEDGMENTS

There are many people that have helped me along the way on this journey. I'm sure I will be forgetting some. For those someone's (and they know who they are)… I'm sorry.

First, I must thank my wife. She put up with countless hours, days, months and years for this book to become a reality. Not to mention all the many questions I sent her way to get her opinion. She was an amazing sounding board and had an immense amount of patience with me.

For the many technical weapons specifications, my author photo, help with the book cover and constant random questions, a massive amount of gratitude has to go to my good friend Emil. He was a consistent support every step of the way.

I also cannot go any further without acknowledging my appreciation to Niko. His assist in the infancy of the idea of writing this novel helped me take an idea and grow it into the B.R.E.A.C.H. you know now.

Many others have helped me along the way. They have been a never-ending source of support during this two-year process. I will be forever grateful for them pushing me to never give up on this dream and to see it through.

www.ingramcontent.com/pod-product-compliance
Lightning Source LLC
Chambersburg PA
CBHW020840020726
47497CB00005B/1189